"You want dessert before or after?" he asked.

"Before or after what?"

"We make love."

Silver just stared at him. She hadn't drunk that much whiskey, had she? "I beg your pardon?"

Rafe leaned back against the counter. "We're going to, you know. You can play all the games you want, try to convince yourself and me you're unwilling, but sooner or later we're going to end up upstairs in that big bed. Things would be a lot simpler if we just accepted that fact."

"What if I say no?"

"You'll change your mind," he said flatly.

"Or you'll change it for me?" she asked, feeling a cold dread in the pit of her stomach, warring with the hot lick of desire that spread through her belly.

Rafe didn't say a word. He didn't have to.

Dear Reader,

No doubt you've noticed the different look to your American Romance novels. Now you're about to discover what's new between the covers.

Come with us and sail the high seas with a swashbuckling modern-day pirate...ride off into the sunset on the back of a motorcycle with a dark and dangerous man...lasso a cowboy Casanova and brand him your own. You can do it all with the *new* American Romance!

In this book, and every book each month, you'll fall in love with our bold American heroes, the sexiest men in the world, as they take you on adventures that make their dreams—and yours—come true.

Enjoy the new American Romance—because love has never been so exciting!

Sincerely,

Debra Matteucci
Senior Editor & Editorial Coordinator
Harlequin Books
300 East 42nd St., 6th floor
New York, NY 10017

# ANNE STUART

## RAFE'S REVENGE

# *Harlequin Books*

TORONTO • NEW YORK • LONDON
AMSTERDAM • PARIS • SYDNEY • HAMBURG
STOCKHOLM • ATHENS • TOKYO • MILAN
MADRID • WARSAW • BUDAPEST • AUCKLAND

For Tahti Carter and Debra Matteucci,
with love and gratitude for the support
they've shown me through all the books,
through all the years.

And for Barbara Keiler,
who's always there when I need her.

Published September 1992

ISBN 0-373-16453-X

RAFE'S REVENGE

Printed in U.S.A.

# Chapter One

Rafael Starret McGinnis could smell the coffee when he stepped into his chrome-and-glass office at half past six in the morning. At that hour there was only one other person present in the rambling building that held the executive offices of Mack Movies: his partner, mentor and the smartest woman in Hollywood. "Bernie," he called out, loosening his silk tie, "I want you to bear my children."

"Too late," Bernadette Thomas said, appearing in the doorway, a mug of coffee in one capable hand. "You should have asked thirty years ago."

He poured himself some coffee. "I know I'm a stud, but even for me seven years old would have been a little young."

Bernie shook her short-cropped gray head. "Nothing's impossible for you, Rafe. Besides, there are any number of sweet young things willing to do your bidding at any hour of the day or night. You don't need me. Anyway, I made this coffee for myself. You're just lucky to get some."

"You're still a wonderful woman," he said with a smile he reserved just for her, his right arm, the woman with the secrets, who'd been in the business longer than he'd been alive. Without her knowledge, her contacts, he wouldn't be where he was, at the top of the heap, founder of one of the most successful independent studios in the history of Hollywood. Together with Bernie and a brilliant young director named Sam Mendelsohn, they'd built the company from scratch and just sold it to Pegasus Pictures for the gross national income of several South American nations. There was a saying—he who died with the most toys won the game of life. Well, he had more toys than anyone he knew of, and one of those toys was Mack Movies. Pegasus might have paid him a fortune for it, but they still had no control over it. He had the protection of one of the few solvent studios left in Southern California, and they had an adequate percentage of the money-making machine he'd created.

On top of that, he had Sam, and most especially he had Bernadette Thomas. They shared the same vision, the same dedication, and she was one of the few people who ever got her own way when it clashed with his.

"Speaking of sweet young things," she added, following him into his office, grabbing her own coffee on the way, "how was your evening with Marcia?"

"So that was her name!" Rafe said, stripping off his tie and shrugging out of his jacket. "I couldn't remember."

"Marcia Allison, twenty-three years old, three featured roles, one lead in a television movie," Bernie cited effortlessly. "I trust you didn't sleep with her if you couldn't remember her name."

"Your trust is misplaced."

"God, Rafe, how do you manage these things? Just an appropriate *darling* here and there?" Bernie said, plopping her ample frame down in a chair and watching with jaundiced eyes as he unbuttoned his shirt.

"Exactly."

"You're impossibly decadent. Does she get the role?"

He tossed the shirt in the trash. It smelled like the woman he'd spent the night with—expensive, sexual and anonymous. "I'm not a casting director," he said, reaching for a fresh shirt and shrugging into it. "It's not up to me."

"She wasn't that good, eh?" Bernie said shrewdly.

"You're a dirty old woman, you know that?" He tucked the shirt in, grabbed the silk-and-wool Armani jacket and sank into his leather chair, reaching for his coffee and stretching out his long legs.

"Or then again, maybe you weren't that good," she added.

"You aren't going to get a reaction out of me, Bernie. I'm in a bad mood, and your little sniping won't affect it."

"I noticed. Maybe I'll just add some fuel to the fire," she said sweetly.

"Oh, yeah? How do you intend to manage that?" he drawled, draining his coffee and reaching for his pack of cigarettes.

"Have you read today's paper?"

"Oh, God, what now?" he said, reaching for it as it lay on his glass-topped desk. "Who died, who's done what to whom?"

"Nothing that simple. Just the review of *Cop for a Day.*"

"Damn, Bernie, you had me worried," he growled. "I thought it was something that mattered. The day I worry about reviews is the day I quit."

"It's S. H. Carlysle."

The name was enough to galvanize him. "Just what I need to make my day perfect," he said with a long-suffering sigh. "What's she saying now?"

"Read it," Bernie said, tapping the newspaper before she headed out the door, "and weep."

Tears were the furthest thing from Rafe's mind as he scanned the review, unless they were tears of rage. S. H. Carlysle had been the bane of his existence, a thorn in his side since she'd started filling in for the revered Clement Walden. Walden had been his own sort of pain—an elitist, elderly pedant who only liked films, pronounced with two syllables. Rafe prided himself on making movies, not films, and he didn't give a damn what someone like Walden said about him.

S. H. Carlysle was a different kettle of fish. The fact that she was obviously a woman was part of it. She reviewed things like a woman, he thought with a satisfyingly sexist contempt. Backbiting, hysterical, more interested in politically correct thinking than whether something worked, damn it. The review was just one more in a long line of scathing reviews that deteriorated into personal attacks on Mack Movies and Rafael McGinnis.

She'd upped the ante this time. In trashing *Cop for a Day,* the third in a line of fabulously successful action movies, she'd added that right-thinking Americans ought to boycott all Mack movies and make their significant others do the same.

"Damn," Rafe said out loud. He'd put up with her for more than a year now, and he was getting sick and tired of her cheap shots. She had every right in the world not to like the kind of movies he made. Hell, sometimes even he didn't like them. But she had no right to tell other people that they shouldn't like them.

"Can you find me a contract killer?" he called to Bernie in her adjoining office. "I want this woman dead."

"Sorry, that's not in my job description," Bernie called back. "You'll have to do it yourself."

"Love to," Rafe said, leaning back in his leather-and-chrome chair and warming his hands on the refilled mug of coffee. "How do you suggest I do that when I don't even know what the woman looks like? Except that I can guess. She's short and squat and ugly and dresses like a man."

"Watch that," Bernie warned, reappearing in the doorway, and belatedly Rafe noticed that Bernie was short and squat and ugly and dressed like a man. "If you lower yourself to attend the premiere tonight she might be there."

"I hate premieres, you know that. Last night was bad enough. I can only stand one Hollywood party a week, max," he said.

"Then it's too bad you're A-list material," Bernie said, completely without sympathy. "It's up to you. There'll be plenty of people around to let you know how things went, but if you want to touch base with the critics..."

"Why do you think I avoid these things in the first place? I hate critics. They're not worth my energy."

"It's not like you to roll over and play dead. However, if you don't mind what S. H. Carlysle says about you..."

"Do I have to have a date?" he asked with sour acquiescence.

"Rafael McGinnis is like the two-thousand-pound gorilla, he doesn't have to do a damned thing he doesn't want to do. However, if you show up unattached you're going to be bombarded by every out-of-work actress in the place, and maybe half the actors."

"You're right." He swiveled around, staring out the window into the early-morning light. The studio was coming awake, early makeup calls and scenery setups already in motion. "The sensible, mature thing to do would be to ignore the provocation, ignore S. H. Carlysle and go home tonight. Wouldn't it?"

"Absolutely. You feel like being sensible and mature for a change?"

"No," he said with a reluctant grin. "And tell Robin when she gets in to give what's her name a call. Marcia. Tell her I'll pick her up at ... what time?"

"Seven. And if she can't make it?"

Rafe looked at her. "Do you really think there's a possibility of that?"

"Depends on how good you were last night," Bernie mused.

"Get out of here, woman," he said. "We've both got work to do."

Bernie moved at her own majestic pace, leaving him alone and quiet for the few minutes before his secretary, attuned to his early hours, made her first appearance. S. H. Carlysle was about the only thing that had piqued his interest in the past few weeks—he almost hated to have his curiosity satisfied. But he wasn't about to let anyone get away with the stuff she had. He needed to plan an effective revenge. And he couldn't think of a more relaxing way to spend the next half hour.

S. H. Carlysle was going to meet her comeuppance. And maybe he'd be able to concentrate a little more on the newest woman in his life, a woman whose name he could hardly remember. She'd certainly been energetic enough last night.

It was a damned shame he couldn't get nearly as excited about her as he was about the prospect of besting Carlysle. It just went to prove how completely cynical he'd become in his old age. And he wondered if he ever, just for a moment, missed his innocence.

"I'M NOT IN THE MOOD for this, Clement," Silver Carlysle said in a quiet voice.

"Dearest, why not?" countered the impossibly dapper little man sitting next to her in the back seat of a pure white Daimler. Clement Walden was an exquisite gentleman of the old school, one who believed that living well was the best revenge. He dressed impeccably, was possessed of a malicious wit that withered most human beings, and he was Silver's best and most trusted friend in the entire world. "You don't get out nearly enough, and besides, if you're going to write about the film business you need to partake of some of the social opportunities. There's nothing like a real Hollywood premiere to teach you about the artificiality of life."

"I've already had more than my share of Hollywood parties and the artificiality of life, Clement," she said scrunching back in the corner of the butter-soft leather seat. "And two Mack Movies in one week is a little more than my stomach can stand."

"I expect you to rise to new and glorious heights in your review," Clement said smoothly, touching a perfectly manicured finger to his snowy-white mustache.

"I don't see why you want me to write it. You've already seen the wretched thing in previews. I don't want to have to go in cold and come to a snap judgment..."

"Silver, darling," Clement said in a cooing voice. "You've already made up your mind about the movie, well before you've seen it. It could be the masterpiece of the decade and you'd trash it.''

''Are you saying I'm unfair?''

''Not in the slightest. I'm saying I've taught you well. You know how to separate gold from dross, and if you're heading into a manure pile you know exactly what you'll find there. Besides, I'm tired of tearing apart McGinnis in print. You provide a fresh take on the man that's charmingly nasty.''

There it was again, Silver thought, that niggling bother of a conscience. She truly despised Rafael McGinnis and Mack Movies, despised them for their cheap emotionalism, their mindless violence, their degradation of women, who were always victims, and gays, who were always caricatures. But she hated to think she had any sort of hidden agenda.

''I'm not dressed for this,'' she said, trying one more tactic, the one most likely to appeal to Clement's fastidious taste.

He wrinkled his elegant nose. ''True enough, darling. If you insist on dressing like an aging hippie, there's nothing I can do about it. I imagine other people will have the distinct bad taste to show up at the premiere in jeans and an old sweater—you won't be the only one. If only—'' he reached forward and flipped at her thick, shaggy hair ''—you could do something about this disreputable mop. I could talk to Marcel. I know he could come up with something quite extraordinary.''

''I like my hair the way it is, Clement. You've been wonderfully helpful in my work, but there's a limit to how far your influence extends,'' she said firmly, tired of an old battle.

"Is there? I wonder," Clement murmured. "We're here, darling. Shoulders back, head up. Remember, you're a queen. If you insist on wearing such tatty clothes, simply think of everyone else as hideously overdressed." He handed her out onto the crowded sidewalk, ushering her into the brightly lighted theater with his usual solicitousness. "We'll sit in the back and make rude comments to each other about the movie, shall we?" he murmured in her ear. "Maybe get some popcorn and throw it."

"You're a devil," Silver said, partially reassured. The theater was jammed with people, but Clement was right. Compared to some of them, even her old jeans and cotton sweater were an improvement. Her mother would have deplored the decay in standards nowadays, just as Clement did. It was a wonder the two of them hated each other so much, when they had such a great deal in common.

She looked down at Clement from her superior height. She was six feet tall in her stocking feet, a fact that her petite mother still bewailed, and while Silver liked being barefoot, she also had a fondness for Western-style boots that added another couple of inches to her already considerable height. It would have been terrific if she'd been model thin, and when she'd been a teenager she'd starved herself, trying to achieve that gaunt-cheeked look.

In her older, wiser twenties she'd given up that notion as a lost cause. She was a healthy woman. Big-boned, curved, undeniably female. Clement might deplore her taste in clothes, but he didn't realize that part of it came from necessity. It was a lot easier to fit into men's clothes, with her long, rangy body, than into women's, even with the handicap of her curves.

There were a lot of tall men in the room, most of them self-absorbed actors looking to be seen by prospective employers. She glanced around her, dismissing them as she and Clement edged their way into the theater, when one tall figure caught her eye, and she groaned, a quiet little sound that nevertheless caught Clement's attention.

"What is it, Silver? Some old flame, risen up to haunt you?"

Clement was unfailingly nasty about her few aborted relationships, and she'd gotten in the habit of ignoring him when he was in one of his acid-tongued moods. But he was wonderful when she was hurting, a shoulder to cry on, an ear to listen, a dinner companion to ply her with exquisite wines and sumptuous foods. She'd learned to take the good with the bad.

"Nothing crucial," she said. "Rafael McGinnis is here."

"Oh, really?" Clement perked up, looking smug. "He seldom comes to these things—I wonder why he's chosen this one. Let me introduce you."

"No!" Her protest came out louder than she would have liked, causing several people around them to turn their heads and watch, ever alert for a new scandal. "I don't want to meet him," she added in a panicked whisper.

"Why ever not? Just because we despise the man's creations doesn't mean we have to dismiss him entirely. He's really too powerful to ignore. Besides, he can be quite charming in an arrogant sort of way."

"I'm not interested in charming arrogance," Silver said, tugging at Clement's arm.

"That's a great deal too bad, darling, because he's headed our way. And I don't think it's me he's interested in."

"Oh, God," Silver moaned, searching about her for a means of escape.

There was none. She was boxed in by the crowds, unable to move, as Rafael McGinnis bore down on them. For McGinnis the crowd parted like magic, for Silver the people remained obstinately in place. There was nothing she could do but remember Clement's words. Shoulders back, head held high, and don't cower. She just couldn't rid herself of the feeling that she was being caught by her teacher in the midst of an indiscretion.

"Clement," McGinnis said, and Silver felt an odd little shiver down her spine as she tried to hide behind the smaller man. She'd certainly seen Rafael McGinnis on television often enough, heard his deep, low voice. It was different in person. Even over the chattering crowd it had its own quiet power.

As did the man himself. He was better-looking in person, younger, although he'd been pretty potent on the tube. He was big—towering over everyone, including her. He wore a charcoal-gray suit, probably Armani, though Silver wasn't enough in tune to know for sure, and his dark hair was pulled back in a queue. His face was all planes and angles, high cheekbones, a strong nose, cool greenish eyes that looked right through you. It was his mouth that dominated his face. Large and sexy, it looked as if it could devour little girls who got in his way.

Not that she was in any way, shape or form a little girl, she reminded herself, stiffening her spine.

"Rafe," Clement said smoothly, with all his legendary charm. "How nice to see you again. And Miss Allison. Very interesting work in *Die for Us.*"

Rafe McGinnis wasn't interested in Clement's social amenities. His gaze was on Silver, and for a moment she felt caught, trapped by its intensity. "Who's your friend, Clement?"

Clement preened slightly, and Silver had the sudden, odd notion that Clement had hoped for this confrontation. "You mean my companion?" he inquired smoothly. "Or S. H. Carlysle?"

"Are we talking about two different people?" he countered, still watching her like a hawk watches a sparrow.

"I should never underestimate you," Clement said with a sigh. "Rafael McGinnis, may I present to you Ms. Silver Carlysle, my associate."

He just looked at her. Silver didn't make the mistake of holding out her hand—he would have ignored it. The gorgeous, impossibly tiny woman beside him was looking at the two of them nervously, as if caught between two angry dogs.

"I've read your work, Ms. Carlysle," he said, all that energy directed at her.

"Have you?" she countered brightly, refusing to be intimidated. "I won't ask whether you liked it or not."

"No, I would say that would be a waste of time." He took a step closer, and in the crowded lobby it was too close. "Obviously you have a problem with me, Ms. Carlysle. I can't imagine what it is—I'm considered a moderately charming individual when I get my own way, and since that's most of the time, I'm usually quite pleasant. Since you don't seem to appreciate my finer qualities, don't you think it might be better if you let someone else, someone impartial, review my movies?''

"It's not a reviewer's job to be impartial. It's to have opinions. And I don't have a problem with you—it's your movies that disgust me.''

He smiled then, a wry upturning of that sexy mouth. "If you say so,'' he said, moving infinitesimally closer, and the closeness of his body was a subtle threat. And an odd, unsettling promise. "It just seems to me that your opinions are preformed ones,'' he murmured, and Silver flushed, remembering that Clement had accused and lauded her for the very same thing.

He touched her then, his long fingers brushing her face, and the heat of his flesh, the feel of his skin, was a shocking invasion, for all its insidious gentleness. "I suggest you keep an open mind, Ms. Carlysle,'' he added, very gently. "Or I might have to do something about it.''

She stared at him, openmouthed in shock at the veiled threat. And then he was gone, moving past her, the gorgeous starlet clinging to his arm, as the crowds parted for him as they wouldn't part for her.

"That overbearing turkey,'' Silver gasped.

"Oh, not a turkey,'' Clement said, taking her arm and patting it with a paternal gesture. "We can be more creative than that, don't you think? But let's save it for the paper tomorrow.'' And he tugged her into the theater as she continued to fume.

Tomorrow, she thought, settling into her seat and ignoring the movie. Tomorrow Rafael McGinnis was going to be tarred and roasted and feathered. She'd never liked the man before, but it had been an artistic difference. Now, with his overt threat, it had become personal. And she was more than ready for a battle.

## Chapter Two

"Any chance I could get your full attention for a moment, Rafe?" Sam Mendelsohn demanded in a long-suffering voice. "Not that my time's worth anything at all in the scheme of things, but yours is, and if you waste your time daydreaming, the gross profits of Mack Movies might drop below a hundred billion, perish the thought."

Rafe smiled faintly. "Don't give me that garbage, Sam. You know the balance sheet as well as Bernie and I do, and you know that it doesn't really matter. I'm sorry, I was thinking about something else. What were you saying?"

"What were you thinking about?" Sam Mendelsohn was the only person Rafe trusted, outside of Bernie. He was short, wiry, intense, an East Coast urbanite, just as Rafe was a deceptively laid-back Californian. The two of them, tempered by Bernie, made a powerful force in Hollywood, one that had wiped out weaker organizations without a backward glance.

"None of your business," Rafe said, reaching for a cigarette.

"Must be a woman," Sam said knowledgeably. "Bernie said you had a burr under your saddle about someone."

"Let me tell you, Sam, that cowboy slang sounds absurd with a New York accent."

"It can't be your ex-wife," Sam mused, not in the slightest bit deterred by Rafe's insult. "You haven't lost a moment's sleep since you got rid of that bimbo. And I can't believe it's that pretty little thing you had clinging to your arm last night."

"Then you'd be wrong," Rafe said. "That's exactly who I was thinking about." He hadn't slept with Marcia Allison the previous night, disentangling himself with single-minded adroitness when he'd brought her back to her house. He'd still felt restless, edgy, with no comforting sense of moral purity to alleviate it. Hell, he should have gone to bed with her after all. If he was damned if he did, damned if he didn't, he might as well do it. Then he wouldn't keep thinking about Silver Carlysle.

"Don't try to kid a kidder, Rafe. I've known you for fifteen years, through good times and bad. Marcia Allison isn't your kind of little prairie flower and you know it."

"God, not another cowboy idiom," Rafe groaned.

"Besides, Bernie clued me in on your little problem," he added.

"Sam, trust me, I have no little problem, apart from what we're going to make next."

"So what's the problem with that? We have a million ideas. *Cop for a Week,* the boxer movie, options on some of the hottest names in Hollywood. Everyone wants to work with us—we're the golden boys. Hell, we can even try a biblical epic. We have so many things in development we couldn't get around to them in this lifetime or the next.''

"That's half the problem. We've got a million ideas, most of them sure money-makers, and I don't give a damn about a single one of them.''

"Don't tell me you're becoming artistic on me all of a sudden!'' Sam made it sound like a dread disease. "We make movies for entertainment, to make money. Not to fulfill your soul.''

"I sold my soul years ago,'' Rafe drawled. "I'm not talking about artistic fulfillment, either. We make movies for entertainment, and they don't entertain me.''

"Well, excuse me. If you don't like them then I guess we'd better find something else to do. Maybe a remake of *Heaven's Gate.*"

Rafe stubbed out the cigarette. Sam's office was a far cry from Rafe's sterile confines. Sam's was chaos personified. Sam matched his office—tie askew, hair askew, food stains on his shirt, his jeans sagging beneath his expanding middle. He was deceptively disorganized just as Rafe was deceptively neat. Neither of them were what they seemed, and that had been part of their strength. "Maybe a Western isn't such a bad idea.''

"Jeez, Rafe, did you hit your head on something? *Dances with Wolves* was a fluke. No one makes money on Westerns anymore. I mean, a tax write-off might come in handy in your income bracket, but I'd just as soon not have my name attached to a flop.''

Rafe watched him for a moment. "It's up to you,'' he said finally. "This one'll be your baby.''

Sam sank into his seat opposite Rafe. "What's the matter with you, buddy?'' he asked in a softer voice.

"If I didn't know you better I'd say you were depressed."

"I don't know the meaning of the word," Rafe protested, the very thought chilling him. His eyes narrowed. "You said Bernie clued you in on my little problem. How did she define it—mid-life crisis?"

"She's lived too long to make such a serious mistake," Sam said. "No, she told me about Silver Carlysle."

"I don't have a problem with Silver Carlysle." He denied it instantly. "Isn't that about the stupidest damn name you've ever heard for a female?"

"Oh, I don't know. I picture someone willowy, with waist-length blond hair and some sort of floaty dress. One that comes off with the first strong gust of wind."

"Maybe you ought to be making movies for the Playboy Channel," Rafe said. "Obviously you've never seen Silver Carlysle. She's about ten feet tall, built like a brick outhouse, and dressed from the Salvation Army."

"You're kidding. I thought she was Clement Walden's protégée. I can't imagine that old dilettante spending time around anyone who isn't as elegant as he is."

"You know more about her than I do," Rafe said. "How come?"

"You tend to ignore provocation until it becomes overwhelming. I like to look into it. She's been riding your tail for almost a year now, and I was curious as to why she had it in for you in particular."

"I hate to tell you this, Sam, but it's not me in particular. She hates our movies. She just hasn't happened to notice you exist."

Sam responded with a rude gesture. "Maybe. You're the one she usually mentions by name, though. Of course, after today's article it's all moot."

"You mean yesterday's."

"I mean today's," Sam said. "Don't tell me you've been lucky enough to have missed it."

"Where is it?" he demanded in a dangerous voice.

"I don't think your blood pressure can stand it, Rafe. Bernie must have decided to spare you." Sam was obviously amused by Rafe's reaction.

"Where's the paper?" he demanded again, rising to his full height and towering over the unabashed Sam.

"On the desk."

Rafe snatched it up, stalking toward the door.

"I guess we'll go ahead with *Cop for a Week* then," Sam called after him. "A Western. Good God, what will he come up with next?"

THERE WEREN'T TOO MANY unsuccessful screenwriters and part-time journalists who lived in Beverly Hills, Silver thought. Of course, she lived above a garage, in the former cook's apartment, and the place smelled like gasoline and car wax and boiled cabbage, but it was Silver's, and that was good enough. If it was up to her mother, she'd be ensconced in the rambling house, in her powder-pink bedroom suite with matching full bath, complete with gold faucets and imported marble. She'd lived in that room from the time she was eleven and her mother left her father to marry her stepfather.

None of that would be remarkable—it happened all the time in the modern era of disposable marriages. The only thing that made it noteworthy was that Silver's mother was Marjorie Carlysle, the minimally talented but quite lovely actress whose career was already on the skids by the mid-sixties. And her father was none other than Sir Benjamin Hatcher, the foremost British writer-director in the history of films, a brilliant, distant man who had no time for wife and daughter, and someone Silver had lost long before Marjorie had taken her and moved from the pseudo-Tudor house they'd shared, lost long before he died two years later in a car crash in England.

Her stepfather was a different kettle of fish entirely. Harry Braddock was an industrialist, with the kind of vast, steady income that was unresponsive to the vagaries of the entertainment industry. Marjorie turned her back on her career, on her old friends, without a moment's hesitation, becoming a wealthy matron, embracing that secure role with more enthusiasm than she'd ever embraced anything in her life, including her only child.

The three of them had made a decent enough family, learning to keep out of one another's way. Harry had worshiped Marjorie, and Marjorie in turn had bestowed most of her affection on the man who bought her. Silver was a ghost figure, wandering through the house, growing taller, more gangly as the years went by.

She suspected her mother had hoped she'd take up where Marjorie had left off. By the time she was five foot eleven that was clearly unlikely, and Marjorie had given up, packing her off to college with brisk efficiency.

She would have liked to find a place of her own when she finally emerged, complete with a master's degree in English literature. She'd wanted to go on for a Ph.D., anything to keep her in the safety of school for a few years longer, but Marjorie had put her foot down. It was time for her daughter to enter society, such as it was, in Beverly Hills, and decide what she wanted to do in life.

It had lasted no more than six months, long enough for Silver to renew her acquaintance with Clement Walden, the elder statesman of film criticism, long enough for Marjorie to decide she really didn't want to have a six-foot-tall daughter in her mid-twenties hanging around, reminding her how old she now was.

The funny thing was, her mother really loved her. Silver had no doubts at all about that. The woman just wished her daughter was a little more charming, a little more feminine, a little smaller.

The long-abandoned apartment over the four-stall garage had been the perfect compromise for both of them. It gave Silver her freedom without having to ask for money from her stepfather. It gave her mother a hold over her without actually having to put up with her.

So Silver had spent the past year and a half in the two rooms over the garage, fixing up old wicker furniture to make it do, spending the last tiny bit of the meager trust fund on a state-of-the-art Macintosh computer. Not for one moment did she regret the expenditure. Her father had been a spendthrift, a charming, energetic man who never worried about tomorrow, or the practicalities of life.

Silver did. She didn't like accepting handouts from her stepfather, even though Harry would have gladly bought her affection. She didn't like debt and things she couldn't afford; she preferred to make do and make her own way.

Her inheritance had paid for six very expensive years at Princeton, two of them in graduate school. She couldn't think of a better way to wipe it out than by buying something to help her write.

Silver considered herself a pragmatic person. She knew the odds against selling a screenplay were astronomical, even if she used her family connections, and she had no intention of doing that. Clement had been kind enough to give her a job, a few hours a week doing research and general office work for him. As the months had gone by he'd taken her under his wing, teaching her so much about films and the heyday of Hollywood that she was truly awestruck. She knew she was a little too reliant on Clement. On her more distant days she could see his prejudices, his little nasty ways. But he showed her more encouragement and affection than anyone had in her entire life, and she would have walked through fire for him.

He was the one who gave her her first chance. She'd happened to see a small French film when she'd been abroad, and he asked her to write a preliminary review of it before he went to see it himself. To her amazement, the review appeared in the paper one week later, complete with her byline and a check that was far more generous than first-time journalists usually received.

Since then the work had been steady. He kept most of the big films for himself, letting Silver sharpen her skills and her wits on the lesser ones. It was only her antipathy for Mack Movies' violent chauvinism in the first place, and Rafe McGinnis himself in the second, that made him decide to pass that lucrative little specialty on to her. Her antagonism amused Clement, who adored maliciousness. He was fond of quoting Alice Roosevelt—"If you don't have something nice to say about anyone then come and sit by me."

Silver flicked off the computer, rubbing a hand across her furrowed brow. This time, however, she might have gone too far. With Clement's encouragement, she had let loose with all the outrage she felt over McGinnis's movies. That would have been acceptable, if it weren't for the fact that she'd allowed her personal fury to creep in. Rafe McGinnis had always stood for everything she detested in the new Hollywood. Slick, soulless peddlers of death and sex and violence, devoid of wit or grace, they were a plague upon the land, and Rafe McGinnis, with his multimillion-dollar studio was the leader of the pack. She'd despised him from afar, but meeting him had been the final straw.

She hated aggressive men. She hated men with long hair tied at the neck. She hated men in cowboy boots and Armani suits and cool, superior expressions and smoldering sensuality that nothing could hide. She hated men with charm who used it at her expense. And there was no denying that Rafe McGinnis had a very lethal brand of charm.

Unfortunately she'd put that hatred into print. Oh, not in its raw emotionalism. She'd put it more delicately, and Clement had passed it along without comment. She'd simply made the point that moviemakers who were obsessed with sex and violence were probably beset by conflicts about those issues in their personal lives.

She really shouldn't be so nervous. She hadn't come right out and said Rafe McGinnis was unsure about his sexuality and used violence to cover it up. She'd simply suggested it. And actually, uncertainty about anything, particularly his sexuality, did not seem to be McGinnis's problem.

It was too late to change it. And she was damned if she was going to apologize for it. She was supposed to appear in the editor in chief's office in half an hour— Clement was coming to fetch her and provide moral support. If she was fired, so be it. More time for her to work on her own projects. If she had to recant, she might be able to manage it. After all, she was uneasily aware that it had been a low blow, one he more than deserved, of course, but perhaps not quite fair.

No one could sue her. She had no money, nothing of value to anyone except the trunk of her father's scripts and notes. They'd been left to her when he died, and she hadn't been able to bring herself to open it until this year. She was going through it like a miser, hoarding the discoveries, and no one even knew of its existence. Marjorie had forgotten long ago.

She heard the Daimler pull up outside, and she rose, forcing herself not to hurry. She glanced at her reflection in the mirror, but no fairy godmother had waltzed by with her magic wand. Still the same long narrow face, blue eyes that gave everything away, strong chin and nose. She looked clever and secretive beneath the thick mop of dark hair, and she felt neither. She felt like a woman in deep trouble. And Clement's doleful expression when she answered the door was no reassurance whatsoever.

"We'll fight this thing, darling," he announced, kissing the air beside her ear. "We won't let them railroad you. McGinnis has gotten away with too much in this town for too long. We're not going to let him crucify you because his macho pride is offended."

"I don't know why he'd want to crucify me," she said miserably, waiting for Clement's chauffeur to open the car door for her. "After all, no one usually reads my stuff anyway. I just fill in for you. If he keeps quiet about it no one will notice."

"I'm afraid that's not quite the case," Clement said sadly. "Your column's been the talk of the town today."

"Don't exaggerate, Clement."

"There's going to be something on *Entertainment Tonight* about it."

"Oh, no!"

"Oh, no, indeed," Clement said, climbing in beside her and waiting while the door was closed silently behind him. "So our only choice is to brazen this out. McGinnis is a barbarian, but he can't come out of this looking like a bully. Even if he doesn't care about public relations, Bernie does. She'll keep him in line."

"Who's Bernie?"

"You really are ignorant, aren't you, darling? And I thought I'd made such advances in your education. Bernie is Bernadette Thomas, one of the most powerful women in Hollywood, and you don't even know who she is."

"Of course I know who Bernadette Thomas is," Silver said irritably. "I just didn't know she was the Bernie you were talking about. She's been around since forever. Long before McGinnis and his horde made their appearance."

"I believe she was a friend of your dear father's."

"Apparently half of Hollywood was," Silver said dryly. "Was she stacked and beautiful?"

"As a matter of fact, Bernie has always been lamentably plain and dumpy."

"Then she must have been the only woman in Hollywood my father didn't sleep with."

"You've been listening to your mother again. Marjorie has such a jaundiced view," Clement said sadly. "Your father was a brilliant man. In this life, the rules don't apply to geniuses."

Silver felt a reluctant grin curve her mouth. "Maybe that's what Rafe McGinnis thinks, too."

"That . . . that mongrel," Clement fumed.

"Oh, come on, Clement, that's not up to your usual style," Silver said lightly. " 'Mongrel'?"

"My mind isn't working at full capacity. I'm worried for you, Silver. I'd hate to think I'd lose you because you were a bit . . . incautious."

"I was furious," she admitted. "Let's call a spade a spade. I suppose I could bring myself to apologize to the man. If I don't choke on the words."

"I imagine, dear heart, that any apology would need to be in print. And I don't think it's going to be that simple."

Silver glanced at him. "You think he's going to want his pound of flesh?"

Clement's faded blue eyes surveyed her with a doubtful expression. "Well, you aren't exactly Madonna, my dear, and he can have his pick of just about anyone . . ."

"I didn't mean that," she said, not at all stung by his disparaging opinion of her natural attractions. She was used to Clement's brutal honesty by now, and her opinion of her own beauty or lack thereof was low enough. "I mean is he going to want to nail my hide to the wall? See me cut down in my prime, never eat lunch in this town again and all that?"

"I really don't know," Clement said in a sepulchral voice. "Let's not anticipate disaster, shall we? I imagine it will find us soon enough."

"How comforting," Silver said faintly as they pulled up outside the *Los Angeles Clarion*.

"I do try to be," Clement replied.

"SO HERE'S THE DEAL, Ms. Carlysle." Jim Steuben, managing editor, pointed a short stubby finger at her. "Mr. McGinnis has decided to be magnanimous about the whole thing."

"Very magnanimous," Royal Penston, features editor, echoed.

"You will apologize in print," Steuben said.

"In print," Penston echoed.

"You will cease to even mention his name or that of any Mack Movie production in future reviews."

"Future reviews," said Penston.

"And you will present yourself, properly attired, at the Beverly Wilton Hotel tomorrow night at a party being thrown in honor of Mack Movies' sale to Pegasus Pictures."

"Outrageous!" Clement sputtered.

"Properly attired as what?" Silver said with deceptive calm. "A waiter? Does he want me to serve his guests? Or no, let me guess. He wants me to jump out of a cake. I certainly hope he can find one big enough."

"This is absurd, insulting..." Clement railed, but Steuben overrode him.

"You're to be an honored guest."

"For what purpose?" she asked warily.

"Mr. McGinnis has made it clear that he doesn't like the nasty innuendo going around, coupled with the gossip."

"If the dear boy doesn't like innuendo and gossip then he shouldn't live in Hollywood," Clement observed.

"Keep out of this, Clement, it doesn't concern you," Steuben said.

"On the contrary, it does indeed. If McGinnis insists we put on a farce as his honored guests I assure you..."

"Not you, Clement," Steuben said. "Just Silver."

There was a moment of silence. "Don't be ridiculous. She won't go, of course," Clement said.

"Yes, she will," Steuben said.

"She will," echoed Penston.

"I would think," Silver finally broke in, "that it would be up to me."

The three men turned to stare at her as if a chair had suddenly begun to talk. "Not really," Steuben said finally. "McGinnis has come up with an offer we can't refuse. You're a film buff, Silver, you should remember that quote. If you do happen to refuse, then I can honestly tell you you're finished in this business."

"You'll never eat lunch in this town again," she muttered under her breath. "Why?"

"Oh, for a number of reasons, Ms. Carlysle," Penston volunteered in a particularly snotty tone of voice. "For one, your so-called review bordered on libelous, and we're just lucky Mr. McGinnis isn't inclined to sue."

"Well, he's certainly got you two on the run," Clement observed blandly. "How did he manage to turn you both into frightened, witless rabbits? And I'm giving rabbits a bad name."

"He threatened to pull all advertising for Mack Movies. And not just from the *Clarion*. From the entire chain of *Clarion*-owned newspapers. Do you comprehend what kind of revenue we're talking about?"

Clement waved an airy hand. "I seldom bother my head with business. Would you really have me believe that McGinnis is that powerful?"

"Believe it," Steuben said. "So here's the deal, Ms. Carlysle. You do everything McGinnis tells you to tomorrow night, the apology goes in print for the Sunday edition, and you may come out of this with your job intact."

"Only may?" Clement asked. "I'm not sure if I can consider that a strong enough guarantee."

"You stay out of this, Walden. Your nose isn't any too clean in all this. You should have checked her copy."

"I still don't think she ought to lower herself..."

"I'll do it," Silver said quite calmly.

"Don't be ridiculous, darling, I won't allow it," Clement said firmly.

"I said I'll do it. After all, it's not as if he's going to expect me to perform odd sexual acts for his friends."

"Silver!" Clement was shocked.

"I'm sure he's just going to do his best to humiliate me. And when it comes right down to it, no one can be humiliated unless they want to. I'll be absolutely fine, Clement."

Her elderly friend looked both petulant and extremely doubtful. "I only hope you know what you're getting into, my dear."

Silver thought back to Rafe McGinnis, with those cool, greenish eyes and his monumental arrogance. Tempered by a streak of truly dangerous charm. She could put up with a few hours of him if it suited her purpose, and she had no intention of losing her job if she could help it.

She'd put up with him, she'd be polite, well-behaved, her mother's daughter, and then she'd keep as far away from Mack Movies and Rafe McGinnis as was humanly possible in such a deceptively small town like Hollywood.

Because the man unsettled her. Pure and simple. And the only way to get past it was to beard the lion in his den. Face him, face her uneasiness, and learn that he was simply an arrogant suit, like so many men she'd known.

And then he wouldn't be any problem at all. Would he? She could only find that she devoutly hoped so. Clement was looking at her with a doubtful expression, one that fed her own uneasiness.

"I'll be absolutely fine," she said again. And she only wished she could believe it.

# Chapter Three

Once the notion of revenge entered Silver's mind there was no dislodging it. No amount of common sense or latent feelings of self-preservation could make any dent in her decision. She spent that evening alone in her apartment, trying to talk herself out of it. By six o'clock the next morning she knew she was going to do it.

It took her the better part of the day to find just the right dress. Even the vintage-clothing stores didn't go in for the level of ghastliness Silver wanted, and it wasn't until she came to the Funky Fifties Resale Shop that she discovered The Dress.

It was an absolute treasure. Clearly designed for someone closer to five feet than six, it was made of bright pink chiffon, adorned with row after row of tiny ruffles that would have made the original wearer of the dress look even plumper than she obviously had to be. It was strapless, with a crinolined skirt that brushed Silver's ankles and stood straight around. It looked like the prom dress for a girl who'd never be asked to a prom, and when Silver tried it on she almost cried with laughter.

The waist came halfway up to her admittedly generous breasts, adding to the wonderfully frumpy look.

The chiffon neckline sagged, making her look even more generously endowed, and the expanse of ankle beneath the frilly hem was the perfect touch.

"Costume party?" the woman with the rhinestone glasses inquired. Silver wanted those glasses too, but she figured that might be going too far.

"You might say so," she murmured. "I don't suppose you have any silver open-toed sandals?"

"Not in your size, dearie. Try a pair of ballet slippers."

"I need heels," Silver said stubbornly, reaching for a rhinestone tiara with several of the stones missing.

"You're going to look choice," the woman said dryly.

"Let's hope so."

Her hair was a challenge. She cut it herself, in a scruffy shag she usually washed and ignored, and she knew from experience nothing on this earth would induce it to curl. She had to make do with her mother's gels and sprays, sneaking into the big house while Marjorie was out playing bridge. The last thing she wanted to do was explain her odd behavior. Marjorie did her best to keep out of the Hollywood mainstream. With luck, she'd never hear about "the hottest feud of the week," as *Entertainment Tonight* had dubbed it.

At the last minute she glanced through her mother's jewelry case. Harry regularly presented his wife with tokens of his devotion, and Marjorie made certain she got exactly what she wanted, but occasionally Harry had gotten his own way. One of the results of that was a monumentally ugly necklace made of diamonds, rubies and emeralds. It was heavy, old and very valuable, a treasured heirloom from Harry's tasteless family. Marjorie was almost pathologically possessive about it, despite the fact she never wore it. Silver held it against her smooth throat. Perfect. The rubies would clash wonderfully with the dress.

She stole her mother's Irish silk cape while she was at it. She needed to make an entrance. If Rafael Mc-Ginnis had any idea what she was about to do to him he might circumvent her, which would be an absolute tragedy when she considered all the effort she'd gone to to look deliciously ghastly for him.

At that point she stopped worrying about her job, her future in the movie industry and her ability to lunch therein, even Clement's concern meant nothing to her. She wanted to embarrass Rafe McGinnis, the powerful, invulnerable head of Mack Movies, and she no longer cared what it cost her.

He was sending a car for her, probably to make sure she showed up. He needn't have worried. She wouldn't have missed this evening for anything.

RAFE DESPISED Hollywood parties. He always had. In the old days they were simply an excuse for excess—sexual, alcoholic and everything else. Deals were made and broken at those parties, deals that never should have been conceived of in the first place. But at least the excesses had kept boredom at bay.

Bernie was right, being on the A-list had its definite drawbacks. Hollywood survived on information—gossip and innuendo included. And the only way to gather that information was at parties. It didn't matter if he was bored to tears, standing in a noisy crowd of over-dressed magpies, smoke clogging his throat, alcohol numbing his brain and sizzling his nerves. He had to be there, particularly when he was the one giving the party.

He stood alone and waited, inviolate, his sunglasses his only protection from the curious crowds.

Tonight was different from all those other nights. Tonight he could tolerate the sheer repetitiveness of it all because he was about to throw everyone a zinger. It had been sheer instinct that had made him deliver his ultimatum to Steuben. His rage at Silver Carlysle had been monumental, a wave of emotion that had left him shaken and curiously refreshed. For the first time in what seemed like years he felt alive.

He'd sounded very reasonable when he'd told Steuben what he wanted, but he didn't think anyone was fooled. He didn't want Silver Carlysle on his arm to convince the Hollywood gossips that there really wasn't a feud. He wanted her there to humiliate her. And he wanted her there because his furious reaction to her sanctimonious scribbling was the first thing he'd felt outside of crashing boredom in months. He wanted to savor it for as long as it lasted.

It wouldn't last long, of course. Silver Carlysle would probably either be so pedantic that he'd tire of the sport, or else she'd become annoyingly attracted to him. Women had a habit of doing that, even women who started out despising him. It had been a useful gift in the past, but occasionally it began to feel like a Midas touch. Just once he'd like a woman to stand up to him without melting. It wasn't as if he had any delusions about himself. Women didn't find him irresistible. They found his power worth lusting after.

"So where's your date?" Sam wandered up to Rafe, a drink in his hand. "Don't tell me you're going stag tonight? Has the beautiful Ms. Allison already gone the way of all flesh?"

Rafe ignored him, glancing out over the crowd. "I have a special guest tonight."

"Listen, Rafe, no one's special to you," Sam said. "At the rate you go through women there'll be no one left. Who's the virgin sacrifice for tonight?"

"You know, Sam," Rafe said in a meditative voice, lighting a cigarette, "maybe that's what I need."

"A virgin? You're in the wrong town for that, buddy."

"Not specifically a virgin. But maybe I need a good woman. A sweet, supportive little woman in an apron, to cook my meals, have my babies, give me back rubs at the end of a long day."

"Donna Reed's dead."

"I'm serious, Sam. Maybe I need a nice woman to clear my palate."

"We're talking about commitment here, Rafe, not lemon sorbet. Bernie would cut your heart out if she heard you."

"Bernie's used to me."

"So what's coming tonight? A bimbo or a fruit ice?"

Rafe's eyes narrowed behind his omnipresent sunglasses as he spotted a tall figure at the end of the room, flanked by his chauffeur. She was dressed decently enough, in a silk cape, and for a moment he felt a sudden sense of disappointment. She must be easily cowed. According to Steuben, she'd agreed to his demand without demur, and here she was, right on time, moving toward him across the crowded room. He watched her, feeling the accustomed boredom settle around him.

"Same old thing," he said to Sam, who was following his gaze.

"Maybe you'd better take off your shades, old man," Sam said dryly. "I think you've underestimated your date for the evening."

There was real glee in Sam's voice. Rafe cast him a startled look, then lifted his shades to get a better look at his reluctant partner.

"Oh my God," he breathed in a shaken voice.

"That's Silver Carlysle, I take it," Sam said. "When you go for a change of pace you don't go half measures. I think I'm going to enjoy this."

"Not half as much as I am," Rafe said, letting his glasses drop back down on his nose.

She reached him, her long legs carrying her across the room with the majesty of a sailing ship. He could see her face beneath the silk hood—the frizz of hair, the slash of bright red lipstick, the unevenly rouged cheeks. He'd had a glimpse of hot-pink ruffles beneath the cape, and he stood there, keeping the smile from his face as he waited.

"Mr. McGinnis," she said, in that throaty, damn-you voice he found himself remembering.

"Call me Rafe," he said, exerting all his charm. "Can I help you with your cape?"

So smug, he thought, watching the smile curve those ruby lips. Reaching up, she unfastened the cape, letting it fall into his chauffeur's hands.

In any other crowd her emergence would have caused a hush to fall. As it was, there was a gasp or two, a smothered giggle, and merely an increase in noise as people immediately digested the full glory of her appearance.

He grinned then. He couldn't help it. "A little predictable," he drawled. "But nice, nonetheless." He reached out with his long fingers and touched the magnificently ugly necklace around her throat. She probably thought she looked dumpy in that horrible dress. She did. But she also looked quite surprisingly luscious with that strapless neckline falling off her.

He felt it, of course. The shiver of reaction that rippled across her warm skin when he touched her. It should have bored him. Instead it fascinated him. Particularly when she looked so defiant and oblivious to the strong sensual thread that spread between them.

"I went to a great deal of trouble to look just right for you," she said, and her husky voice sent shivers down his spine.

That bothered him. It was one thing to be amused by her, fascinated by her, even attracted to her. It was another to feel such an intense pull.

"You succeeded admirably," he murmured, drawing her bare arm through his. Her skin felt hot and sleek beneath his fingertips, and he had the sudden notion that it was going to be a long night. And far too short. "Let me introduce you around. I'm certain people are dying to find out who my mysterious guest is."

It hit her then. He wondered how long it would take her to realize the magnitude of what she'd done. She'd been out to embarrass him, and she'd never considered what it would do to her own credibility.

He could take pity on her. Introduce her simply as Silver, and most people would have no idea she was the infamous S. H. Carlysle who'd trashed him so effectively in the *Clarion*.

But he hadn't brought her out to be merciful. "I know the other guests are dying to know who is my exotic companion. They'll be even more interested to find out you're my nemesis from the *Clarion*. Not to mention Clement Walden's protégée."

He felt her flinch. She hadn't thought about that aspect of it, either—that her admirably tacky appearance would reflect on the so-perfect Walden. "Uh..." she said, suddenly hesitant. "Do you suppose you could do me a favor?"

"Now why would I want to?"

She didn't look daunted, simply more determined. The effect oddly beguiling in her bizarre apparel. "I can't imagine why. Nevertheless, I'd appreciate it if you didn't mention my connection to Clement. Most people here are smart enough to figure that out—there's no need to remind them."

"Did he approve of your little outfit?"

"He doesn't know."

"I thought as much. I think you overestimate my guests. Most of them haven't got the brains of three maggots put together."

"If you don't like them why did you invite them?" she asked with a certain charming ingenuousness.

"But Silver," he countered gently, "you don't think I like you, do you?"

He waited for her to flinch. Instead she surprised him again by managing a rueful smile. "Good point," she conceded.

"Aren't you going to introduce us?" Sam had reappeared, Bernie in tow. Bernie was looking frankly disapproving, but Rafe didn't make the mistake of thinking that disapproval was for Silver's outrageous attire. He never made the mistake of underestimating Bernie. She would know exactly who Silver Carlysle was, and assume by her apparel that she wasn't there willingly.

"Silver Carlysle, may I introduce my associates, Bernie Thomas and Sam Mendelsohn?"

"What's going on here, Rafe?" Bernie demanded.

"Nothing at all, Bernie," he said blandly. "I thought I'd try to charm Silver over to our way of thinking."

"Sure you did," Bernie said, glaring at him. "Don't let him intimidate you, Silver. He's an arrogant SOB, but he's not evil. I knew your father." She changed the subject with her customary abruptness.

The effect on Silver Carlysle was instantaneous. Wary, hopeful, pleased all at once. "Did you?" she countered neutrally, but Rafe could feel the tension in the arm he had tucked beneath his.

"He was a good man. One of the best," Bernie said.

There was no mistaking the shy smile on Silver's carmined lips. It changed her whole face, softening it beneath the outrageous makeup, and the curious tightening in Rafe's gut increased. "I thought so," she said shyly.

"Who's her father?" Sam asked the question before Rafe could.

"Nobody you knew," Bernie said repressively.

Rafe didn't bother to pursue it. He knew Bernie in that kind of mood—nothing would elicit the information if she wasn't ready to give it.

Silver Carlysle was a different matter. He had the unnerving feeling that she was a Hollywood rarity—a real innocent. She wouldn't stand a chance against him.

He steered her around the crowded room, pausing long enough to give her a glass of champagne she insisted she didn't want, introducing her to a few choice people. People who wouldn't fail to make the connection, even if he didn't point it out.

She was miserably aware of it, too. By the time an umpteenth person said, "Oh, you write for the *Clarion*," and accompanied it with a knowing leer in Rafe's direction, her credibility was effectively sabotaged. He wondered whether he ought to feel the slightest bit guilty, then dismissed the notion. She'd started it, she'd upped the ante. Now it was time to pay the piper.

She held up with surprising stamina. Once she realized she couldn't free herself by tugging her arm loose, she accepted his possessive grip. She didn't know anyone in the room, another surprise, given the size and cross section of the gathering, and the fact that her father was someone who'd once been important to Bernie.

He'd caught on to that right away. Bernie was the least sentimental person he knew, and yet she still felt something for Silver Carlysle's mysterious father.

"Ready to leave?" he asked pleasantly enough a couple of hours later.

He looked down at her, caught for a moment by the deep blue of her eyes. She looked tense, exhausted and edgy, all at the same time. And he wondered what she'd look like in bed, all that edginess wiped away.

"Leave? Is the party over?" She glanced around her.

"It is for me."

"I thought I was only supposed to come to the party."

"Think again. We're going to dinner next."

"Alone?" Her voice was husky, tinged with an odd nervousness.

"In a public restaurant. You're safe with me," he said dryly.

"Why?"

"Why are you safe with me?"

"No. Why do you want me to have dinner with you? Haven't you humiliated me enough for one night?"

"Darlin'," he said, allowing a Western drawl to sneak into his voice, "I've only just begun."

SHE REALLY HATED HIM. She wasn't someone who hated easily—she tried to accept people, faults and all. She didn't care much for her stepfather, or her first boyfriend, or her physics professor in college, but she didn't hate them, or anybody else.

Except Rafael McGinnis. With his sunglasses at the dead of night and his condescending smile and his Armani suits and his strong, powerful body, she despised him from the bottom of her heart. It didn't help matters that her act of petty vengeance had backfired, causing embarrassment only to herself. It only made her detest him more.

He was watching her from behind those sunglasses, coolly, as if her response didn't matter in the slightest. She'd like to tell him where he could put his dinner invitation, but she'd come this far, she might as well go the whole way. He couldn't very well introduce her to everyone at the restaurant, maybe she still had a chance of giving him just a taste of embarrassment. Besides, she was curious as to what he'd say to her, once they no longer had an audience.

The chauffeured Bentley was waiting for them. Once more she climbed into the spacious back seat, only to find that it wasn't as spacious as she'd thought it was, when McGinnis crammed his six foot plus frame in beside her.

Apparently the evening had been planned ahead of time. Rafe leaned back beside her, as the car moved smoothly into traffic, and the smoked-glass partition kept the chauffeur well isolated.

The light was dim in the back seat, deliberately so, she knew. She wasn't a peasant, she'd been driven in Bentleys before. In just about every luxury car known to Hollywood as well. She eyed Rafe nervously as she edged away from him across the black leather seat.

"There's not that much room on the seat," he observed, making no effort to move after her. But of course, why should he? He was right, she was a captive audience.

"You don't really want me to go out to dinner with you," she said, having had enough. "You've accomplished what you set out to do in the first place. Everyone at the party knew who I was without you even introducing me."

"I shouldn't have underestimated them," he agreed. "Hollywood partygoers are like sharks when there's blood in the water. They can sniff out scandal anywhere."

"You didn't need to cling to me in such a...a friendly way," she continued. "Your plan was very successful. They assume we're sleeping together, and that my recent reviews of your disgusting movies were simply the result of personal pique."

"They do believe that, don't they?" he said, unmoved by her wrath.

"My credibility has been destroyed. People will think I let my emotions and prejudices color my reviews."

"Don't you?"

She glared at him. Not that he could see it, hidden behind those damned sunglasses. Unfortunately she wasn't able to come up with the words to refute his uncomfortable charge.

"I wouldn't worry about it if I were you," he continued smoothly. "Your credibility might be destroyed, but your career will flourish. People love scandal, they love malice, and if they think sex is behind it, so much the better.''

"Sex has nothing to do with it!''

At that he lifted his sunglasses. His eyes were very dark, almost black in the dimly lighted comfort of the back seat, and they surveyed her with far too much acumen. "Sex has something to do with everything," he said. "You know, that dress backfired.''

"I'm well aware of it. I'm the one who looked like a fool, not you.''

"I wouldn't say that. At least you showed everyone that you weren't cowed by me. That's rare. But that wasn't what I was referring to. Obviously you chose that dress in the hope that you'd look impossibly frumpy and thereby keep my animal urges at bay. I'm afraid it's not working. The dress is remarkably frumpy. It's also surprisingly... luscious.''

She stared at him in total astonishment. "You can't be attracted to me," she said bluntly.

"Oh, but I could," he murmured. "I am.'' And he reached for her, pulling her back across the seat and into his arms while she was still too shocked to resist.

## Chapter Four

His mouth was hard against hers, hot and wet. He kissed her with a thoroughness that should have been insulting, but instead simply devastated her. He used one hand beneath her chin, holding her head still for his openmouthed kiss. The other was at the sagging neckline of her strapless dress, tugging it down.

For a moment her brain simply went numb, awash with the undeniably wonderful physical sensations of his hands and mouth. It had been so long since she'd been touched, even in friendship. So long since she'd been kissed like that. As a matter of fact, she didn't think she'd ever been kissed like that.

They used to talk about soul kisses. That's what this one was. Not simply a matter of mouths and lips and tongues. It was heart and mind and soul, it was something so powerful that it wiped out all her defenses, her judgment, her self-preservation.

For a moment the struggle was inside her, fighting against the insidious gentleness of his mouth on hers, wooing, seducing, fighting against the hands on her body, holding her but not restraining her. She lost that fight with a deep, inward sigh, giving in to the unbearable temptation to kiss him back, to let her lips soften beneath his, to touch his tongue with hers, to start on that downward slide of desire that could end in places she'd never been before.

It wasn't until she realized he was pushing her down on the wide leather seat, until she felt the coolness of the air, the heat of his skin against her bare breasts, that her sense of self-preservation surfaced again, and this time the struggle was outward, as she realized what she was doing. And with whom.

She shoved, hard, using her hands, her knees, and he released her with a less-than-flattering acceptance. He fell back on the bench seat opposite her, and his eyes glittered in the darkness.

"Didn't you like it?" he said, his voice a faint whiskey drawl.

She wanted to slap him. She wanted to screech "How dare you?" like a proper, outraged heroine. She had the self-control to do neither, struggling to a sitting position and yanking the sagging dress up around her. "What was that for? Just to see if I'd do it?" she countered. It was just too bad that her shaky voice gave away her reaction.

He shrugged, reaching for his sunglasses on the floor, and she wanted to stomp on them. "It was worth a try," he murmured, unrepentant.

"Why? To humiliate me further?"

"No, actually, it was just spur of the moment. I wanted to." His smile was rueful, disarming. Silver refused to be disarmed.

"Stop the car."

"Oh, God, don't go all melodramatic on me," he sighed. "I swear, I won't touch you again. Scout's honor."

"Stop the car," she said between clenched teeth, "or I'll jump out of it while it's still moving."

For a moment he didn't say a word. She couldn't see his reaction behind the glasses, but she could imagine it. He rapped on the window. "Stop the car," he ordered the driver.

The huge, boatlike limousine cruised to a stately halt. Before she could leap out, Rafe was ahead of her, opening the door for her and stepping into the brightly lighted street.

To her covert relief they were on the edge of Beverly Hills, only six or seven blocks from her mother's house. She could slip off her hellishly uncomfortable spike heels and walk home barefoot in no time.

She spurned his offered arm as she stepped down from the limo, but she'd underestimated him. He caught her arm as she tried to jerk away, and she stumbled, coming up against him in the street.

"Be reasonable, Silver," he said. "Get back in the car and I'll drive you home. I'll do my best to resist my animal passions."

She could feel his heart beating rapidly beneath his shirtfront, belying the bored expression on his half-hidden face. She didn't trust him, but most of all she didn't trust herself, didn't trust what had almost happened. "I can walk," she said, yanking herself away from him.

He let her go. "Don't bother to thank me for a lovely evening," he said. "The pleasure was all mine."

"I'm sure it was." She started down the street, head held high, her mother's silk cape over one arm, when his deep, slow voice trailed after her.

"I have just one question, Silver. Who exactly is your father?"

She was glad he couldn't see her. She couldn't keep her spine from stiffening in alarm, but there was no way her face would give her away. She ignored him, continuing to trudge down the sidewalk, half expecting him to follow her. A moment later she heard the car door slam, and the limo drove off.

She turned to watch him leave, feeling curiously deflated. She hadn't wanted to waste another breath on him. For one thing, she didn't want to discuss her father, but she put no faith whatsoever in her ability to keep his identity away from McGinnis. He'd keep at it until he found out what he wanted to know.

Not that it should matter. She'd gone by her mother's name since she was twelve, when her father had agreed to let her stepfather adopt her. There was no way she'd take *his* name, and no way she'd continue to have the name of the father who no longer wanted her. Her mother was at least making an effort, and she'd been Silver Carlysle ever since, and very few people had made the connection. It wasn't as if she was petite and ravishing like her mother. She favored her father—tall, rangy, long-legged, and handsome rather than pretty.

Rafe was right, though. This was a town of gossips, a town where there were no secrets if someone was determined enough to find the truth. Her mother had been moderately well-known—if someone just put the name Carlysle together with Marjorie, the late Benjamin Hatcher would be the next obvious step.

She just hoped no one would take it. The divorce had been messy, painful, but not as bad as the fact that her father had been completely willing to let her go. He'd given her nothing but a trunk full of papers and enough money for a useless education. She wasn't about to trade on his name in a name-conscious place like Hollywood.

She turned the corner, slipping off her shoes and letting her stockinged feet wiggle on the cement sidewalk. People seldom walked in that area of town—they relied on their chauffeurs and their indoor exercise tracks. She'd probably make it back to the house without passing a single soul, but she pulled the silk cape around her anyway, tying it round her bare throat. She'd made it through the evening without it ending in complete disaster. She'd made a fool of herself, but she wasn't possessed of such overwhelming dignity that she couldn't survive it. The worst part of the evening was the end of it. When Rafe McGinnis had taken it into his head to kiss her.

She still couldn't quite figure out why. His romantic exploits had been legendary—only Warren Beatty seemed to go through more gorgeous women. She didn't for one minute believe he'd truly been attracted to her. At her best she'd fall far short of his usual standard of beauty. Dressed in frumpy nylon with frizzy hair, she'd been a disaster.

His heart had been beating fast, though. Even through her own besotted reaction she could see that he hadn't been unmoved by her. But why had he kissed her? If it was part of some grand scheme of revenge, why hadn't he done it in public?

There was no way she was going to make any sense of it. No way she even wanted to. She needed to put his kiss from her mind. After all, it was no surprise that it was the most powerful kiss she'd ever had in her life. He'd certainly had enough experience, if the tabloids were to be believed. One had to pick up a certain amount of skill.

Her mother had guests in. Silver trudged up the driveway, her feet hurting, her dress still drooping embarrassingly low as she crept past the multitude of Daimlers, Bentleys and Cadillacs. She kept to the bushes, waving at the chauffeur who was serving as security.

Wilkers waved back, used to her by now, as she climbed to her apartment above the garage. Her answering machine was blinking, but for once she didn't succumb to temptation and rush to see who'd called her. It was probably just Clement, wanting to know how the evening went. She wasn't quite ready to tell him all the gory details. And she certainly wasn't going to tell him the truth about how the evening ended.

She dumped the silk cape on the wicker sofa and headed for the kitchen, grabbing her staple of caffeine-free cola and draining half the can. She needed a shower and a good night's sleep to put things in perspective. She was heading toward the bedroom when she stopped, unable to resist, in front of the huge mirror her mother had banished from her own bedroom before her most recent face-lift.

Luscious, he'd said. The man was crazy. Her usually thick straight black hair was frizzed around her narrow face, her blue eyes were absurd beneath the heavy makeup, her lipstick was smeared across her slightly swollen mouth. And then she remembered why her lipstick was smeared, and she put a tentative hand up to her lips.

Luscious? Absurd. Exotic, perhaps. Not quite the plain Jane as she tended to think of herself. But surely not luscious.

She didn't trust him. Didn't trust a word the man said. But still, as she ran a tentative hand across the broad expanse of bare skin that ran from her neck to the top of the silly pink dress, she thought in this case he might just be right.

"ARE YOU STILL PLANNING on dinner, sir?"

Rafe stretched out in the limo, rousing himself from his abstraction. "Not tonight, Jimmy. Drive me home."

"Yes, sir." The answer, polite as always, nevertheless suggested a certain level of disapproval. Jimmy had been driving him for the past ten years, before that he'd been employed by Pegasus Pictures to drive all their most important executives. He was as old and almost as savvy as Bernie, and he figured it gave him some privileges.

"Okay, out with it," Rafe said with a sigh, sliding the glass partition open.

"Out with what, sir?" Jimmy said stiffly.

"I can sense your disapproval a mile away. You think I'm a turkey, don't you?"

"I wouldn't put it quite that way, sir," Jimmy said. Centuries ago he'd been born in England, and he still clung to an artificially correct way of speaking that Rafe usually found humorous. Tonight, however, his sense of humor was slightly impaired.

"How would you put it?" he asked in a deceptively gentle voice.

Jimmy knew him well enough to hear the edge beneath the seeming amiability. He also knew him well enough not to be cowed by it. "A cad," he offered. "A bounder, though that's a bit archaic."

"You must have been talking to Bernie," Rafe grumbled.

"No, sir. Reading your mind."

"You're too smart for your own britches, Jimmy."

"Yes, sir."

The interior of the Bentley, Jimmy's favored mode of transportation, was silent for a moment. "Where does she live?" Rafe asked suddenly.

"Where does who live?"

"Don't be obtuse, Jimmy. Where did you pick her up?"

"She won't have far to walk, if you suddenly remembered a gentlemanly concern for her well-being."

"I can always fire you."

Jimmy's derisive sniff was answer enough.

"Does she live with Clement Walden? I know that's highly unlikely, but she is his protégée."

"Mr. Walden lives in Holmby Hills."

"If you think Steuben at the *Clarion* won't tell me, you'd better think again."

Jimmy's long-suffering sigh conveyed a world of disappointment in him. But he gave him the address in a flat voice.

Rafe let out a whistle. "Pretty fancy neighborhood."

"She lives over the garage." He pronounced it in the British manner, accent on the first syllable, and Rafe gritted his teeth, controlling the urge to remind Jimmy he'd been in L.A. for more than fifty years.

"People who live in that area don't need to rent out apartments," he said instead. "Who owns the place?"

"I couldn't say, sir."

"You're a pain in the butt, Jimmy."

"Yes, sir."

"And you know I won't be able to get anything out of Bernie, either."

"Ms. Thomas has a most excellent sense of discretion."

"And why does she have to be discreet about a second-string reviewer for a local newspaper?"

"I couldn't say, sir."

Rafe's reaction was satisfyingly obscene. Jimmy merely clucked disapprovingly in the back of his throat as Rafe slammed the dividing window shut.

Jimmy must have been put up to it by Bernie. The two of them were as thick as thieves, and whenever he saw them with their heads together his blood ran cold. It usually boded something unpleasant for him.

But what was the big secret about Silver Carlysle? Obviously she came from old Hollywood stock. Bernie had no respect for the nouveau film types, and it was clear that Silver merited her highest approval simply on account of her lineage. But the address didn't give anything away. He knew Beverly Hills very well, and no one of any consequence lived in the area where Silver Carlysle did. There were mainly bankers and businessmen, the plutocrats of California with their manicured lawns and elitist life-style. Maybe Silver was the daughter of a banker.

No, Bernie hated bankers and businessmen as much as he did. If his associate thought she'd keep him from finding out everything he could about Silver Carlysle, then she'd certainly gone about it the wrong way. Everything she'd said and done had simply piqued his interest. He wasn't going to be able to get the woman out of his mind until he found out everything he wanted to know about her.

And he did want to get her out of his mind. Her mouth had been soft, startled beneath his, her reaction to his deliberately overwhelming kiss had been both unpracticed and disturbingly...endearing. He usually found the chase to be the most interesting part of his romantic entanglements, and he tended to get bored once things got settled.

But Silver Carlysle's hands had dug into his shoulders for a moment, and her untutored mouth had kissed him back, and he'd been more powerfully aroused than he could remember.

That was dangerous. He found his life eminently agreeable. A little boring, maybe, but that's why he had his sports car. He didn't want to take risks when it came to other human beings.

No, he wanted to get Silver Carlysle settled into a safe little niche in his mind, so he could forget about her. As long as there were unresolved questions about her, she'd linger. And she was just too damned distracting for his peace of mind.

He glanced out the smoked windows of the Bentley as Jimmy sailed through the nighttime streets of L.A. He could always lean forward, rap on the window again and have Jimmy take a detour to Marcia Allison's bungalow. Jimmy's disapproval would reach monumental proportions, but that was the least of his worries. It would get Silver Carlysle off his mind.

He had no doubts about his welcome. And that was half the problem. It wouldn't matter to Marcia that he'd just hosted a large party and she hadn't been invited. It wouldn't matter that he'd slept with her once, rejected her the second time. And it was that knowledge that kept him from rapping on the window.

He had a videotape of *Cop for a Day,* the movie Silver had trashed with stunning effectiveness. He'd sat through it on several occasions, not paying much attention, but he made a practice of having all the new releases transferred to his own personal videotape. Maybe he'd go home, pour himself a drink and watch the stupid movie. And remind himself what an elitist Silver Carlysle really was. Even if she did have wounded eyes.

But if he expected comfort he should have known better. He was a man who'd stripped comfort from his life, and there was none to be had when he needed it. His house, constantly under renovation, greeted him in dark silence when he entered. He'd bought it on an impulse, falling for its absurd Moorish outlines. It had been built sometime in the late 1920s, and it hadn't aged well. He'd been pouring money into it nonstop since he bought the place, and the end wasn't in sight. It was too small, too impractical, and about as far from the rustic simplicity of the log cabin in Colorado where he'd spent the first fifteen years of his life as he could find. And bizarre as it was, it was the only place he really felt at home.

He poured himself two fingers of single malt, ignoring the conventional wisdom that he shouldn't drink alone. Even with his mother's history as a bad example, he wasn't about to forgo his nightly drink. Especially when he had so damned much to sort through.

Three hours later he sat alone in the darkened living room. The television was a bright blue light, the videotape long ended, but Rafe didn't move.

So all right, it wasn't the finest movie ever made. It wasn't going to win Oscars or even Golden Globes, but it was going to make an obscene amount of money, millions of people were going to see it, and what the hell did it matter if a bunch of film snobs didn't find it socially redeeming?

It didn't matter, he decided finally. What mattered was that he hated it, too.

He rose, kicking over the coffee table, knocking his empty glass to the floor, and stalked to the bay of windows that looked out over the valley. There were too many lights, too many people, too many years gone by.

He thought about his father, dead on a mountain pass in a Colorado blizzard. His mother, quietly drinking herself to death afterward. And he wondered whether it would hurt if he smashed his fist through the thick plate glass.

He turned on his heel, moving back through the darkened house with unerring instinct. The Lotus started immediately, with a throaty rumble, and he tore off into the night, not even bothering to lock his house.

He needed to drive away his demons, as fast and as hard as the highly tuned Lotus could take him. He needed to wipe out his lingering sense of depression caused by that stupid movie. Depression was for weaklings. He needed to wipe out the memory of his parents and his lost childhood. He needed to wipe out the memory of Colorado, the sweet, clean mountain air, the mountains, the stillness, both outer and inner, that you could find there. And he needed to wipe out the memory of Silver Carlysle. The last innocent in Hollywood.

"WHAT DOES THIS MEAN, 'the bizarrely costumed Ms. Carlysle'?" Clement demanded.

Silver blindly reached for a coffee, wishing she'd ignored the pounding on her door. If her head hadn't hurt so damned much she would have simply pretended to be asleep, or in a coma or in Siberia. But Clement's pounding had been fiendishly in time with the pounding in her head, and if she didn't get some aspirin she was going to die, so she'd thrown an ancient chenille bathrobe over her huge T-shirt and straggled to the door. Only to be greeted by an upraised newspaper that could only contain bad news.

"I don't know," she said wearily, tossing two pills in her mouth and washing them down. "Are you sure I can't get you some coffee?"

"Instant's only fit for pigs," Clement said with a sniff.

"Oink," said Silver weakly. She didn't dare look at her reflection in the mirror. She'd stumbled into the shower and stood there for an hour last night, then fallen into bed. For all she knew her makeup was still streaked on her face.

"What happened last night, Silver?" Clement demanded in a slightly more reasonable voice. "Was it a total disaster? I should have insisted on coming, I know I should have."

"It was fine," she said for the fourth time since he'd arrived. Clement had seated himself on one of her wicker sofas after brushing away imaginary dust, and his expression was doubtful.

"You still haven't explained the 'bizarrely costumed' part. And how was McGinnis? I hope he had the good sense to treat you like a lady."

"He was a perfect gentleman," Silver said without a blush, remembering his cool hands against her breasts.

"Are we talking about the same man?"

"Don't, Clement," she said, draining her coffee. It did taste nasty, but she had burned out her last two coffeemakers and decided she was too scatterbrained for ground coffee.

"So he's made a convert, has he? The legendary McGinnis charm. I suppose if you like all that crude sexuality then he might have something to recommend him. And he's a very powerful man in the movie business. They do say power is the greatest aphrodisiac of all. Did you sleep with him?"

"Give me a break, Clement!" she pleaded. "Am I the sort of woman to be seduced by power? Am I the sort of woman to be seduced by someone like Rafe McGinnis, for that matter? Apart from the fact that he has the most beautiful, talented women in the world at his feet, what could I possibly find attractive about such an arrogant, soulless schlockmeister?"

"You've been reading my reviews," Clement murmured, obviously pleased. "I'm sorry I underestimated you, my dear. I should have known you wouldn't be bowled over by his tawdry sexuality. You're too much of a lady for that. Still the man does have his charm."

"Does he? I hadn't noticed," she lied.

"Didn't you?" Clement sounded skeptical. "Well, now that you've appeased the monster, maybe we can get back to work. I was thinking of a series of articles on the modern taste for sex and violence combined. You write so well on those subjects."

"Clement, I've promised I wouldn't write about Mack Movies anymore. And I couldn't write about sex and violence in modern Hollywood without mentioning Mack Movies," she said flatly.

"You didn't promise, darling. It was presented to you, and you didn't say anything one way or the other. Of course, if you're going to bow to corporate pressure, you can always concentrate on reviewing the cartoon tie-ins."

Silver shuddered with heartfelt horror. "I haven't bowed to corporate pressure, Clement."

"Of course you haven't, darling. Rafael McGinnis is going to forget your existence in a matter of days, if he hasn't already. You can write anything you want about him. We just have to be circumspect for a while."

His words made a certain depressing sense. She'd definitely gone too far in that last article, and it was only her lingering sense of guilt that had made her give in to McGinnis's outrageous demand.

But that didn't mean she was going to roll over and play dead. She had every right in the world to her opinion, and if the *Clarion* wouldn't let her express it, she had no doubt she'd find another outlet. She wasn't going to let the man bully her. Not with his power, his money, his prestige.

Not with his body, his hands, his mouth.

She looked up at Clement's smooth, faintly smug face, and pushed her tangled hair back. "I'm looking forward to it," she said, hoping to retrieve some of her righteous anger. But all she felt was hollow inside.

## Chapter Five

"You ought to be ashamed of yourself," Bernie greeted him not that many hours later when he strolled into his office.

"I've already had Jimmy read me the riot act," he said wearily. "I don't need you as well. What is this, the Preservation of Silver Carlysle Society? She can take care of herself—she doesn't need you and Jimmy as guardian angels."

Bernie was glaring at him. She had her own cup of coffee, and she was pointedly refusing to offer him any. "Did you take her to bed last night?"

"Obviously you haven't checked in with your cohort or you'd know the answer to that. And anyway, my sex life is none of your damned business." He stared longingly at her coffee. "And besides, what do you mean by 'take her to bed'? Who says I take anyone anywhere? What if we're simply talking about a mutually pleasurable experience?"

"I thought we weren't talking about it," Bernie shot back. "Did you?"

"Did I what?"

"Have a mutually pleasurable experience?"

"Not with Silver Carlysle. As a matter of fact, my time was spent both alone and unpleasantly. Have you seen *Cop for A Day?*"

"On numerous occasions," she said dryly. "It doesn't improve on closer examination."

"Is it as lousy as I thought it was?" He poured himself a cup of coffee and drained it, scalding and black and wonderful.

"No. It's stupid, mindless violence, but it's fairly good stupid, mindless violence, if you enjoy that sort of thing. It gives the public a vicarious thrill, watching people mutilate each other. So why didn't you seduce her?"

"Latent nobility?" he suggested.

"I doubt it. If you've ever had a noble urge in your life you've managed to suppress it."

He refilled his mug, then took a measured sip of his coffee as he stalled for time. "I'll tell you about Silver Carlysle," he said, "if you tell me who her father was."

Bernie didn't bat an eye. "How should I know?"

"For one thing, you know everything. For another, you told her you knew her father in my presence. So give over, Bernie. Who was he?"

"Jack the Ripper. What's on the agenda for the day?"

"Don't change the subject. Don't you want to know what happened between Clement Walden's protégée and me last night? Oh, God..." A sudden, horrific thought struck him. "Clement's not her father, is he?"

"Not likely," Bernie said dryly.

"Well, you never know...."

"In this case I do know."

"And you're not going to tell me?"

"You got it right the first time. It doesn't really matter, Rafe. He wasn't anybody you've ever met, or cared about. Just an old Hollywood legend, forgotten by most."

Rafe had known Bernie since he and Sam first arrived in Hollywood from NYU, a prize-winning independent film under their belts, looking for the right opportunity. She'd shown him the ropes, taught him all he needed to know, and when things took off he took her along with him, giving her the power and opportunities she'd always deserved. But he knew her very well after all these years, and he knew when he was going to find out what he needed to know. And when it would just be a waste of breath to keep asking.

"You knew most of the old legends, worked with them. Were you in love with this one?" he asked instead. "Is that why you're feeling so protective of his daughter?"

Bernie made a face. "If I was in love with him, and I'm only saying 'if,' then it was a long, long time ago and it no longer matters to anyone. I'm not the femme fatale type, and the man was married. What mattered between us was friendship. I trusted him, Rafe. Trusted him as a man, trusted him as a creative force. In honor of that trust I'm going to make sure you keep your cotton-picking hands off his daughter."

Rafe held up his cotton-picking hands in a gesture of surrender. "She's safe from me. Just satisfy my curiosity and I'll never even think of her again."

"If you have so much extra time on your hands I have a suggestion for you," Bernie said.

"I'll just bet you do."

"It's on your desk."

He didn't move for a moment. Bernie wasn't the type to put things in writing. She was a scrapper, a dealer, a talker, just like he was. And there was a nervous edge to her, one that betrayed the fact that whatever was waiting for him on his desk mattered to her. More than she wanted him to see.

"What is it?"

"A story treatment. From an old novel from the fifties. Pegasus Pictures bought the rights back then, and I don't think they've reverted. No one's done anything with it, it's just sitting there, waiting. You might find it interesting."

"I might," he said carefully, knowing damned well that anything that important to Bernie was interesting indeed.

"It'll be nothing but trouble for you. Production was started in the sixties and then dropped when the director died. But there was some preliminary work on it, and God knows where that is, or whether the director's heirs have any claim to it. Or whether the original writer or his heirs have a claim to it."

"Great," he grumbled.

"As I said, it wouldn't be easy. But you've been in such a foul mood I figured you needed a challenge. Go to it, sport. At least it'll keep your mind above your waist and off of Silver Carlysle."

"What makes you think my mind's below my waist when I think of Silver Carlysle? She's not my idea of a fox, Bernie."

"I know. But I have the utmost faith in your ultimate good taste. Leave Silver alone, Rafe. You'd be too much for her."

He paused in the doorway, watching her. He knew perfectly well he ought to take her advice. There was nothing he wanted more than to leave Silver alone. Unfortunately the more Bernie warned him, the more stubborn he became.

He managed a tight smile. "I'll go read your mysterious proposal, and maybe I'll waste my time with it. What is it? Whodunit? Action picture? Not, God help me, a psychological drama?"

"None of the above," Bernie said. "It's a Western."

"WE DO IT."

Bernie looked up, pushing her reading glasses high on her forehead. "That fast?" she said, but there was no disguising the satisfaction in her faded brown eyes.

"Have you ever known me to hesitate when something's right?" Rafe said, dropping down in the chair opposite her. "You knew perfectly well I'd react this way. You've worked with me long enough, we share the same tastes. This is going to make *Lonesome Dove* look like a Saturday afternoon serial."

"Or it's going to make *Heaven's Gate* look like a minor error in judgment," Bernie pointed out wryly. "You're not impervious to mistakes, Rafe, and neither am I. Are you willing to take a chance on surpassing the most notorious flop in movie history?"

Rafe grinned. "What do you think, Bernie? Aren't you getting a little tired of playing it safe?"

She just stared at him for a moment. And then she nodded. "It won't be easy," she warned.

"So you said before. Who says I like things easy? What's the big problem with this? The preliminary treatment says Pegasus Pictures. You've probably already got the legal department on the trail . . ."

"I do."

"So what's the problem?"

"Did you read everything I gave you?"

"I read enough. The treatment, started the novel, which, by the way, is terrific. I don't suppose the writer's still alive?"

Bernie shook her head. "I don't think so. He was an old recluse living out in Colorado somewhere. I imagine he's dead by now."

"And of course I noticed that Benjamin Hatcher himself was going to write and direct. I can't believe it."

"Can't believe what?" There was a careful edge to Bernie's voice, one that fascinated Rafe.

"Can't believe that a legend like Hatcher would leave behind an unfinished project and no one would pick it up. The man's one of the few truly great ones in this business, Bernie. We'll probably have film scholars crawling all over us when we do this."

"Probably."

"So what's the problem? Why didn't Pegasus ever finish the project?"

"I don't know. I have my own theory, of course. Sir Benjamin's death took everyone by shock. He died in a car accident in England, you know. When the dust settled, his papers had all been disposed of. Including the work he did on *Black Canyon*. The studio didn't have enough to go on, and without Hatcher's vision there was no one to push it through."

Rafe leaned back in the chair and propped his booted feet on her desk. She frowned at him, but she was used to it, and she didn't object. "So tell me, Bernie, my angel," he drawled. "You know a hell of a lot more about all this than you've told me so far. I remember that you were working with Hatcher when he died. You must know what he had in mind for *Black Canyon*. Why didn't you push it?"

"Who would have listened to me?" She said it without bitterness. "No one gave me a chance in this business. Except you."

"And now you're giving it to me. Why, Bernie? You must have known about this for years, thought about it for years. It's too good, too exciting to forget about."

"The time felt right. You're sick of the easy action movies, and I think the movie-going audience is ready for a change."

"Bernie," he said, entirely ready to play devil's advocate. "*Cop for a Day* just broke opening-weekend grosses. We're making money hand over fist. We'll probably take a bath on *Black Canyon*."

"Probably. Do you care?"

He didn't even hesitate. "Not in the slightest. I could do with a tax write-off. So where does this thing stand, legally? Does Pegasus own it or not?"

"Yes and no."

He shut his eyes for an impatient moment. "Stop pulling my chain, Bernie."

"Technically the option lapsed. But the book is out of print, the writer can't be traced, so it's a free project. The only problem is the work Hatcher had already done on it."

"You said it had disappeared."

"It was passed on to his heirs. I imagine you'll have to negotiate with them."

Rafe reached for his crumpled pack of cigarettes. He was down to five a day, and the last few in the pack were stale, but he didn't care. He lighted one, taking his time, and watched Bernie's nervous gestures through the haze of smoke. "Who are his heirs, Bernie?" he asked softly.

"Why do you think I'd know that?" Bernie protested weakly.

"We've already agreed that you know everything. Let's see, if my memory serves me, Hatcher wasn't married when he died. He'd been married two...three times."

"Twice," Bernie mumbled. "First to a girl in England who died in a fire. Then to a second-rate American actress who divorced him for his infidelities and remarried a businessman." She stopped, waiting for the penny to drop.

"I'm sorry, Bernie, if I'm being obtuse. I haven't memorized Hollywood lineages. What was the actress's name?" If *Black Canyon* wasn't so damned good he'd be bored by all this. As it was, he was merely irritated.

"Marjorie Carlysle."

For a moment he didn't move as everything fell into place. "I don't like being jerked around," he said, very softly.

Even Bernie could be intimidated when he used that tone of voice. "What was I supposed to do, say here's a hot prospect that belongs to the woman you're having a very public feud with?" she countered.

"Yes. Then I wouldn't have wasted my time." He dropped his booted feet to the floor and rose, starting for the door.

"I didn't know you were a quitter, Rafe," Bernie fired after him.

He paused, looking back over his shoulder. "What's next, Bernie? You gonna double dare me?"

"I double dare you," she said.

He turned, pausing in her doorway. "What makes you think Silver Carlysle owns it?"

"She doesn't necessarily own it. She just thinks she owns it," Bernie said. "The rights aren't clear."

"What makes you think she even knows of its existence?"

"Because she's been offering her screenplay of it around. Through Clement Walden's agent. She's offered it at Touchstone. And at Regis."

"Over my dead body," he said flatly. "She'll wimp out the men, she'll soften the violence, she'll turn it into some new-age bullshit. And I'm sure as hell not letting Regis have it. Have they shown any interest?"

"Rafe, I really don't know everything. The last I heard, it's just been sitting on a desk. She didn't put her father's name on it, and no one pays attention to a screenplay by a nobody."

"Get legal going," Rafe said abruptly. "We're getting those rights."

"You think Silver's going to agree?"

"I don't give a damn. We're getting it. There's just one thing that mystifies me, Bernie."

She still had that wary expression on her lined face. "What's that?"

"I thought you were watching out for the poor defenseless lady. How come you're throwing her to the wolves?"

"I don't want you seducing and abandoning her, Rafe. For Benjamin's sake, I don't want to see his daughter destroyed by your powerhouse habits. But when it comes to her father's work, it's a different matter. My first loyalty is to Hatcher's artistic legacy. And to you."

"I'm glad you added that," he said dryly. "I suppose you're going to want a credit to Hatcher?"

"I want it dedicated to him," Bernie said flatly.

"You *were* in love with him, weren't you?"

"None of your damned business. I might give you a bit of advice when it comes to dealing with his daughter, though."

His eyes narrowed as he took a drag off his stale cigarette. "And what's that?"

"An old southern saying. You can catch more flies with honey than you can with vinegar."

A sudden, totally bizarre thought strayed into his mind. If he didn't know Bernie so well he'd think she was trying to throw him together with Silver Carlysle. "Are you suggesting I try to seduce the rights out of her, Bernie?"

"Hell, no. I'm just saying she might be willing to listen to reason if you behave like a decent human being for a change. You may be able to melt other women's brains, but I suspect Silver Carlysle is going to be a tougher nut to crack. She's not going to fall apart if you put your hands on her."

That was exactly what she'd done. For a brief, delicious moment in the back of his limousine. But she'd pulled herself together far too quickly for his peace of mind, just when she should have been surrendering. And if she had surrendered, this whole issue would be academic. Women seldom denied him anything.

"So let's get this straight. I'm supposed to wrest her father's legacy from her, something she's put her own work into, and I'm supposed to do it like a gentleman. I hate to tell you this, Bernie, but I don't conduct business like a gentleman."

"I have faith in you, Rafe. You can do anything, get anything, you set your mind to."

"True enough. But I won't necessarily do it your way. I don't have your patience." He pushed away from the doorjamb and headed back toward his office suite.

"Rafe." Bernie's voice called him back.

"Yeah?"

"You won't hurt her, will you?" There was sudden doubt in Bernie's voice. "Maybe we should just forget about *Black Canyon*. There are a million ideas out there..."

"Too late, Bernie," he said softly. "I want this one. And I'm going to get it. No matter what the price."

"I WISH you'd let me come up for a while," Clement said in what Silver had come to think of as his dry white whine. She usually gave in to him when he used that tone of voice. For one thing, it was extraordinarily annoying, and if she didn't acquiesce it would continue as punishment for days. For another, it always made her feel guilty. She'd been a disaster as far as her mother and father were concerned. At least Clement approved of her, supported her. She owed him her loyalty in return.

But not tonight. "I'm sorry, Clement. I haven't been sleeping well, and I'm exhausted."

"Then let me take you out to dinner. It's still early— only nine o'clock, and I happen to know for a fact that you haven't eaten anything but stale doughnuts since breakfast."

"Clement, my jeans are split at the knee, I'm not wearing a bra, and my running shoes are falling apart. Any place you'd consider worthy of patronizing wouldn't allow me into their parking lot."

"You underestimate my consequence," Clement said blandly. "I could get you into Buckingham Palace dressed like that, if I wanted to."

She managed a tired grin at the thought as they sailed toward her mother's house in the back of Clement's

Daimler. "I'm just not hungry, Clement. Give me a rain check?"

What Clement gave her was a case of the sulks, leaning back against the white leather and crossing his white-linened arms across his narrow chest. She considered giving in, then decided against it. Clement got his way far too often, and she'd be lousy company in her current state of mind.

She could always try to charm him out of his bad temper, but she didn't even have the energy for that. All she wanted to do was climb the narrow stairs up to her apartment, nuke herself a gourmet frozen dinner and tumble into bed.

"I don't know about that article, Clement," she said instead, deliberately changing the subject.

It was enough to distract him. "What don't you know, my precious? We've worked long and hard on it for the past three days, and it's absolutely splendid. The most wickedly ripe invective. You've outdone yourself."

His words just made her feel even more unsettled. "I don't know that ripe invective is my forte. Yours, perhaps."

"And yours, too, dear. You've really torn the action-movie industry apart this time, and it's been long overdue. If you're worried about your promise not to mention Rafe McGinnis, you can just leave it to me. Both our names are going to be on the series of articles. I'll just say I wrote the stuff about McGinnis."

"It's not that," she said, despite the fact that a small, edgy part of her felt a certain cowardly concern. "It just wasn't... fun anymore."

The moment the words were out she knew she'd made a major mistake. There were few things Clement Walden considered more enjoyable than slashing apart pretension and mediocrity wherever he discovered them. It was his devastating wit that had made him a household name for almost three decades.

For Silver, half the pleasure was in finding some rare jewel of a movie, or finding the gold amidst the dross, the small perfect part of a larger, weaker movie. Clement would tease her, telling her she was a disgusting optimist, but she really did find that she got more pleasure out of celebrating beauty than decrying ugliness.

And she'd wallowed in ugliness for the past three days. Ever since that disturbing evening with Rafe McGinnis, she'd followed Clement's lead, immersing herself in movies with a higher body count than the Gulf War. And every night she felt soiled, depressed and angry. And the only person she could direct that anger at was Rafe McGinnis.

As Clement had told her, he'd simply forgotten her existence. He'd had his revenge, humiliated her, forced his professional will on her and then dismissed her as he went on to pursue other things. Not that he would have pursued her, of course. That kiss in the back of his limousine was just a spur-of-the-moment impulse for him. It had nothing to do with his real taste in women, which doubtless ran to tiny blondes like Marcia Allison and away from dark-haired Valkyries like herself.

Not that she wanted him to be attracted to her. God forbid. That kiss had been disturbing enough. He knew how to get past a woman's defenses. If he could get her to kiss him back, even for a moment, then his powers were formidable indeed, and she didn't want to be exposed to them any more than necessary.

No, she was glad he'd forgotten about her, and she trusted Clement when he said McGinnis wouldn't even notice the latest series of articles.

She just wished she hadn't been quite that easy to dismiss. Silly pride on her part, of course. But alone in her apartment, late at night, there was no denying her feelings. Or at least some of them.

The Daimler slid silently up to the garage. Clement sat still, sulking, as the chauffeur opened the door before Silver could do it for herself. "You left your lights on," he said peevishly. "I thought you were so concerned about the environment."

Silver glanced up as she climbed out of the car. "Mother probably sent one of the maids down to do it. She worries about me when I'm out late."

"Your mother doesn't worry about anything but her new face-lift," Clement said waspishly.

Silver sighed. "I'm sorry, Clement," she said humbly. "Forgive me?"

He brightened an infinitesimal amount. "I suppose so. Though why I bother with you is beyond my comprehension."

"Because you love me?" she suggested.

"Hardly. Because you'll do all my dirty work and accept a pittance for a salary."

"There's that, too," Silver said, smiling. "See you tomorrow, darling."

Clement managed only an aggrieved harrumph as the chauffeur closed the door behind her. The garage was only half full when she let herself in. Her mother's limousine was out, as was her own disreputable rattletrap. Every now and then her mother tried to make it disappear, presenting something new and expensive in its place. Silver always managed to resist temptation, even when Marjorie had upped the ante to a Jaguar. She wondered what her mother would come up with this time.

There'd been a Lotus parked halfway up the driveway, but it had plates on it already. Besides, even her mother wouldn't go so far as to buy her a Lotus. Not her style at all. It had gotten to the point where she might have agreed to that other symbol of Hollywood trendy-ism, a four-wheel-drive Jeep. But her mother hadn't offered, and since Silver hadn't gotten away from the city in months, it didn't seem that dire a necessity. Maybe when Christmas drew closer she might drop a hint.

She climbed the stairs slowly, still thinking about Clement's temper tantrum and the nasty tone of the articles. Maybe she ought to have a tantrum of her own. Put a halt to the article, or at least demand a rewrite. It wasn't going in the paper for another week—she had more than enough time to tone it down, just a little.

She didn't even notice the music until she'd opened her unlocked door. Someone had turned on her CD player, and the undeniably sensuous sounds of Sam Cooke filled the apartment.

Silver didn't hesitate. Her mother had a habit of treating the apartment as her own, and she showed up at any time of the day or night, full of suggestions and advice, going through her cupboards and drawers, turning on her stereo. Though Sam Cooke was an odd choice for Marjorie.

"Mother?" Silver called, closing the door behind her.

The one light in the room had left most of it in shadows. Rafe McGinnis rose from her sofa, stretching to his full height as Silver stared in shock.

"Not exactly," he said in a wry tone of voice. "It's your worst nightmare."

And Silver, staring at him, could only agree.

## Chapter Six

"What are you doing here?" Silver demanded.

"You should know better than to leave your doors unlocked," Rafe said easily. "You never know who might turn up."

Silver leaned back against the closed door, all trace of her earlier weariness gone. In its place was a kind of blazing excitement, fueled by anger, and something else she was afraid to analyze. "You must have had a pretty good reason to break into my home," she said evenly. "What is it?"

"I didn't break in. The door was unlocked, remember?" He had a drink in one hand, and he gestured toward it. "Can I get you one?"

"You can get the hell out of my apartment," she said flatly.

His smile was just a faint upturning of his mouth. "Not until we talk."

"I can call the police."

"Why should you do that?" he asked calmly, not at all distressed by her threat.

"Because I asked you to leave and you wouldn't. Think of the scandal."

"No, Silver. You think of the scandal," he said, his raspy voice only slightly threatening. "It'll backfire on you, just as your designer costume backfired on you. You really think it would do my reputation any harm? I'm a bad boy to begin with—it would only add to my legend. Whereas for you, it would be disaster."

He was right, of course. There was no denying it. And her mother, with her passionate concern for her safe conservative life-style, would have hysterics. Besides, she didn't necessarily want him to leave. Not without telling her what he'd come for.

He certainly couldn't have come for her. She tried not to think about her disheveled appearance, but the moment it entered her mind there was no dislodging it. He was standing just a few feet away from her, and she was acutely aware of the difference between the two of them.

He was wearing jeans, too. Faded ones, that looked like they were tailored to his long legs. Not ratty ones like hers. He wore a T-shirt, a pale color that should have looked wimpy on him. It only made him sexier. And the rumpled linen jacket that hung on his frame looked like it was made to be wrinkled. Whenever she wore wrinkled clothing it looked like she'd slept in it.

Even his long hair was tied back, ridiculously neat after a long day, while hers tangled about her face in silky strands, making her look like an overgrown elf. She felt unkempt, childish and inept in front of him. And quite intensely bra-less.

"What do you want, McGinnis?" she asked, suddenly tired again. She wanted to cross her arms in front of her chest, but she was afraid it would only draw his attention to that untrammeled part of her anatomy. "State your business and leave."

"There's no reason why we can't be civilized about this. Have a drink," he said again.

"McGinnis..." Her voice carried a warning.

"Rafe," he supplied with a charming smile that she didn't trust for one moment. "I know, it's your house. Why don't you offer me a refill?"

"I don't think you need one. I suppose your chauffeur told you where I live. I don't think the people I rent this place from will take kindly to your Lotus parked in their driveway. That is your Lotus, isn't it?"

"If your mother has any objections she can take them up with me," he said gently.

It was like a fist to her stomach. If he knew Marjorie was her mother, then it stood to reason he knew who her father was, too. Clement could never understand why she wanted that kept secret. It wasn't just an unwillingness to trade on her father's stellar reputation. It was the fact that he'd turned his back on her when she was most needy. She didn't want to accept his help when it was no longer up to him to grant or deny it.

She walked past him, into her kitchenette, and poured herself a meager glass from the bottle of scotch he'd found. She took a deep sip, forcing herself not to cough as it burned its way down her throat. There were tears in her eyes when she turned back to him, tears from the scotch and nothing else.

"All right," she said. "What do you want from me?"

She didn't believe that small, sexual smile, or the way his eyes slid gently down her body. It was an automatic instinct on his part, his stock in trade, and she wasn't going to succumb to it, even as she felt her nipples harden in reaction, even as she felt the fiery warmth in her stomach that wasn't the scotch.

"I want you to come to dinner with me."

"Forget it."

"Trust me, I'm absolutely harmless," he said, and she wondered whether the man had any acting experience. She could almost believe him, which was surely insanity on her part.

"I don't want to go to dinner with you, I don't want to talk to you, I don't want to have anything to do with you," she said fiercely.

"Why not?"

It was a simple question, impossible to answer. Not without admitting how irrationally vulnerable she was to him. Instead she settled for the obvious. "I don't trust you."

If she'd hoped to wound him she failed. He simply looked amused. "No one trusts anyone in Hollywood," he said. "It's part of our job description."

"Go away."

"I didn't get where I am today by taking no for an answer. I can be very tenacious."

"And I can be very stubborn," she shot back. "Tell me what you want and then leave."

"I have something for you," he said.

"I don't want anything from you," she parried. "Besides, I don't believe you. I've been around long enough to know the truth. You want something from me. What is it?"

He sat on her overstuffed wicker sofa again, stretching his long legs out in front of him and propping his booted feet on the scarred and battered coffee table. He looked completely incongruous surrounded by her makeshift belongings. Even the lumpy, comfortable old sofa, covered with an ancient Indian-print bedspread, looked absurdly tacky beneath his casually upscale frame. It didn't matter that he was making himself at home. He made the home surrounding him seem suddenly shabby.

"I want your father's papers."

It was the last thing she expected. Or was it? "Why?" she said bluntly, wandering around the room, nervously straightening a stack of old newspapers that she hadn't bothered to throw out in weeks. "I've had them for seventeen years, and no one's ever shown any interest in them before."

"I'm thinking of producing a version of something he was working on when he died."

*"Black Canyon,"* she said flatly, not liking the sick feeling in the pit of her stomach. Another woman might jump to the flattering conclusion that he'd heard of her own work on the Western. Another woman might assume her big break was just around the corner. Not Silver.

"Exactly. I gather you've done some work on it yourself. Of course we'd be interested in seeing it, but I should warn you from the outset that I expect we'll be using a screenwriter with a track record. One who'd be more likely to share our vision."

"Your male vision," Silver said.

Rafe shrugged, obviously not the slightest bit uncomfortable with his outrageous demand. "I'm a man," he said. "What can I say?"

"You can say goodbye, Mr. McGinnis."

He didn't even flinch. "You're forgetting something, Silver," he said in that dangerously sexy voice of his. "Your father was working for Pegasus Pictures when he died. He was under contract. Therefore, any works in progress technically belong to Pegasus. And since I'm now a major force in Pegasus Pictures, they belong to me.''

"Over my dead body."

"Be reasonable about this. You can't possibly hope to win. I've sent word to the various studios that have your screenplay, informing them there's a question of copyright infringement. You know how touchy studios can be. I expect your manuscripts will be back in a matter of days, if not hours. If you want it to be considered, send it over to my office."

"I'd burn it first."

"That might be for the best."

"Is this part of your grand scheme for revenge?" she asked, holding herself very still. "I dared insult the great Rafe McGinnis and in return I get destroyed?"

"Don't be ridiculous. I could care less about your little snipings in the paper. I admit I was irritated, but that's a minor issue compared to *Black Canyon*. I want it, and I intend to have it."

"You arrogant, ruthless bastard," she said, her voice trembling with fury. "I'll see you in hell first."

He rose then, unmoved by her fury, crossing the room to stand in front of her. "Anyone with power in this town is an arrogant, ruthless bastard," he said in a damnably calm tone. "Why does *Black Canyon* matter so much to you? If it's financial, that's easily remedied. I'm sure our lawyers could come up with something mutually agreeable."

"Money hasn't got a damned thing to do with it," she said fiercely.

"Well, it can't be out of memory for your father. The man was a genius, but he couldn't have been the finest parent. According to Bernie, he gave you up quite readily when your mother ditched him. Surely you can't think you owe him anything more than a way to make a living."

It shouldn't have been so devastating. It was nothing more than she'd said to herself a thousand times. Coming from his cool, cynical mouth, though, it was shockingly painful.

"It has nothing to do with my father. It's mine. I put my heart and soul into that screenplay, and it belongs to me. You can't have it. I won't let Mack Movies turn it into some stupid sex-and-violence extravaganza where the women exist only to be murdered so the hero can be tormented. I won't let you have it!"

He simply watched her for a long, unfathomable moment. "You won't have any say in the matter," he said finally. "I always get what I want."

"Not this time."

And then suddenly she was aware of what was going on beneath the anger. She was dangerously close to the man. Her shabby apartment was dimly lighted, shadowed, and he was watching her out of hooded, unreadable eyes, eyes that saw far too much.

"Most particularly," he said, "this time." And with seemingly effortless expertise, he put his hand behind her neck, beneath her close-cropped hair, and pulled her against him.

She tumbled, off balance, falling against him, too startled to react. And then it was too late, much too late, for he was kissing her again, his mouth hungry against hers, as his arm went around her back and held her body tight against him.

The small part of her mind that was working expected another all-out assault. That she could have combated. But this time it was different. There was no hurry, no particular demand in his kiss this time. No sensual tussle in the back seat of a limousine. He kissed her slowly, deliberately, as if he had all the time in the world to savor her mouth, to taste the trembling softness of her lips. She could taste the scotch on his tongue, and she wanted more.

And then he lifted his head, looking down at her in the shadowy room. "I told myself I wasn't going to do that again," he said. "You have the most destructive effect on my willpower." He kissed her again, a brief, hard kiss. "But then, I seem to have the same effect on you."

"You have no effect on me whatsoever," Silver said in a tight little voice, rigid in his arms.

"Oh, yeah?" he said lazily. "Then why are your nipples hard?"

She shoved him away then, and he let her go, watching her as she scrambled back across the room. She wanted to wipe the taste of him off her mouth, but she decided that would be going too far. "I know you think every woman in Hollywood is ready to fall at your feet, McGinnis," she said in an admirably cool voice. "But I'm not one of them. I don't deny that you know how to kiss. You've probably had a great deal of practice at it. But I don't need to sleep with you to benefit my career."

His eyes narrowed, and his smile was thin. "That, of course, being the only reason for my heralded success between the sheets?"

"Oh, I expect any number of women actually find you attractive," she said. "With your masculine swagger and your arrogant cowboy manner, you might be very appealing to some people. Not to me."

He rose then, crossing the room toward her, stalking her like a predator, and Silver knew a direct streak of panic sliding down her ramrod-straight backbone. It took every ounce of courage not to take a step backward, away from him.

"You sound like Clement Walden," he said softly. "I think you've been spending too much time with him. Not that you have to worry about sleeping with him to get to the top. As long as he can control your sex life he doesn't actually need to participate. As to whether you find me attractive or not," he added, cupping her chin in one hard hand, "you'll find that life is a lot easier if you don't lie to yourself. Lie to everyone else—your boss, your mother, your tax accountant, your lover. But don't lie to yourself. You want me, Silver, and that's what scares you. You want me as much as I want you. And it doesn't make any sense to either of us. It's too soon, too illogical. But it exists, no matter how much you try to deny it."

She opened her mouth to protest, but he stopped the words, kissing her. She told herself it didn't mean anything, didn't move her at all, as she melted against him, her breasts flattening against the hardness of his chest, her hips reaching up toward his, her mouth slanting beneath his. Even the hungry little moan must have been a moan of irritation, as his hands slid up under her loose cotton T-shirt and touched her breasts, and then she wanted it, wanted him, with a mindless ferocity that frightened her, and she knew she was going to do anything he wanted, do it there, do it then, and sanity and self-preservation had vanished with the touch of his hands and the taste of his mouth. Her hands were shaking, she could barely stand, and all she wanted to do was sink into him, lose herself with the man who was the greatest danger she'd ever faced in her life.

She heard the pounding of her heart. The pounding of his heart, against her. And the pounding on her door.

"Maybe you'd better let him in," Rafe whispered in her ear, nibbling on her lobe.

She stared up at him in hazy confusion. "Who?"

"I expect it's Clement Walden," Rafe said with a half smile. "Come to make sure I'm not debauching the virgin princess of Hollywood."

She disentangled herself from his arms, his body, and the only thing that came to her mind was, "There are no virgins in Hollywood."

"You come damn close, honey," he replied. And she wondered what he'd do if she slapped him.

She didn't need to go to the door. By the time Clement remembered that she never locked it and let himself in, she was already halfway across the room from Rafe, her flaming face in the shadows.

"What's going on here?" Clement demanded, stepping into her apartment with his usual fastidious shudder. "Are you all right, Silver?"

"Why shouldn't she be?" Rafe drawled. "What brings you out here at such a late hour, Clement? Isn't it a little past the time for social visits?"

"I could say the same thing to you," Clement said in a bored voice. "I was halfway back to my house before I realized why that Lotus looked so familiar. For a moment I thought . . . well, that doesn't matter. I knew Silver was much too tired to have to deal with any unwelcome guests, so I'm here to make sure you get on your way."

"What makes you think I'm unwanted?" Rafe murmured.

"I know Silver. She's a lady, and you're a hooligan. A low-class upstart with more testosterone than brains, and she's never been fool enough to fall for your sort. If Silver wanted company she would have accepted my dinner invitation. As it is, I'm sure she'll be very happy if you'd leave."

"Clement," Silver said wearily, finally finding her voice. "I can handle this."

"You haven't been doing a very good job of it," Clement observed. "Haven't I warned you about men like McGinnis?"

"Oh, we have you to blame for it," Rafe murmured. "I should have known. Maybe your little protégée was in the mood for a hooligan. Maybe she was interested in a walk on the wild side . . ."

"Don't be disgusting," Clement said. "You don't know who you're dealing with. I'd like you to leave. Now."

Silver had been trying to make Rafe leave for half an hour. It made no sense that she resented Clement asking the same thing.

"We were discussing business, Clement," she said pointedly.

"Were you, indeed? Is that why your face is whisker-burned? Really, Rafe, if you're going to make out with a woman you ought to consider shaving before you show up at her apartment."

"Go away, Clement," Silver said. "And go away, Rafe. I don't have anything to say to either of you."

"But Silver," Clement began in his well-bred whine.

But Rafe had finally accepted his dismissal. He put one strong hand under Clement's arm and pulled him toward the door. "We've had our marching orders." He glanced back at Silver, standing motionless in the middle of the room. "We'll finish this later."

"There's nothing to finish. Nothing to discuss. You can't have it."

"Can't have what?" Clement said in a fretful voice. "What in heaven's name is going on here? I demand to know..."

Rafe silenced Clement by the simple expedient of shoving him out the door and locking it behind him, leaning against it to prevent Clement from reentering.

"It's not a bad question, Silver," he said, his voice a seductive murmur in the dim room. "Can't have what? The rights to *Black Canyon?* Or you?"

A cynical smile curved her mouth. "You can't have the only thing that really interests you. The rights to *Black Canyon* are mine, and you'll never get them."

For a moment he didn't move, oblivious to the sounds of Clement's pounding behind his back. "I play hardball, Silver. I always win. I fight dirty, and I'll use everything I can to get what I want. Give it up, before you get crushed."

"I'm tougher than you think."

"Maybe," he said in a meditative voice. "You're going to have to be. Don't say I didn't warn you." He moved away from the door, opening it and letting Clement stumble back in, the little man quivering in rage.

"We're out of here, Walden," he said calmly, dragging the fuming Clement with him. "I've given Silver an offer she can't refuse. She needs some time to think about it."

The door slammed behind them. Silver watched them go, then realized she was holding her breath. She let it go in a whoosh, them moved over to the windows overlooking the drive, peering through the thin-slatted blinds.

Clement's Daimler was already out the driveway. Nothing and no one but an immovable force like Rafe McGinnis could have kept Clement from hassling her further, and she knew a sudden feeling of desperation. If Clement couldn't hold out against his inexorable will, how could she?

Because it mattered too much. She wasn't going to give him *Black Canyon* and let him turn it into a piece of garbage. It was too important to her, to her heart and soul. She wasn't going to let him destroy it.

She was in for a battle, she knew that. If she was very, very lucky, that battle would be legal. Rafe McGinnis would keep away from her, letting his formidable lawyers do all the dirty work. And dirty work it would be, she had no doubts about that whatsoever. Rafe was right, he hadn't gotten where he was by being gentlemanly, decent, merciful.

But she had one thing on her side that was entirely lacking on his. A simple matter of right. And a dream. And for that right, for that dream, she was willing to fight for as long and as hard as she could. If in the end she lost, so be it. She'd make the victory taste like ashes in Rafe McGinnis's mouth.

His mouth. Damn, why had she kissed him back? For that matter, why did he kiss her? Simply because he knew how much it upset her? Even he couldn't be that ruthless, could he?

He was climbing into his Lotus, folding his long, lanky body into the tiny cockpit. At the last minute he looked up to her darkened window. He couldn't see her, she knew that, and yet his eyes looked directly into hers.

He smiled then, and it was different. Not the mocking sexual conquest. Not the cynical Hollywood grin. It was a small, rueful upturning of his mouth. As if, impossible as it seemed, he'd been caught in his own trap.

And then he slammed the door, speeding out of her mother's deserted driveway with a reckless disregard for anybody else's safety.

She watched him go. And for one mad, wild moment she wished to God that Clement had never shown up, never interrupted what had been about to happen.

Not that it would have made any difference to Rafe. It wouldn't have changed his plans for *Black Canyon*, and it wouldn't have changed her determination to stop him. But even as her mind rebelled, her body longed for him with a reckless disregard for her well-being.

Enmity was her safest choice as far as Rafe Mc-Ginnis was concerned. She had to remember that. From now on it would be war—simple, straightforward and openly declared. The lawyers would do battle, and the two of them need never confront each other again.

If only she could believe it was going to be that easy.

## Chapter Seven

Rafe didn't bother to turn on the lights when he let himself into his house. Instead he walked straight through the darkened rooms, moving with unerring instinct, stripping off his clothes as he went, dropping the little package he'd never had a chance to deliver to her on the coffee table. When he reached the terrace he was nude, and he dived into the tile-lined swimming pool with one clean leap, slicing beneath the warm water without a splash.

He swam hard, lap after lap, moving through the pool at a mind-blanking pace. He didn't want to think about her, didn't want to think about what he was doing. He wanted only the water, the night sky overhead, his blood pumping, his breathing deep and measured, his body tingling with energy. And then he wanted to sleep.

But even the butterfly stroke at eleven at night couldn't keep his quicksilver mind at a comforting black. Finally he stopped at the deep end of the pool, treading water while he measured his pulse rate, and once again Silver Carlysle was back.

He leaned his shoulders against the blue tile, looking around him. The moon overhead was bright, shimmer-

ing down on his unlighted house, and in the darkness he
could see the ridiculous Moorish roofline of his preten-
tious house. He never did understand why he hadn't
picked something a little more rustic, a little more real.
Some glass-and-wood cabin, with clean lines and tex-
tures instead of a romantic anomaly like this. On top of
everything else, the house was in terrible shape, the tiles
falling off, the roof leaking, the plumbing ridiculous,
and it was too damned small. He told himself he lived
there for some sort of cosmic joke, but the truth of the
matter was, he loved it. And of all the people who knew
his house, and were mystified by it, only Bernie under-
stood.

He should have invited Silver Carlysle up here. Not
that she would have come willingly, of course, but that
was a minor issue. Once she saw this absurd place she'd
be even more confused by her worst enemy. And he
liked keeping her confused.

He pushed off against the tiled pool, floating on his
back into the middle of the water. He knew what he was
going to do. He didn't like it. Didn't much like himself
for doing it. But once he'd realized the weapon he had,
he knew he had to use it. Or face his own unacceptable
reasons why he might be inclined to show mercy.

If you started accepting other people as vulnerable,
then you started making adjustments. He'd meant it
when he told Silver that anyone with power in Hollywood was ruthless and arrogant. If he showed mercy, it
stood to reason he'd lose some of that power, and that
was the one thing that was completely unacceptable.

He knew what he had to do. The longer he floated
around in his pool, staring up at the stars, the longer it
would take to put his next step into motion. He'd never

been a man to hesitate. There was no reason to hesitate now.

He glanced back at the pool as he headed into the house. He was about to deliver the cruelest blow he could think of to the far too vulnerable Silver Carlysle, simply for the sake of getting what he wanted. It was ridiculously optimistic to think of her in that pool, naked, the moonlight silvering the water on her body.

But then, he hadn't gotten where he was today by accepting any limitations. Just because he was doing his best to shatter her didn't mean he still didn't want her in bed. And anger could be a powerful aphrodisiac.

He didn't want to listen to that little voice in his head that told him to leave her alone. Maybe they'd both be better off if he did. There was no way he was ever going to find out. He'd set this play in motion, and he had every intention of seeing it through to the end. He was determined to get the rights to *Black Canyon,* and he was just as determined to get Silver Carlysle. The only difference was, he intended to keep *Black Canyon.*

He flicked on the light, stepping over the debris the carpenters had left that morning, heading toward the state-of-the-art phone system in his office. It took him exactly two minutes to get what he wanted. When he hung up the phone he stood there, looking at nothing, including the sterile confines of the only finished room in the old house. And then he went in and poured himself a very stiff drink.

"YOU AREN'T GOING to like this, Silver."

Silver looked up from her computer screen. She was sitting in the little office space Clement had forced the *Clarion* to provide for her, trying to concentrate on her work, when Clement had loomed up behind her. If anyone who barely topped five foot four could be said to loom.

She turned with a sigh, deliberately darkening the screen from his prying eyes. "I imagine not," she said. "What's up?"

"I've been reading this week's edition of the *Nosy Parker*."

Silver could feel the first tendrils of uneasiness churn in her stomach. "I'm surprised at you, Clement. The *Nosy Parker* is the sleaziest of all the sleazy supermarket tabloids. I didn't realize you had a subscription."

"It isn't a joking matter, Silver. Someone saw fit to send me an advance copy. There's no way I can soften the blow for you, my dear."

She forced herself to smile brightly. "It can't be that bad, Clement. So they've run a picture of me at Rafe McGinnis's party. I warned you I looked atrocious. And I imagine they've come up with all sorts of salacious details. If the world wants to think I'm sleeping with the man, it's hardly my concern."

"The article isn't about you and McGinnis, or at least, only marginally. It's about your family background." He dropped the brightly colored tabloid onto her desk, and she stared at it numbly, for a moment the screaming headlines not making any sense.

"Did you ever play that game, Clement?" she asked absently, staring at the paper. "The one where you make up the most absurd tabloid headlines you can think of? I won once, when I came up with 'Man Rips Out Own Heart, Stomps On It.' I never thought I'd be the subject of one." She turned away from it. "I don't think I have the stomach to read it."

"It's not bad as these things go. They haven't come up with some bizarre sex angle."

"How about my latest diet?" she asked with a lame attempt at humor.

Clement surveyed her with a critical eye. "I don't think anyone would be interested, my dear. They mainly take the tack of the impoverished daughter of a screen legend, forced to live over her mother's garage and eke out an existence as a second-string reporter."

"It could be worse, I suppose," she said glumly. "Mother's going to have a fit."

"You've stood up to her fits before. If she gives you any trouble I'll talk to her. In the meantime, we have more important considerations."

"Such as?"

"Such as the fact that the pictures of you and McGinnis leave no doubt at all that you're having the affair of the week. Such as the fact that everyone in Hollywood now knows who your father was, knows you have access to his work, knows you're trying to sell something connected with him."

"He put that in too, did he?" she said in a bitter undertone.

"The article was written by a woman."

"It was instigated by a man."

"You don't think McGinnis had anything to do with it? The man's a swine, but he wouldn't sink this low. How would the article benefit him?"

"There are no limits to how low he'd sink," Silver said. "He warned me two nights ago that he uses dirty tricks. He's merely running true to form. He wants to see me crushed and humiliated. I don't know if it's just an oversize ego demanding revenge, or whether he really wants *Black Canyon*. And I don't care."

"Revenge I can understand," Clement mused. "After all, I'm an expert at it. But we're not going to let him get away with this. I can talk to my lawyers..."

"What can I do about it?" Silver interrupted his fuming. "It's not libelous, is it?"

"I consider any article that says you're sleeping with a pig like Rafe McGinnis to be libel. Look at this." He leaned past Silver and flipped open the newspaper to the center. "You look like a besotted tramp."

She leaned forward reluctantly, staring at the picture. She certainly didn't look like Silver Carlysle. The fluffy pink dress rode low on her chest, her ridiculous hair looked bed-mussed, and her eyes as she stared up at Rafe McGinnis were definitely filled with emotion. Hatred, she told herself. But that wasn't what the photograph had picked up.

There was an old photo of her parents beside it, her father tall and elegant, her mother petite and beautiful, with a tiny squalling mass of humanity in her arms as she strove to look maternal. Silver had never seen that particular photo before, never seen her father looking down at the baby with a sort of surprised affection.

A lie. He'd never had time for her—he'd simply taken advantage of the publicity offered and managed to look like a doting father. It was all a damned lie.

"Don't!" Clement protested, but he was too late, as she crumpled the paper, ripping it with cold, shaking fingers. "It's not going to hit the newsstands for another couple of days, and we need to prepare our defense against the gossip."

"There is no defense against gossip," Silver said in a numb voice. "Nothing outside of murder."

The telephone beside her computer buzzed, and she jumped, unaccountably nervous. "Don't answer it," Clement ordered.

"Why not? I thought you said it wouldn't be out for another couple of days."

"That doesn't mean everyone hasn't already heard about it. You're not ready to deal with it. Let me take you out to lunch and we'll plan our strategy."

She reached for the telephone. "My strategy, Clement. You don't need to be tarnished by this mess."

"Silver..."

But she'd already picked up the receiver. She knew who was going to be on the other end—there'd never been the slightest doubt. "Silver Carlysle," she said, her voice husky with suppressed rage.

"I warned you."

"So you did." For some reason she didn't want the avidly eavesdropping Clement to know she was speaking to the enemy himself. "I shouldn't have doubted you."

"Who is it?" Clement demanded.

Silver put her hand over the mouthpiece. "Just an old friend. I'll come see you in a minute."

She waited, pointedly, as Clement made no move to leave her. She could be infinitely patient. She didn't mind how long Rafe McGinnis had to wait on the other end of the line, she didn't mind how long Clement stood there, frustrated. She simply waited.

"Don't be long," Clement said finally, turning on his heel and walking away.

She waited until he disappeared into his office before removing her hand. "What did you want?"

"It's nice to know I'm your old friend. I never realized you cared. I imagine that was your mentor?"

"What do you want, Rafe?" she asked again. "Haven't you done enough?"

"Are you ready to relinquish the rights to *Black Canyon?*" He sounded no more than lazily interested. She could picture him on the other end of the line, leaning back in some impossibly expensive leather chair, one custom-made to fit his body, his long legs propped up on his desk, his big hand holding the telephone, his mouth close to the receiver, his mouth...

She had to be insane to be distracted by erotic thoughts.

"Are you still there?" he drawled.

"I'm still here. Why should I give up the rights to *Black Canyon?* You've already taken your best shot, and I'm still here. Still telling you to go straight to hell."

"You think that was my best shot, Silver? You underestimate me. I can get a lot nastier if I set my mind to it. You can still walk away now, bloody but unbowed. Don't make me get really mean."

"I've got a hell of an imagination, McGinnis, and I can't fathom how you can get meaner."

"Seen your mother's necklace recently?"

She felt like she'd been blindsided. Her hand went to her neck, to the loose-knit collar of her T-shirt, as horror swept through her.

She'd never missed it. She'd clasped the ugly, outrageously expensive thing around her neck before leaving for the party, and she'd never thought about it again.

It took everything she had to keep from hyperventilating. She held her breath, long enough to quiet the first panic, and her voice was admirably cool. "I didn't know you were a thief, McGinnis."

"I'm every bad thing you can think of. It took me a moment to remember who'd worn such an outrageously ugly piece of jewelry. I almost tossed it, thinking it couldn't be real, until I found out who your parents were. And sure enough, those are real diamonds and emeralds and rubies. Does your mother know you borrowed it?"

"What makes you think it's my mother's?"

"Not your style, sweetie. Not hers, either, but her husband never had much taste. You want it back?"

"I can call the police, McGinnis."

"You wouldn't want to do that," he said. "For one thing, you'd have to prove ownership. For another, I wouldn't put up a fight, once it caused enough publicity. I just sort of thought you'd had enough of seeing your name in the paper for the time being."

"I'm not giving you the rights to *Black Canyon* for a stolen piece of jewelry."

"Did your mother steal it? I hadn't thought she was that kind of woman. She always seemed so staunchly Republican to me."

"You stole it. And you're not blackmailing me into giving you the rights."

"No," he agreed. "I'm not. I'm blackmailing you into coming out to my house and picking it up."

He wouldn't have made the mistake of thinking she'd be relieved by his suggestion. "Why?"

"So we can discuss this. You know how these things work, Silver, even if you haven't spent much time with power brokers. I make an offer, you make a counteroffer, I sweeten the deal, you hold out for more. In the end we both get what we want. Satisfaction guaranteed."

He was talking about *Black Canyon*. There was no reason to think he was talking about sex, except for the fact that she was momentarily obsessed with it. "Bring it to the office and we'll talk," she said.

"Nope. For one thing, we'd have Clement breathing down our necks, and he's not one of my favorite people. For another, we're going to do this my way. I'm the one holding all the cards. I was ready to give it to you the other night, but you managed to distract me. Now we'll do it on my terms."

"My apartment," she suggested, regretting it. Her apartment wasn't demonstrably safer than his place.

"My house, Silver. Four thousand Hemdale Drive. I'll send my car for you."

"No."

"No? I can always call your mother and explain the situation," he said gently.

"I'll drive my own car. I can be there in about twenty minutes."

"Sorry. Some of us have to work for a living," he said, and Silver gritted her teeth. "Tonight. Nine o'clock. For dinner."

"I'd rather eat nails."

"I don't think my cook knows how to prepare those."

"I'm not coming, McGinnis."

"Then you're not getting your mother's necklace. Come on, Silver, it won't hurt you to talk. It won't hurt you to consider other alternatives to our little impasse. Nine o'clock. I'll be waiting."

He hung up before she could protest again. Not that it would have done her any good. She simply would have told him she wasn't coming. And he simply would have ignored her.

She had no choice. Marjorie loved her, in her own self-absorbed way. And Marjorie hated that ugly, expensive necklace that was doubtless covered by a very effective insurance policy.

None of that mattered. If she discovered her slightly scatterbrained daughter had helped herself to a piece of gaudy jewelry worth well into the six figures, she'd go berserk. And Silver would be paying for it, emotionally, for the next decade.

She was going to go. She wasn't some talentless actress on the make, willing to use the casting couch to get what she wanted. She was a mature adult, one who found Rafe McGinnis inexplicably attractive. That didn't mean he was similarly afflicted, even if he did have an unfortunate tendency to kiss her every time they were alone. She didn't have to succumb. This time she'd be prepared. She'd use every weapon she possessed to keep him at a distance. Because once he came close enough, her brain melted, her resolve vanished, and she'd probably give him just about anything he asked for.

"Who was that?" Clement had waited only moments before hustling back to her desk.

"No one that matters," she said. The last thing she needed was Clement interfering. She was going to have a hard enough time keeping Rafe McGinnis at bay. Clement would only complicate matters.

"What are we going to do about McGinnis?" Clement said. Another man would have leaned against her desk, lounged in the doorway. Clement stood still, his small, spare figure upright and alert with malice.

"I don't think there's anything we can do. At least for now, all we can do is wait and see."

Clement didn't look pleased with the notion. "What's between the two of you? Is this just more revenge for your articles? I can spread the word around among the journalism community, and that man will wish he'd never interfered...."

"It doesn't have anything to do with my work. Not anymore. He wants *Black Canyon*."

Clement blinked. "How extraordinary. Not that he shouldn't, of course. It's a very nice little piece of work for a first effort, given that you started with a Western, for heaven's sake." He made it sound as if she'd worked on a comic book. "I'm simply surprised that McGinnis is that enthralled with it. It's not as if anyone has shown a great deal of interest so far. But then, where's the problem? If McGinnis wants it, you should be celebrating."

"Clement," she said wearily, "you're missing a couple of points. For one thing, we're talking about Mack Movies here. What do you think they'd do to *Black Canyon* if they got their hands on it?"

Clement nodded sagely. "A good point. Not that you'd have any guarantees anywhere else. The movie industry nowadays writes in committees, and you know what committees are like. Not much of your original vision is likely to remain in any case."

"It doesn't have anything to do with it," Silver said. "Because he doesn't want my screenplay. He hasn't even seen it. He simply wants the rights to the novel, and my father's preproduction work on it."

"How much is he offering?"

"Clement!" Silver was horrified. "Do you think I'd sell my birthright?"

"There's not much room for sentiment in Hollywood nowadays," he pointed out.

"What about honor and decency? What about matters of principle?" she said fiercely.

"Not much room for them either, darling. You're going to fight him on this?"

"What do you think precipitated the article? I'm not going to let him have it. I'll burn my father's papers before I let him have it."

"You can't stop him from getting the rights if he's determined."

"He thinks he already owns them. Father was under contract to Pegasus Pictures when he started developing *Black Canyon*. Therefore Rafe thinks it still belongs to them."

"I wonder who brought this to his attention," Clement mused. "It's not the sort of thing he'd be likely to run across unless he had a little help."

"Does that matter?"

"It might. You're right, Silver. For the time being we won't do a thing. Who knows, one of the other studios might come up with an offer if they know Mack Movies is interested. In the meantime, let me see what my contacts can come up with. We might be able to turn this thing around. I would love, simply love, to be able to put one in the eye of Rafe McGinnis."

Silver stared at the dapper little man who'd been more of a father to her than anyone in her life. She wished she could simply dump the whole problem into his hands and forget it.

But there was the problem of the necklace. And the problem of her pride. She didn't want to be rescued, much as a small, weak part of her was tempted by the notion. She didn't want Clement and Rafe making deals while she sat meekly on the sidelines.

As a matter of fact, if someone was going to do battle with Rafe McGinnis, she wanted that someone to be her.

That night, at nine o'clock, she was going into battle, fully prepared for full-scale war. She needed to be ruthless, determined and completely merciless. Rafe McGinnis was the kind of man who would take no prisoners.

She needed to be just as cold-blooded. Particularly when it came to a man like Rafe. Because the fact of the matter was, he made her blood run hot. Feverishly so.

And she had the unpleasant conviction that he knew it.

## Chapter Eight

There was absolutely nothing to worry about, Silver told herself. He had a cook, he probably had a raft of servants besides, he probably lived in a house similar to her mother's. He wasn't going to go chasing her over manicured lawns. It would all be well lighted, supervised, civilized. He'd probably flirt, but then, he did that as naturally as he breathed. She didn't have to show her undeniable response.

She dressed carefully, unearthing one of the simple black dresses her mother regularly bestowed upon her. This one was demure enough, even if it showed too much black-stockinged leg, and she even searched through the tackle box that held her seldom-used jewelry and found a pair of diamond studs that had been a gift from her stepfather on her sixteenth birthday. She'd never worn them, but tonight they were just the right touch. They gave her an illusion of sophistication, of being in charge. Maybe she could trade the diamonds for the tacky necklace.

Having lived in Hollywood most of her life, she was vaguely familiar with the hilly area of Hemdale Drive. She couldn't remember any spacious estate—the houses up there tended to be smaller, more idiosyncratic, but then, with the kind of money Rafe McGinnis had made during his meteoric career, he'd no doubt bulldozed half a neighborhood and put up an ostentatious mansion.

She ought to go all out, take her mother's Rolls and chauffeur and arrive there in style. It would be one more person to turn to, if things got a little sticky.

Problem was, she didn't know if she wanted someone there to rescue her. Rafe certainly wasn't going to force her to do anything she didn't want to. There was no denying he came on to her every chance he got. Each time she'd been alone with him he'd kissed her, and it hadn't been the casual Hollywood clinking of cheekbones.

But she still couldn't really believe he wanted her. It was instinct on his part, second nature. What was that song about if you can't have someone you want, want someone you have?

If she wasn't so ridiculously vulnerable, she could steer him away from such dangerous ground. The problem was, every time he touched her, every time he looked at her, she reacted with an inexplicable longing.

Logically it made no sense. She despised everything Rafe McGinnis stood for. The violent, stupid, obscenely profitable movies, the fast-lane, indiscriminate life-style, the arrogant sexuality.

But there was something about him. Something beneath the arrogance, beneath the cool, dare-you attitude that drew her. A streak of dangerous charm, a touch of vulnerability in his green eyes. Not to mention that he was undoubtably the sexiest man she'd seen in her entire life.

But she'd spent a lifetime, twenty-nine years in fact, not succumbing to sexy men. She'd learned early on that men weren't to be trusted. Hollywood taught you that lesson early, and in the ensuing years she hadn't had any reason to change her mind. During the past few years, when she'd begun to make her way, to grow up, she'd thought of reaching out. There'd been men, kind men, gentle men, and she'd considered falling in love.

But Clement was there, protecting her best interests. If it wasn't for Clement, she'd probably be living in a bungalow in Encino, facing a life married to a very nice man who absolutely bored her to tears.

Still, she might have been happy with Tom in that bungalow. Even if the few times they'd gone to bed together hadn't been world-shaking, she couldn't really blame him. After all, she'd been an elderly virgin, uneasy with sexuality, and he'd been patient.

Clement had hated to tell her the truth about Tom, about his ex-wife and his sleaziness with child support. Just as it had pained Clement to tell her about Dennis's managing to court her as he was trying to climb her stepfather's corporate ladder. At least in the case of Dennis it hadn't gotten as far as the bedroom.

With Rafe she knew exactly what he wanted from her. Not the perfect housewife with no demands. Not a fast track up the corporate ladder. He wanted her birthright, pure and simple. He'd do anything, honorable or not, to get it. And she'd do anything she could to stop him.

The honesty was part of what she found so refreshing in Rafe. The knowledge that the cards were on the table, along with the stakes. Winner take all. And he was so damned certain he was going to win.

She had every intention of showing him otherwise. The article in the *Nosy Parker* hadn't even hit the stands yet, but word had spread. The gossip about the McGinnis-Carlysle feud had died down just as quickly as

Clement had predicted, but this would add new fuel to the fire.

She supposed there was a chance her mother wouldn't find out about it, but she doubted it. Once Marjorie's youthful face adorned the tabloids, all hell would break loose. And it would take all of Silver's emotional reserves to hold out against her.

She surveyed her appearance in the front mirror in her apartment. If there was one thing her two rooms had, it was mirrors. Marjorie was very select in her placement of mirrors, not liking to be presented with her reflection in less than flattering conditions, and she'd sent half of her collection down to Silver. Silver didn't mind being presented with her reflection every time she turned around. For one thing, she considered herself singularly lacking in vanity, for another, the mirrors lightened the area, giving it an illusion of spaciousness.

She put a hand to her close-cropped hair, ruffling it slightly. She didn't look like Silver Carlysle. For that matter, she looked more like her British father's daughter. Tall, long-legged, broad-shouldered, with her simple black dress and her sparkling diamonds, she looked like old Hollywood money. If someone was perceptive they might see the shadow of uneasiness in her wide blue eyes, the faint edginess playing around her mouth. But Rafe was hardly a perceptive, sensitive person. With any luck, he'd believe the package she presented. If anything could intimidate an upstart like Rafe McGinnis, this persona in the mirror could.

However, she had no hope at all that anyone on this earth could intimidate McGinnis. The best she could hope for was to hold her own. It was already nine, and it would probably take her a good fifteen minutes to find his house up in the hills. She'd end up making a conspicuous entrance, which would bring its own set of problems.

She climbed into her aging Toyota and pulled out into the quiet streets. Of course there was no guarantee that Rafe would have invited anyone else, but half of his strategy seemed to involve public humiliation. She could hardly be backed into a corner with curious witnesses. She'd meant it when she told him he'd done his worst. She had no other secrets to hide. No shameful affair, no sleazy business dealings, no dysfunctional family apart from the one he'd already exposed. With Silver Carlysle, what you saw was what you got. Sort of like Popeye. I yam what I yam and that's all what I yam. And if Rafe McGinnis expected something more he was going to be disappointed.

McGinnis himself was another matter, she thought some twenty minutes later as she sat in her car outside four thousand Hemdale Drive, staring at the Moorish turrets of the house that had to be his. His choice of residence made no sense whatsoever, but the Lotus parked out front, the only car in sight, proved that it was indeed.

She was certain she'd find something made of glass and wood, something starkly modern and huge. Instead the kitschy outlines of the Moorish-style cottage were small and muted against the moonlit sky. The gardens were a tangle of overgrowth, and there was construction debris littering the tiled walkway as she made her way toward the front door, moving carefully on the tallest heels she'd possessed.

The door was open. She called his name, quietly at first, afraid of what she'd find inside.

"McGinnis?" she called in a husky voice. Absolute silence. "McGinnis?" She stepped inside, stumbling slightly on a broken tile. The place had a myriad of smells: fresh lumber, the faint trace of chlorine from a swimming pool, the aroma of grilled chicken. He had to be there, lying in wait. She closed the door behind her, wondering if he was going to jump out at her and scare her.

"Rafe," she said, a little louder this time.

"That's better." His voice carried from the dimly lighted interior. "I'm in here."

She followed the sound of his voice into the darkened living room. She could see him stretched out on the couch, wearing dark clothes, his feet bare. The only light in the room came from the big-screen television, sending flickering images around the room.

She deliberately kept her gaze away from what he was watching, half expecting something deliberately erotic. He'd muted the sound and stilled the frame, but she still expected the worst. "Sorry I'm late," she said with proper carelessness. "Did the other guests go home?"

"You're the only guest, Silver." His voice was a lazy drawl across the darkened room. "We can start any time you're ready."

"Start what? I came for my mother's necklace."

"You'll get it. Eventually. When I'm good and ready. In the meantime, come and sit down."

"Why?"

"Because you're wearing the tallest heels I've ever seen, and your feet must hurt."

"They don't."

"That's probably because you put them on in my honor. How tall are you?"

She gritted her teeth. This wasn't going the way she wanted. For one thing, it was too dark in the room. She couldn't see him clearly, could only see the dark clothes and the outline of his shape against the pale-colored sofa. For another, she felt uncomfortable, exposed. She wanted to tug the hemline down on her dress, she wanted to pull the neckline up. She kept her hands at her side.

"Five eleven and a half," she answered instead. "In my bare feet."

"Those heels probably put you about six two. Impressive, but I'm six four. You're still going to have to look up to me."

"Not if I keep standing."

"Don't be a pain, Silver. You agreed to come for dinner, I agreed to hand over the necklace, and we agreed to talk business. We can't do all that if you keep standing in the middle of my living room looking like an oversize socialite."

The term rankled, and he'd meant it to. She crossed the room slowly, her body radiating elegant disdain, and sank at the far end of his sofa. Since it was the only piece of furniture in the room, she didn't have any other choice.

She kept her face averted from the screen. "What are you watching?"

His laugh was dry. "Obviously you think I've lured you up here to show you pornography. Such a dirty mind you have, Silver. As a matter of fact, this is all part of my seduction plan."

That caught her. She glanced at the screen unwillingly, and her brow knotted in confusion as she recognized it. *"Angels from Hell?"* she said in a soft voice. Her favorite of all her father's movies, though a surprisingly obscure choice for Rafe. "How did you get this? I wasn't aware that it was out on videotape."

"Pegasus owns it. I had them make me a copy a few months ago. It's one of my favorite movies."

"It was very special to my father. Though it's not my idea of an erotic movie."

"Who's talking about eroticism? You must have a one-track mind, Silver," he said lazily, stretching out beside her. "I'm not talking about seducing your body, though the notion has very definite appeal to me. We're talking about seducing you away from your elitist principles about movies versus films. That isn't a film on the screen, it's a movie. Your father made movies. I make movies. If you try to turn *Black Canyon* into a film you'll destroy it."

"It's mine to destroy."

"The hell it is." His voice sharpened for a moment, then relaxed. "The problem is, I know you. I know the kind of person you are. Deliberately, downwardly mobile. With your depressing little apartment and your ratty clothes, you're playing at turning your back on everything you were born with. Life is a game to you, Silver. You write your elegant, malicious little reviews, you rebel against your parents when you're too damned old to be indulging in such behavior, and you trail around a spiteful creep like Clement. But we all know that in a couple of years you'll forget all about it, marry some rising executive in your stepfather's business, and become the perfect conservative wife, just like your mother."

She'd almost done exactly that, with Dennis, so she couldn't refute it. "Is there a point to this?" she questioned coolly, leaning back against the cushions with a ramrod-straight spine.

"You don't need *Black Canyon*. No one else will touch it, and five years from now it won't mean anything more to you than a nostalgic memory of when you were young and foolish. Sooner or later you'll probably be ashamed of it, just as you're already ashamed of who your father was."

She could see him clearly now, in the light reflected by the wide-screen television. He was dressed in soft black pants, with a black shirt open at the neck. His long hair was tied back, his feet were bare, and he was looking at her with a kind of sorrowful contempt that lashed her soul.

"I loved my father," she shot back. "I was proud of him. I just don't like to trade on his name."

"Which just goes to prove you don't belong in the movie business. If you want to get a film done, you trade on everything you can if it'll bring in the backers. The industry isn't a place for ladies and gentlemen. You know as well as I do the rights to *Black Canyon* aren't yours. If you have some notion about seeing it produced as a testament to your father, then stop fighting me. I'm the one who'll see it produced. I'm one of the few people in Hollywood to do exactly what I want."

"Not this time."

She waited for his explosion. It didn't come, and she knew the beginnings of despair. No matter how adamant she was, he could hold out. In this battle they seemed equally matched, he by his calm ruthlessness, she by her angry determination. But one of them was going to fall, and she couldn't imagine it was going to be the mighty Rafe McGinnis.

His words echoed her thoughts with eerie exactness. "You're going to lose, Silver. Sooner or later, you're going to have to admit defeat. You can't stop me. The book exists, and even if we don't have your father's pretreatment stuff we can go ahead on our own. I have access to the best in the business. I can make it any way I damned please, and I shouldn't be wasting my time on you."

"Then why are you?"

"I really don't know. No, scratch that. One reason is your father. Your father was one of the finest craftsmen who ever lived, but he didn't make films for the likes of Clement Walden. He aimed for the masses, and he hit, time and again. If there's a living, viable part of his artistry left, then I want it."

There was a sudden silence in the room, as the unwilling thought came to her, echoed in his words before she'd even completed the notion. "But then, you're it, aren't you? The living, viable part of his talent."

"Hardly," she denied, ignoring her own sudden longing. "Don't get confused at this point, McGinnis. You don't want me. You don't even want my father's ideas—you want your own. You just want the cachet of having Sir Benjamin Hatcher's last work as part of Mack Movies."

She didn't expect him to deny it, and he didn't. "It gets a little more complicated than that," he said instead. "You don't know about Bernie. She used to work with your father. She was obviously in love with him."

"She and the entire female population of California," Silver said. "What's that got to do with anything?" She wiggled her foot inside the uncomfortable shoe, and realized with an element of shock that she'd snuggled into the overstuffed corner of the couch. As far away from Rafe as she could manage, so she told herself she could feel safe.

"She was the one who brought the script to my attention. She wants it made, she wants it made in his image, and she wants it dedicated to him."

"So what does that matter? You don't listen to anybody else, why should you listen to a woman?" She wiggled her foot again, and before she realized it he'd caught it in one hand, stripped off the shoe and sent it sailing across the room. A moment later the other one followed suit, before she could tuck her long legs up underneath her.

"Bernie knows more about the business than anyone I've ever met. Her instincts are infallible. If she wants to do something, she does it. I have complete faith in her."

"So I have her to thank for this?" He still had hold of her foot, holding it in one large, strong hand, his fingers massaging the silk-covered arch.

He shrugged in the shadows. "It would have come up sooner or later. Five years ago it wouldn't have mattered, five years from now you won't care. It just happened to come up at the wrong time, when you already had a grudge against me. Be reasonable, Silver. This is the best chance for your father's final work to be produced. Bernie'll make sure it doesn't get mucked up, and you'll get a nice enough piece of change that you can move into a place of your own."

"What makes you think I can't do that already?" She wanted to yank her foot away. But his hand was unbelievably deft and soothing, melting her resistance. In the background the muted scene went on, reminding her of her father's passionate love for what was, undeniably, a mass-market movie.

"Your stepfather would give you anything you want, but you refuse to take it. You spent the last of your father's meager trust fund on college. That's the problem with screen legends—they weren't very good at handling their money. I'm offering you a chance to make more than most executives make in a year, plus points. Consider it your first sale. We'll buy your screenplay, burn it, and you can keep your self-respect."

"What makes you so sure you wouldn't want to do my screenplay?" He'd shifted to the other foot, and for a moment his fingers stopped working.

"Do you want me to see it?" he asked finally.

"No. I wouldn't sell it to you if you were on your knees, pleading. You sound very reasonable. But I'm not giving in. You can't have it. You can't have my father's notes, and you can't have the rights to it."

He didn't say anything more. He didn't release her foot, simply sat there as *Angels from Hell* moved to its inevitable conclusion. She didn't want to see the brief love scene, one that was nothing more than a hurried kiss in an airplane hangar and yet was somehow more erotic than any Mickey Rourke movie. She didn't want to see the battle between the aging pilot and the young upstart. It reminded her too painfully of her father's work being trashed by the brash man who still caressed her foot.

And the heroine picked up a gun, started firing it and stopped the stupid male battles. She'd always loved that part, fantasized about that part. But this wasn't an old movie. She was the combatant, not some pigheaded male, butting her head against the mightiest force in Hollywood today. And she was going to lose.

She yanked her foot away from him, pulling herself off the sofa as the credits rolled. "I came for my mother's necklace."

"You came for dinner."

"I'm not hungry."

He shrugged, unmoved by her distance. "You want to hear numbers?" He mentioned one that almost made her faint.

It didn't make her resolution waver. "No."

"Do you want a drink?"

"No."

"Do you want to go to bed with me?" The question hung in the air, shocking, abrupt. Silver knew with sudden clarity that he meant it. And that she wanted to. Very badly.

"No."

"I could change your mind."

"Not in this lifetime, McGinnis."

He rose, a sudden graceful surge that made her stumble backward, her stockinged feet slippery on the tile floor. "Is that a challenge? You'd better watch yourself, Silver. That's not the way to keep me away from you. I'm not a man who could ever resist a challenge."

She held her ground. "I want my mother's necklace," she said. "And then I want to leave."

"Certainly," he said coolly, crossing the darkened room to her side, and she kept herself from backing away with an effort. "You'll have to get it."

"Don't tell me," she said cynically. "It's in your bed."

"There goes your dirty mind again, Silver. Why are you so obsessed with my bed?"

"Where is the necklace?"

Even in the murky light she could see his wide, innocent smile. "Someplace you'll have no trouble finding it."

"I'm tired of playing games, McGinnis," she said, trying hard to keep her voice from shaking. "Don't you have any lights around here? It's weeks before Halloween, and I want to get on with my life. Where is the necklace?"

"Out there," he said, nodding in the direction of the sheltered terrace.

"Out there?" she echoed, not liking this.

"At the bottom of the swimming pool. You'll have to swim for it, Silver. Do you want a bathing suit or do you want to go au naturel?"

She looked at him for a long moment, considering, and then stared out at the shimmering, moon-silvered depths of the pool. "You're a bastard, McGinnis," she said tightly.

"Bathing suits are in the cabana," he said, reading her rage correctly. "I'll be waiting."

She wished she had the colossal nerve to call his bluff. To go out to the pool, strip off all her clothes and dive in with magnificent disdain for his schoolboy pranks. But she didn't.

She couldn't simply walk away, either. She had to get her mother's necklace back. Things were going to be bad enough when her mother heard about the tabloid—if she found her gaudy piece of jewelry was gone too, all hell would break loose.

If she wanted the necklace, she was going to have to go into the pool and get it. And she was going in decently clothed.

"I'm going to get even," she said calmly enough, heading for the terrace doors. "I want you to know that. Sooner or later I'm going to have my revenge."

She could feel his eyes on her, as physical as a touch. "I'm counting on it," he murmured.

And in the warm night air, Silver shivered.

## Chapter Nine

Rafe took his time. He knew Silver Carlysle. At times he thought he knew her better than she knew herself. She was going to storm into that cabana and be confronted with a daunting choice of bathing suits. He'd seen the fury flash in her eyes, had known she'd wanted to simply pull off that elegant, unlikely little dress of hers and dive into his pool, impervious to his goading.

It was a wise thing she hadn't. She knew a predator when she saw one, even if she still couldn't quite believe he was after her. He couldn't imagine where she'd gotten such a mistaken notion of her own attractions. With her tall, rangy body, her mane of close-cropped dark hair, her wide mouth and to-hell-with-you blue eyes, she was absolutely magnificent. More woman than he'd dealt with in a long time. And she seemed to have no notion of it.

He knew who to thank for that diffidence, and it wasn't the obvious choice of an insensitive ex-husband or lover. He stripped down to his bathing suit as he followed Silver onto the terrace, grabbing a towel while he was at it. He could see Clement Walden's work in Silver's abysmal sexual self-esteem. Indeed, it made perfect sense. As long as Clement convinced Silver that sex wasn't a viable part of her life, then she'd remain his humble little acolyte, with no other man as a rival for her time and attention.

Of course it was part of her attraction. The sleeping-beauty touch was irresistible, particularly when he was used to such flamingly aggressive women. He should be too old and wise to be seduced by innocence. But there was something about her that he wanted, needed. Maybe just to wipe that innocence away, to force her to face the world as it really was.

Flipping on the underwater lights, he slid into the warm water. The ugly necklace lay on the bottom in the center of the pool, fully illuminated. He wondered lazily whether he'd be able to entice her to stay in with him, surrounded by the warm, sensual lap of the water. Or whether she was going to dive in, grab the jewelry and run. Doing her best to drown him on the way.

He didn't bother wondering why he'd set this up. It had all been instinct on his part. He'd wanted her in his house, he'd fantasized about having her in the pool. He didn't really know what he expected to accomplish. Just to make her mad again. And to remind her that he could make her do what he wanted.

He wasn't about to get her into bed at any time in the near future, he'd accepted that with a certain amount of fatalism. His assault on her stern defenses was going to be a long drawn-out affair, and if he rushed, it would only take that much longer. It was a delicate thing, inciting her rage while he kept her senses stirred. She hated the fact that he got to her. But she hadn't figured out how to make herself immune.

Of course he could always do the gentlemanly thing, he thought, taking a few lazy strokes through the water. He could give her back the rights to *Black Canyon*, even put in a word at Regis or Touchstone and push it toward getting produced. She'd probably fall into his bed in gratitude, another love slave who'd do it for the sake of her career.

That wasn't what he wanted from her. For one thing, *Black Canyon* had come to mean too much to him. The disillusionment, the jaded cynicism had grown over the past five years, so that he didn't give a damn about the movies he made, the work he did. Even the money didn't matter.

*Black Canyon* did. It would bring his heart back, make things matter once more, and he wasn't about to give up that dream for anything, up to and including the most desirable woman he'd met in years.

And he didn't just want Silver Carlysle, grateful and compliant, lying on her back. He wanted her to come to him because she couldn't help herself. He wanted her to know it was the worst thing she could do, and to do it anyway. He wanted her to want him so much that common sense and all those impeccable defenses disappeared. And he wasn't going to stop until he got her.

If there'd been a door on the cabana she would have slammed it. As it was, she strode out, her body radiating a fiery rage that almost wiped out her self-consciousness. Treading water, he stared at her as she dumped her clothes on a nearby chaise longue and stomped toward the water, and he wondered whether he might have made a major miscalculation.

She'd managed to find the one demure maillot amid the various bikinis. At least it should have been demure. But it was made for a woman half a foot shorter and a lot skinnier. The silky black material molded itself to Silver Carlysle's hitherto unseen flesh, and the effect was more powerful than if she'd chosen one of the skimpy bikinis.

She had hips. Definitely she had hips, a flare of body that emphasized the smallness of her waist. She had breasts, God, she had breasts. The kind of breasts that would have ruled the world in the fifties, the kind of breasts that he knew made her self-conscious in the shapeless nineties. He'd never considered himself the kind of man to be transfixed by body parts. Maybe he was changing his ways.

And her legs. They went on forever. Long, lithe, luscious. He wanted those legs wrapped around him, he wanted her unbelievably sexy body entwined with his.

Treading water, he moved deeper, keeping his face impassive. "Coward," he taunted her softly. If she didn't look beneath the crystal clear water, she wouldn't see how even her demure choice of bathing suit affected him.

She ignored his taunt, jumping into the shallow end of the pool with a reckless disregard for her hair, her diamond earrings and the untested depth of the water. She swam toward him, with long, graceful strokes, all the time keeping her face out of water, and if she was troubled by his proximity, she managed to hide it.

"Where is it?" she demanded tightly.

"At your feet." She glanced down, looking at the plastic bag at the bottom of the tiled pool. The pool was six feet deep at that point, and the decorative tile lining made the gaudy jewels blend in a bit with the background, but he had no doubt she saw them.

What he didn't understand was why she didn't simply dive down and get them.

She moved away from him, treading water, and for the first time her concentration wasn't on him at all. It was on the hideous piece of jewelry lying within reach. Something she wanted very much, and yet made no move to retrieve.

Since she wasn't about to move, he decided to probe a little. "I take it your mother didn't know you helped yourself to her necklace," he said, moving toward her through the warm water. "Hasn't she missed it yet?"

She didn't even realize danger was moving closer. "My mother has good taste," she said absently, staring at the bottom of the pool. "She never wears the ugly thing. It may be months before she notices it's missing. I can't take that risk."

"Why didn't you ask her?"

"None of your business," she said, moving away from him in the water, backward, toward the side of the pool. "We don't necessarily see eye to eye on things."

"And she would have known you shared her same conventional good taste. The only reason you would have worn the necklace was if you wanted to look tacky." His voice was dry.

He'd managed to sting her into reacting. "I don't share my mother's taste. Besides, what's wrong with having good taste?"

"I don't believe in it. Good taste is the natural enemy of art."

"Since you don't seem to have even a passing acquaintance with either, I wouldn't think it would matter to you," she shot back.

"Don't be predictable, Silver. I was waiting for that one." She was still retreating, he was still advancing. He couldn't figure out why she didn't simply dive for the jewels and make a run for it, but he didn't fool himself into thinking it had anything to do with him. There was some other issue at stake here, and until she came to terms with it she was going to stay in the water with him, her luscious, overwhelming body a distracting few inches away.

The moon was bright overhead, the night was as still and silent as a night in the hills of Hollywood could be. He could hear the faint lap of water against her body, the quiet catch of her breathing, and he wanted to hear her make those same sounds out of the water, when she was lying in his bed.

Damn, he was making himself crazy! This was backfiring on him—at this rate he'd be the one suffering, not her. "So tell me, Silver," he said softly, and his voice was the only soft thing about him, "what's the problem?"

She looked up from her perusal of the pool floor, momentary surprise darkening her eyes, and once again he knew he was temporarily the lesser of her worries. "Problem?" she echoed. "You mean apart from you?"

"Apart from me," he said, and he was almost touching her. If he simply let his body drift it would brush against hers. And he wasn't sure if he could simply let it drift back again. "Why don't you go get the necklace?"

"I will," she said stubbornly. "Just give me a minute."

He didn't know why he hadn't realized it sooner. "You're afraid of the water," he said flatly.

It would have been a waste of time for Silver to deny it, and she wasn't a woman who believed in wasting her time. "Yes."

"You can swim," he said. "You grew up in Beverly Hills. It's against the law for a house in Beverly Hills to be without a swimming pool."

"We had a swimming pool," she said. "We always had a swimming pool."

"Downwardly mobile, what did I tell you?" Rafe said. "So what's the problem? Some childhood trauma? Don't tell me—you nearly drowned when you were five years old and you haven't been able to put your head under water ever since."

She glared at him, and to his amusement she called him a name he wouldn't have thought she'd know. "I was seven," she snapped. "And it isn't a laughing matter."

"No, I suppose it's not. But you aren't the kind of woman who'd succumb to a childhood trauma. I can't imagine you giving in to any weakness."

"You don't even know me," she said, a touch of panic in her voice. "How can you make judgments about the kind of person I am, when you haven't the faintest idea who that is?"

"I've told you, I know you far better than you think. I know that all you have to do is make your mind up and you can face anything, including deep water and overbearing film producers. So why are you hesitating?"

She didn't move. "Don't rush me," she said. "I'll do it eventually."

That was when he realized he'd been wrong about her. It wasn't a case of self-indulgent neurosis. She was deeply afraid of the water, so afraid that his nearness, his opinion, no longer mattered. She was going to stay in his pool till her body temperature dropped, her lips turned blue, and she still wasn't going to be able to dive down and get that damned necklace.

Suddenly he felt like a fool. As long as Silver Carlysle fought back, he could revel in the battle, even knowing the outcome was preordained from the beginning. But the panic in her eyes, the paleness of her lips, the very real fear made him momentarily ashamed of himself.

He didn't like that feeling. He swore, then dived down without a word, snatching the necklace from the tile floor and surfacing again in a matter of seconds.

If he expected the light of gratitude to fill her eyes he'd deluded himself. She was watching him warily, knowing he was going to name his price.

Which of course he was. Only he didn't like the fact that she realized it. He pushed away, moving into the middle of the pool, keeping his expression enigmatic. "All right, Silver," he murmured. "Come and get it."

She may have been afraid of water, but ravening movie producers were child's play in comparison. She came after him, her strokes strong and sure, and he knew the effort that much proficiency must have cost her. She'd conquered her terror of the water. She just couldn't bring herself to put her head under the water.

She caught up with him near the deep end of the pool, reaching for the plastic bag. He caught her wrist before she could grab it, pulling her body up against his, and she felt strong, vibrant against his water-slick skin. "Forfeit," he murmured, sliding one hand beneath her wet hair and holding her head still as he tossed the plastic bag onto the tiled walkway beside the pool.

Her mouth was wet from the water, cool and startled. He used his tongue, pushing into her, his anger and frustration overriding his better judgment.

Her hands caught his shoulders, her fingers digging in, and her eyes fluttered closed in instant acquiescence. He knew what she was doing. She was paying the forfeit, hoping to get off lightly.

He lifted his head to look down at her as they drifted into the center of the pool. "It's not going to be so easy," he muttered. And he kissed her again, his mouth covering hers, his arms wrapped around her body, as he pushed them down below the surface of the water.

She struggled for a moment, panic suffusing her body, and her fingers dug into his shoulders. But he pushed his hips against hers, held her mouth still beneath his, and she held her breath, sinking with him, letting him kiss her, letting his mouth seal hers away from the suffocating water, letting his aroused body press against hers. And then her generous breasts pressed against his chest, only that thin layer of spandex separating their flesh; and her tongue touched his, for a brief moment her terror of the water overridden by her reaction to him.

His foot touched the tile floor, and he pushed off again, rising upward, his mouth still clamped to hers, until they shot out of the water, surfacing into the moon-gilded night.

She hit him then, her fists pounding at him as she tore her mouth away, taking in deep, furious gulps of air.

But he was too strong for her, too determined. He kissed her again, pulling her beneath the surface, and her fear channeled into a rage so powerful it was a wonder the water around them didn't boil.

Up they came again, and she tried to knee him, but he stopped her, pushing her up against the side of the pool, and kissed her again. And this time when they slid beneath the pearly water she kissed him back.

The water surrounded them, a cocoon of sensation, rich and cool and velvety, caressing them, pushing them tight together beneath the surface. He could feel the tremor beneath her skin, a tremor that had nothing to do with fear, and his hands slid up her arms to the straps of the thin maillot, pulling the spandex down to her waist.

Somehow they'd moved into shallower water. When his feet touched the tile his head and shoulders were in the night air. He hauled her up against him, and she was pliant, warm against him, as he wrapped her legs around his waist.

She sank against him, her face against his shoulder, her soft breasts against his chest, and he took a deep breath, struggling for some lost remnant of control. "Do you make a habit of this?" she asked in little more than a whisper. "Drown a woman into compliance?"

He wouldn't have thought she had that much fight left in her. She startled a laugh from him. "Only if I have to," he said. He was rapidly reaching the point of no return. The sweet, heavy weight of her breasts against his chest, the sleekness of her thighs around his hips, the taste of her mouth still lingering on his, were pushing him to a point he didn't remember reaching before. He'd never been so aroused that he couldn't pull back. He was almost there now, and if he moved his hands between them, cupped her breasts, he'd be lost.

For a moment he contemplated going for it. He could have her, he knew it, despite her best judgment. He could strip off the rest of her bathing suit and make love to her in the pool, and she wouldn't even notice if they came under water.

But much as his body screamed for it, what little remained of his self-control told him no. She wasn't ready to give in completely. He could make love to her until she was a pleasured little mass of desire, but half an hour later she'd be fighting again.

He needed her acquiescence, her defeat on all fronts. If he took her body now, she'd still be able to fight back. He needed to wait until she was ready to give up everything. It was the only way he could ensure getting exactly what he wanted. And he never settled for less. He never had, he never would show that kind of weakness. Especially for a woman.

It was physically painful, releasing her, and he wondered if he was being a complete fool. But the moment his grip loosened she pushed away, and her dazed expression sharpened into awareness once more as she stumbled away from him in the waist-deep water.

"The necklace is over there." He jerked his head carelessly in the direction he'd thrown it, and watched with undimmed appreciation as she climbed out of the water.

She hadn't realized her bathing suit was at her waist. She yanked it up, her back to him, and he knew a moment's regret that he hadn't been able to see her. When he finally had her, he wanted it to be in broad daylight, on a bed uncluttered with sheets or covers of any sort. He wanted to lose himself in her glorious body. He had the strong suspicion that no one had appreciated it sufficiently before. He intended to remedy that error in judgment on the male part of the species.

She grabbed her clothes from the chaise, scooped up the wet plastic bag, and stalked toward the house. "Are you stealing my bathing suit, Silver?" he called lazily, hiding the sharp tang of need that was still eating at his gut.

"It wouldn't fit you. You're not getting *Black Canyon*, McGinnis. And you're not putting your hands on me again," she said fiercely.

He pushed off, floating on his back in the pool, and there was no way she could miss how aroused he was if she cared to look. Chances are she was too upset to notice. "Don't count on it, Silver," he said. "I've told you before, I always get what I want, by fair means or foul."

"I should have listened," she said bitterly, pausing in the doorway. "I thought you'd played your dirtiest trick. I should have known you could sink even lower."

"Literally," he said in a lazy voice. "I take it you don't like the idea of being seduced into giving up the rights? Why don't you just sell them to me and I'll leave you alone? If that's what you really want."

"Sexual harassment is an ugly term, McGinnis."

"Silver, you wound me," he protested. "And I thought you liked my kisses. If you don't, you shouldn't kiss me back."

She exploded. "I hope you drown, McGinnis. I hope you die a slow, painful death. You're the most despicable, contemptible, sexist, macho turkey I have ever met in a long, miserable life, and if you smashed yourself up in that ridiculous sports car I would dance on your grave. I'd—"

He surged out of the pool, coming after her. "I wish I knew what I'd done to make you so crazy," he said dryly. "It's not my fault that I find you completely gorgeous."

"Liar."

"Am I going to have to prove it again?" he said in a silken voice, stalking her around the edge of the pool.

She ran from him. The bold, inimitable Ms. Silver Carlysle turned and ran, her clothes clutched against her, her wet bare feet making footprints on the pale tile, and it took all his self-control not to go after her.

"Later," he murmured, a promise to his needful body. "Later," he said again, when he heard the noisy muffler of her car as she tore out of the driveway, and this time he was making a promise to some deep, irrational part of him that was only partly sexual.

He ignored his own, irrational uneasiness. There was a part of him that wanted Silver Carlysle, needed her, on a level even more profound that his physical craving for her. A need that powerful was hard to shake, hard to control, and if he had any sense of self-preservation at all he'd back away, run like hell, and not even worry about *Black Canyon*. Hell, there was nothing wrong with making *Cop for a Day II*.

But he knew he wasn't going to. It had gone too far already, and Rafe McGinnis never backed down from a threat. He could get Silver Carlysle in bed, take *Black Canyon* from her, and then walk away, without even a twinge of conscience.

Couldn't he?

## Chapter Ten

It was a conceptual impossibility, Silver thought. The day simply couldn't have gotten worse. Starting with that god-awful article in the tabloid, with her family history laid out in maudlin detail, only to be compounded and surpassed by the time spent with Rafe McGinnis. She had the necklace, but that was about the only triumph she was able to wrest from a day of complete disaster. She needed to keep away from him. He unsettled her, shook her to her very core, and her formidable defenses were useless against him.

No, scratch that. She wasn't an infant, to blame other people for her own problems. The issue wasn't Rafe McGinnis and whatever mystical, sexual powers he had. The issue was her weak-minded reaction to him.

She hated to admit her weakness. Hated to accept the fact that she simply couldn't deal with him. She, who'd always prided herself on her tough-minded defenses, was defenseless when it came to a man like Rafe. She despised herself for it. But she couldn't change it.

Fortunately there was no longer any reason to deal with him. She had the necklace, she wouldn't give him the rights to *Black Canyon*. Two simple issues resolved, at least to her mind. If he wanted to keep after her, he'd have to do it through lawyers.

And if only the night had ended on that firm note, she would have counted herself lucky. She should have known fate had more in store for her. Nothing could equal being kissed by Rafe McGinnis, her body wrapped tight in his, sinking beneath the cool depths of his pool and no longer caring if she drowned.

But being stopped for speeding, wearing nothing but a too small bathing suit and bare feet, with an out-of-date license and a car with a taillight missing, certainly came a close second in the scale of disasters. It didn't help that the police made her climb out of her car and walk a straight line dressed only in that skimpy bathing suit. In the end she gave in to weakness, bursting into noisy tears, loud enough to convince the patrolman that she could drive herself home as long as she put on her spiked heels.

The problem was, once she started crying, she couldn't stop. She had to keep wiping the blinding tears from her face as she drove at a sedate enough pace through the wide, elegant streets of Beverly Hills to her mother's mansion. She didn't even bother to consider why she was crying, she who cried approximately once every eighteen months. She just knew she needed to cry, and every time she thought of Rafe McGinnis, which was far too often, she simply cried harder.

She needed a shower, she told herself as she pulled up the winding driveway and stopped outside the closed garage. She needed to wash the chlorine from her hair and skin, she needed to wash the taste of him from her mouth, the feel of him from her breasts. And then she needed to crawl into her bed, wrap the covers around her and not wake up until she damned well wanted to.

She kicked off the heels, grabbing her clothes and heading up the flight of stairs. She came to an abrupt stop on the landing, as she realized she wasn't alone.

"Uh, good evening, miss." Wilkers, her mother's chauffeur, rose from a crouching position by her door, his normally bluff face darkened with embarrassment.

Silver didn't move, as dread shot through her. "What's going on, Wilkers? I know you're not trying to break into my apartment. For one thing, you already have a key to everything here, and for another, I never lock it. So what's up?"

"Your mother."

It was answer enough. Silver climbed the remaining flight of stairs, pushing past him, into the tiny section of peace that had been the best home she'd ever had. It was empty, her makeshift furniture gone, the mirrors off the walls, the rugs rolled up. Her last remaining comfort had been ripped away, and she felt raped.

"Your mother had us bring all your stuff up to the big house. I was just putting a lock on the door," Wilkers said miserably, torn between the woman who signed his paychecks and the one who'd been his friend for the twelve years he'd worked there.

Silver didn't move. It was never cold in Los Angeles. The wet bathing suit and the night air had to be responsible for the desolate chill that swept up her spine. "Did she happen to mention what precipitated this?"

"Something about a newspaper article," Wilkers said. "She was in a rare mood, miss. She's up there, waiting for you."

Silver didn't bother to glance toward the house. "You know, Wilkers," she said in a meditative voice, "I'm not in the mood. Would you take her this?" She dropped the waterlogged plastic bag into his hand. "And tell her I'll be in touch."

"But, miss . . ." he protested. "You haven't a change of clothes. You can't just walk away. Where will you go?"

She managed a wry smile. "Believe it or not, Wilkers, I have possibilities. I have friends, and I have a gold credit card compliments of my stepfather that I have so far refrained from using. I'm afraid I'm going to have to lower my standards for the next month. But I'll be fine. Just fine."

"Do you want me to see if I can sneak out one of your suitcases?"

"And put your job on the line? No, Wilkers, much as I appreciate the offer. My mother can be a holy terror, and I don't want you getting in the middle. Just tell her I'll be in touch." She took one last, sorrow-filled glance around her denuded living room. "She even took my computer?" she asked in a mournful voice.

"Everything, miss."

"Well—" she forced some brightness into her voice "—I needed to upgrade. And I needed a break from L.A.—too much smog and hot wind this time of year. Take care of yourself, Wilkers. And watch out for Mother. She doesn't like to lose battles, and she's losing this one."

Suddenly she couldn't bear to stay in the empty apartment a moment longer. Without a backward glance she headed out, running back down the stairs as fast as her bare feet could carry her.

She didn't bother to slip on the heels again as she took off into the gathering night. Chances of her being stopped twice, even with a broken taillight, were unlikely.

She turned on the heat full blast as she drove through the wide, clear streets, and the little-used system kicked out an oily smell that turned her stomach even as it warmed her exposed flesh.

She stopped in a parking lot long enough to tug the skimpy black dress over the damp bathing suit, ignoring the fact that the straps showed.

L.A. was a big city, catering to people's whims, and it didn't take her long to find a clothing store that stayed open all night long. She bought indiscriminately, for the first time not stopping to consider price, suitability or even what she planned to do for the next twenty-four hours. She bought everything that caught her eye and looked big enough for her tall figure, using her stepfather's gold card wherever she went.

When she'd filled the back of her Toyota and her feet hurt too much to walk anymore, she gave up, heading for the nearest anonymous hotel. She hadn't lied to Wilkers—she did have any number of friends who'd put her up for the night, for the week, forever, if she asked it. Clement would be beside himself with glee—he'd been trying to get her to move into his palatial French provincial town house for the past year.

He'd ply her with Earl Grey tea and Courvoisier, he'd soothe her and murmur deliciously malicious things about both her mother and Rafe McGinnis, he'd give her back her pride and self-respect, he'd take care of her.

But she'd already had a taste of the price he'd exact from her. Clement wanted unwavering loyalty, no diverging opinions, and a slavish audience to listen to his pronouncements. She'd had no trouble providing those requirements in the past, but in the last few weeks she'd begun to change. She still adored Clement, but occasionally, just occasionally, he could be wrong.

He'd pointed out her errors in judgment when it came to men, pointed them out in such a way that she had no choice but to turn her back on the possible relationships. She'd always been grateful he'd rescued her from making an utter fool of herself. But she was coming to the point where she was ready to risk it.

Hell, she'd done more than risk it. She had only to get near Rafe McGinnis for her brain to go into core meltdown. Clement knew it, even though she denied it to his face. If she went to Clement for shelter she'd be treated to a vicious, impossibly clever diatribe on just how pathetic Rafe McGinnis really was.

She didn't want to hear it. She didn't want to be told that the enemy, the man who was effectively destroying everything she'd worked so hard on, was unworthy. She'd imbued him with almost superhuman attributes. If he really was an ordinary mortal, then her powerlessness was that much more shameful.

She'd finished the series of articles. She had money in her account, she had a back seat full of new clothes, she had a gold credit card with a stratospheric credit limit. What she needed was a break from everyone and everything. And that was what she was going to get.

She didn't sleep well in the queen-size bed that smelled of stale cigarettes. She checked out by six the next morning, dressed in a pair of baggy black pants and a T-shirt that somehow managed to look impossibly elegant. Not that it shouldn't, when she considered the price tag she'd ripped off and thrown into the trash. The new black leather running shoes were a relief after hobbling around on high heels, but she kept her diamond earrings in. She spared herself a startled glance in her rearview mirror as she pulled into the beginnings of rush hour. Lord, even the fastidious Clement might approve.

It hadn't taken her long to decide where she was going. Or where she was going to stop along the way. She'd done a cursory amount of research into Rafael McGinnis, stopping abruptly when he became too interesting. She knew he came from Colorado originally, knew he'd gone through the University of Michigan as an undergraduate, then taken a graduate degree at NYU. He'd gotten into the movie business almost by accident, something Clement had always maintained was obvious if you saw one of his productions, and his work habits were legendary. He was at his studios by six every morning. She knew just where to find him.

She also knew going to see him one last time had to be far from the smartest thing she'd ever done. It was weakness, pure and simple, a longing on her part for some sort of resolution. Or at least a final glance.

Apparently the other employees of Mack Movies shared his zeal for overwork. The place was already busy when she pulled up to the gate at 6:45, and she paused, wondering whether she was going to have any trouble getting onto the lot to face her nemesis.

"Can I help you?" The genial gatekeeper was unlike anyone she'd ever seen in security before, with his Hawaiian shirt, baseball cap and long hair.

"I want to see Rafe McGinnis," she said, momentarily startled.

"You and half of Hollywood. I don't suppose you have an appointment?"

"I'm afraid not."

"Go home and make one."

"I'm on my way out of town. He'll see me, I'm pretty sure of it, if you could just give him my name."

The guard shook his head. "Can't do that."

Silver felt frustration building inside. Coming to see Rafe wasn't her brightest idea in recent years, but now that she'd gone this far she intended to see it through to the end. "Why not?" she demanded, trying to keep the truculence out of her voice.

He smiled sweetly. "Because I don't know what your name is."

Silver growled, low in her throat like a rabid cocker spaniel. "Silver Carlysle."

"One moment." He picked up the phone inside the booth, spoke into it briefly, and Silver knew a sudden hope that he'd come back, chastened and apologetic.

It was too much to hope for in such a casual operation. "Go ahead," he said cheerfully, raising the gate. "Second building on the right, walk in and turn left. Have a nice day."

Silver growled again, gunning the motor and zooming past him. The sooner she got out of this town, away from sun-addled surfers, the happier she'd be.

The Lotus was nowhere in sight, but she didn't let that bother her. She already knew Rafe was just as likely to be carried around by the Bentley parked outside the building, and if the man had a Lotus he probably owned several other cars besides, including the Ferrari parked beside the door.

She shoved her short-cropped hair behind her ears and climbed out of her aging Toyota. It didn't belong in such august company, but she no longer gave a damn. She was coming in for her final confrontation, and the financial inequity just solidified her determination.

The secretary wasn't any more standard than the gatekeeper. She was young, with long hair hanging to her waist, dressed in spandex biking shorts of a particularly bilious shade of green. "Miss Carlysle? First door on your left. What do you take in your coffee?"

"No coffee, thank you," she said, though the words nearly choked her. She needed caffeine even more than she needed peace of mind. The only thing more important was keeping Rafe away from her, and if she accepted his hospitality, even in a cup of coffee, she'd be giving him an advantage.

The door was ajar to his office, and beyond she could hear the quiet murmur of voices. At least he wasn't alone. If there were witnesses he wouldn't touch her, wouldn't kiss her, and she just might possibly make it through what she counted on being her final meeting with him. Taking a deep, determined breath, she pushed open the door and walked in. And then came to an abrupt halt.

Rafe wasn't there. Sitting behind his desk was a plain, ageless woman in dark-rimmed glasses, and it took Silver a moment to remember her name. Bernadette Thomas. The woman who'd brought all this about.

Bernie rose with a graciousness worthy of Marjorie Carlysle at her most elegant. "We're so glad you came by, Silver," she said, her rough voice matching her no-nonsense exterior. "You remember Sam Mendelsohn, don't you?"

Silver glanced at him warily, her initial relief fading into uneasiness. "I was looking for Rafe," she said baldly.

"Damned if I know where he is," Sam said genially. "He's usually here at the crack of dawn, setting a lousy example for all of us. He must have had quite a night of it. I wonder if we have Marcia Allison to thank for it, or someone new. He goes through women so fast you need a scorecard.''

Silver drew herself up to her full height, towering over the smaller man. "If that information is directed at me it's nothing I don't already know. And I certainly don't give a damn. I wanted to talk to Mr. McGinnis about a business matter.''

"Don't pay any attention to Sam—he's a jerk half the time, and brilliant the other half. You're catching him in his jerk mode," Bernie said. "Let me get you some coffee.''

"No coffee," Silver said again. The damnable thing was, she liked Bernie Thomas. She liked her frank manner, she liked her work, she liked everything about her. It was all she could do to summon her anger. "I gather I have you to thank for this current mess.''

"I don't blame you for being angry," Bernie said wryly. "I don't suppose it would help if I said I was sorry.''

"Not unless you can call Rafe off.''

"No one can call him off when he's got his mind set on something," Sam said. "Besides, I don't know if I'd let him. I read the book, and it's got terrific possibilities. I'd give ten years of my life to see what Hatcher had in mind for it. The man was a legend.''

Unwillingly Silver's eyes met Bernie's. "A legend," Silver echoed stiffly. "Forgive me if I'm not that enthusiastic.''

"Why don't you just hand over the papers?" Sam pushed it. "We'll keep Rafe out of it completely if you don't want to feel like you're giving in to him. I promise you, I'll treat the whole thing like the solid gold it is. You'll lose in the end, Miss Carlysle. Why don't you give in with dignity, not make this thing unbearably unpleasant?''

"I didn't come here to argue about it," she said.

"Then why did you come?" Bernie asked, with real curiosity.

"To tell Rafe that I'm going out of town. He may be one of the most powerful men in Hollywood, but I have an advantage over him. I have my father's papers, and I know where the original author of *Black Canyon* came from. I intend to find him, if he's still living, or his closest relatives and heirs. By the time I come back here there won't be any more question about who owns the rights to it. I will.''

"It's been thirty years, Silver. What makes you think you'll find any trace of him?"

Silver merely smiled. "If D. Maven is still alive, I'll find him.''

"Where?" Sam demanded.

"None of your business," she said with ultimate sweetness. "Just tell Rafe he's wasting his time."

"Don't you want to wait?" Bernie said with surprising urgency. "He'll be here any time now."

"I don't think so." Silver could feel her resolve weakening. She'd come for one reason, and one reason alone. To warn him away from her. Since he was gone, she was spared, and with luck she'd be able to return with the proof she needed.

She left the room with unruffled grace, moving slowly until she was out of their eyesight. And then she ran for it, jumping in her car and tearing out of the lot at a dangerous speed, considering the baldness of her tires.

It was a close call. His Lotus was pulling up to the building just as she was peeling away. She didn't have any illusions that he might have missed her, and she knew a moment's panic, that he might come after her. The aging engine of her poor Toyota would be no match for the Lotus, but apparently he didn't think her worthy of pursuit.

She glanced in the rearview mirror, almost sideswiping a building as she sped away from him. He was standing by the car, staring after her, dressed in black jeans and a T-shirt. And it didn't help her unsettled state of mind to realize their clothes were almost an exact match.

She was past the sprawling, endless city limits of greater Los Angeles in forty-five minutes, deftly avoiding gridlock, the army of traffic heading in the opposite direction. She had no idea how long it would take her to get to the tiny town of Elkmate, Colorado, and she didn't particularly care. D. Maven had waited for the past thirty years. He could wait another day or two.

She happened to own the only car in the greater Los Angeles area without air-conditioning. She rolled down the window, letting the fresh autumn breeze blow through her short-cropped hair, blow through her soul. In twenty-nine years she hadn't been able to break the invisible golden apron strings that had tied her to her mother's whims. Finally, thankfully, Marjorie had gone too far. And she was blessedly, completely free.

Except for the unsettling specter of Rafe McGinnis haunting her dreams. And she had every intention of exorcising that final ghost by the time she was finished in Colorado.

"WHY DIDN'T YOU keep her here?" Rafe demanded, stalking into his office.

"There's a law against detaining people against their will," Sam said from his spot on the leather sofa. "She came, she saw, she conquered, she left."

"What did she want?" He turned to Bernie, knowing he wasn't going to get a sensible answer from Sam in his current mood.

"I'm not quite sure. What's going on between the two of you, anyway?" Bernie asked. "I've never known you to be so gauche in handling women. I would have thought she'd be eating out of your hand right now. If I thought you were going to have any real trouble getting the rights to *Black Canyon* then I never would have brought it up."

"I'm not having trouble," he said with gritted teeth. "Silver Carlysle happens to be one of the most pig-headed, frustrating females I've ever met."

"Yeah, you're used to having 'em roll over and play dead, aren't you?" Sam piped up. "Maybe I ought to see if she goes for the short, rumpled type. I mean, someone in this world has got to prefer me to you."

"It's possible. But not in this case. That's part of the problem. If Silver was a man the issue would be straightforward and between our lawyers."

"I never thought to see the day when a woman would get the better of you," Bernie mused.

Rafe knew perfectly well she'd said it to goad him. It still didn't keep him from reacting. "The day she gets the better of me will be the day *Cop for a Day* wins an Oscar," he snapped. "Where was she going?"

"Out of town, buddy boy," Sam chortled. "You're going to have to sit here and twiddle your thumbs for the next few days until she decides to turn up, and then it might be too late. She says she's going after the old codger who wrote the book, and she's coming back with the deal signed, sealed and delivered."

"What are you sounding so cheerful about? I thought you were as committed to *Black Canyon* as I was?" Rafe said.

"Oh, I am. I admit, I'm torn. On the one hand, I really want to do that Western. Anything that's got both you and Bernie in such a snit is powerful stuff indeed. The book's fantastic, and the possibilities are endless. On the other hand, I really enjoy watching you squirm."

"Thanks," he said morosely. "What about you, Bernie? You got us into this. Do you have any suggestions, or are you just going to sit around and watch me tear my hair?"

"I've got a very good suggestion," she said tranquilly. "Beat her to it."

"What the hell do you think I've been trying to do for the past few days? How can I beat her to it when I don't know where she's going?"

"Elkmate, Colorado," Bernie said.

Rafe just looked at her. Life couldn't be that twisted, could it? He stalled for time. "How do you know she went there?"

"I was in on the original development, remember? D. Maven had to be the most reclusive writer Hollywood has ever known, but I remember Elkmate. You can make it out there faster than she can, beat her at her own game."

"You got a problem with that?" Sam asked, his eyes narrowed in the early-morning light.

"Why should I have a problem with it?" he shot back.

"I don't know. You just don't look too pleased with the idea of returning to your native state. Ever been to Elkmate?"

"No."

"Ever heard of it?"

He wasn't a man who believed in exhibiting his problems. "I've heard of it. It was about thirty miles from where I grew up."

"Thirty miles away and you've never been there?" Bernie said.

He glared at her. Bernie knew as much about his childhood as anyone, and she knew enough not to question him about it. "Want to make something of it?"

She held up a hand. "I wouldn't think of it. If you don't want to go back to Colorado you don't have to, Rafe. D. Maven has probably been dead for the past twenty years, and all she'll find is an empty cabin on a hillside. You can stay right here and wait for her to come back. If she does."

"Why wouldn't she?"

"Word travels fast. Her mother heard about the tabloid article and kicked her out of the house. Or at least, that's what I was told. I don't know if she has anything to come back to."

"Sure she does," Rafe said in a sour voice. "She has Clement Walden."

Sam shuddered. "So what's it gonna be, buddy? *Cop for a Day—the Revenge* or *Black Canyon?*"

"What the hell do you *think* I'm going to do?" he said wearily. "I'm taking the next flight to Denver."

Bernie smiled, and he never realized how sphinxlike she could be. "I thought so," she said in a deceptively tranquil voice. And once again he wondered what was going on in her razor-sharp mind.

And what the hell it had to do with Silver Carlysle. And him.

## Chapter Eleven

Rafe could have taken the company plane. Even in the current economic climate of trying to scale back sky-rocketing costs, Pegasus Pictures owned two Lear jets and half a dozen propeller planes. He could have commandeered any one of them, but he didn't. If he had to go back to Colorado, and it certainly seemed as if he had no choice in the matter, then he preferred to do it without a raft of witnesses.

In Hollywood he was an easily recognizable figure. Out in the real world he was much more anonymous. His height drew people's attention, but in Colorado a lot of men were tall. He'd learned early on that women tended to notice him, and he'd used that to his advantage over the years. He'd also learned how to ignore it.

When he took his first-class seat on the commercial airline several hours later, it would have taken even a Hollywood ferret like Clement Walden a great deal of trouble to recognize him. Gone was the Armani suit, the Rolex, the accoutrements of power. He was wearing old jeans, Western boots that came from Texas not some trendy boutique in Hollywood, a heavy denim shirt and a Stetson that was probably older than his quarry. His shearling-lined coat was dumped in the bin overhead, his shades covered his face, and he leaned back in his seat, one large hand around a glass of whiskey, as he shut out the world.

He didn't want to be there. He would have given ten years of his life, half his annual income, even his beloved Lotus, not to have to go back to Colorado. The one thing he wouldn't give up was Silver Carlysle.

His grip tightened on the glass of whiskey as the silver plane carried him and a hundred others closer to Colorado. It wasn't Silver Carlysle he wanted, he reminded himself, draining the glass. At least, not more than temporarily. It was a matter of pride, a matter of power, a matter of control. He'd decided he wanted to do *Black Canyon,* and nothing under the sun, most particularly not a defensive, luscious society amazon was going to get in his way.

And if he had to go back home to do it, the one place he'd assiduously avoided for the past fifteen years, then do it he would.

The flight into Stapleton airport was bumpy but brief. It was a simple enough matter to rent a four-wheel-drive vehicle. He even could have hired a Range Rover in that moneyed city, and for a moment he was tempted. In a Range Rover he'd remember who he was, who he'd become. It was a trendy symbol of power, and it would help keep the memories at bay.

But he'd left his Armani suit behind and dressed in denim. He could have rented a Rolls and he'd still know where he'd come from. In the end he rented a four-wheel-drive pickup, taking off into the mountains while the woman behind the Hertz counter still tried to remember where she'd heard his name before.

He knew he had plenty of time. Silver was driving that rattletrap of a car—she wouldn't make the Colorado state line until sometime tomorrow, if she didn't stop to rest. He could take his time, maybe head out to Aspen to see if there was some early skiing.

He wasn't going to do that. He knew where he was headed, the pickup practically driving itself. He was going to drive over Red Mountain Pass, past the spot where his father had gone over the edge. And then he was going home.

It was almost midnight by the time he pulled up to the little cabin that had seen the first fourteen years of his life. Even through the bright headlights he could see the changes his money had wrought. During the long, intervening years, when he'd lived with his aunt and uncle, then in foster care, then on to college and making his own way, the cabin had been sold to hunters, used and abused for years, open to the weather and even stray grizzlies. When he'd made his first real money he'd bought it back, sight unseen, a lawyer handling the transaction, and he never did figure out why. Maybe because a place that had witnessed that much pain needed to be held on to. And maybe because, while he'd turned his back on Colorado, on his past, it was still a part of him. A big part.

He stared straight ahead, looking at it. His money had been spent well. Over the years high-priced contractors had fixed it up, redoing the roof, putting in new airtight windows, a sprawling addition. Inside, the amenities were all they should be, including two bathrooms, a state-of-the-art kitchen, even a hot tub. It was now the mountain home his mother had always dreamed about, the place she'd wanted to live, instead of a tumbledown shack with no electricity or running water. But she was long gone, drinking herself to death with quiet despair after his father had gone off that cliff. And Rafe had never even been back.

Why the hell did it have to be Elkmate? Why couldn't D. Maven have come from up north, around Steamboat? Or even better, how about Wyoming or Montana? Why did he have to hail from Rafe's backyard?

Not that it mattered. Mack Movies and Pegasus Pictures had resources Silver Carlysle could only dream about. Bernie had come up with a death certificate with surprising ease, once push came to shove. D. Maven had died in 1973 of cirrhosis of the liver, complicated by pneumonia, at the ripe old age of seventy-seven. He'd left no will, and no heirs.

Which meant *Black Canyon* was up in the air. No, it meant *Black Canyon* belonged to him, if he wanted it. Sir Benjamin Hatcher had negotiated for the rights. Hatcher had worked for Pegasus, Pegasus had paid the pittance a 1950s movie option was worth. Therefore, it was his.

He switched off the engine, grabbing his duffel bag from the back of the truck and heading toward the cabin as he considered how life was arranged for him. He could see a thin plume of smoke coming from the chimney, and he knew Bernie had seen to it that someone had come in, stoked the fires, turned on the heat, made sure the refrigerator and freezer were well stocked. He could remember back to the times when his mother would struggle with the fires, her hands clumsy in the cold air, her movements slowed by the vodka she was drinking in increasing amounts.

He had all the money, all the amenities, and it couldn't change the past. It couldn't make his mother's life any easier, it couldn't stop his father from going out in a blizzard, heading over a mountain pass that was treacherous even in midsummer. And it couldn't stop him from remembering.

He shut the door behind him, shutting out the autumn chill, and stared at the rustic interior. Thank God they hadn't sent a California decorator out to oversee the place. Whoever had been hired, and Rafe had never bothered to find out who, had done the job right. It looked real and solid, comfortable and homey.

And no wonder. Whether he liked it or not, wanted it or not, beneath the Indian rugs and the bird's-eye maple furniture, beneath the modern plumbing and state-of-the-art electronics, it was his home. Always had been. Always would be.

He cooked himself a frozen steak over the fancy grill in the kitchen, made himself a pot of strong coffee, nuked himself a potato and poured himself a whiskey. It didn't take much time to get the fire blazing, sending out heat into the room. He sat in front of it, kicking off his boots as he alternated between the whiskey and the coffee, and he told himself he should have brought a woman to warm the king-size bed in the master bedroom overhead. He certainly wasn't going to get Silver Carlysle in there, and he needed distraction.

He told himself he should be feeling angry, crazy, tormented by a past he'd never bothered to come to terms with. He told himself coming to Colorado was the worst idea he'd ever had in his entire life.

But when it came right down to it, with the food in his belly, the coffee and the whiskey warming him, the sound of the fire crackling, he knew a peace he hadn't felt in years. Maybe never.

And the only thing that would have made it better wasn't a faceless, inventive bed partner imported from L.A.

It was Silver Carlysle.

A DAY AND A HALF after she left Los Angeles, Silver sat in the front seat of her Toyota, her hands clenched tightly on the steering wheel. The little cabin at the end of the narrow, twisting road hadn't seen any life in maybe a decade. The windows were nothing more than gaping holes in the rough planking, the porch sagged into the dirt, the front door was long gone. The rusting frame of an old pickup decorated what might once have been called a front yard, but age and weather had made its vintage impossible to identify. It might have belonged to D. Maven, or his grandfather. Or his grandchild.

The one thing that was indisputable—D. Maven was long gone. The directions on the notes in her father's trunk were clear and precise, written in a stranger's hand, presumably one of his assistants. Or one of his mistresses. D. Maven was a recluse—he didn't have a telephone, and he despised mail. It apparently had taken all of Hatcher's legendary charm to pry the rights to *Black Canyon* out of the old codger, and it had probably required several trips and a prodigious amount of whiskey to accomplish it. Though there was no mention as to whether her father and his assistant had actually ended up making that trip.

And now his daughter had followed his path, tracking down the house where Maven had lived. Long, long ago, if the condition of the place was any indication. It had all been a wild-goose chase.

She leaned forward, sinking her head against the steering wheel. She'd told herself she should take her time, stop and rest along the way, but she hadn't. Except for a brief four-hour nap at a motel, she'd been on the road since she'd left. Reaching Denver had been straightforward enough, traveling the broad super-highways. Finding this tiny, deserted cabin, up in the stark mountainous passes was another matter alto-gether. Particularly when the sky had darkened into a premature black, and the rain that was just starting had a bite to it that didn't augur well for her bald summer tires.

She heard an ominous clacking sound, and she sat back, shaking herself out of her momentary torpor. Self-pity had its place in this life, but that place was very small. She'd done her best, and failed. Now the smartest thing she could do would be to get back up that nar-row, twisting road and drive the hell out of the moun-tains.

Elkmate, Colorado was in the middle of nowhere. No towns, no motels, hardly even a gas station to enliven the mountainous region. She started the car, backing around with more speed than care, and felt the first initial slipping.

Except for her years at an East Coast college, when she hadn't even owned a car, Silver had lived her entire life in California. She had never driven through even a mild case of flurries. She looked at the wet, white stuff coming out of the early-afternoon sky, and felt a fear deep in the pit of her stomach, something that made Rafe McGinnis, her mother and even *Black Canyon* pale in comparison.

"I have a bad feeling about this," she said out loud, quoting a line used in almost every action movie since talkies began. Her only answer was the clicking sound of the freezing rain as it bounced against her wind-shield.

RAFE FIGURED he had plenty of time. After all, it took a certain amount of time to get from the West Coast of California to the western slopes of Colorado, and she'd have to stop along the way. He'd beaten her by taking the airplane—he could take his time before he went after Maven's cabin. Bernie's directions had been very precise, almost suspiciously so for a woman who could still manage to get lost on Hollywood Boulevard. She was hiding something, he was sure of it. But he couldn't begin to imagine what.

He slept late the next morning, in no particular hurry to do a thing. He busied himself splitting firewood and carrying some in, he drank a quart of black coffee that wasn't any particular brew, he ate steak and eggs and listened to country music on the radio and read old Louis L'Amour Westerns that some visitor had left behind.

It wasn't as if the cabin had been empty all this time. He'd always told himself he was a practical man, without an ounce of sentiment. The cabin had been available for anyone who'd asked. Sam had been out here several times, so had various friends and business associates. He'd justified its upkeep by offering it to anyone who needed a break from L.A. Some of Mack Movies' most lucrative films had been written in that little cabin. Also, some of the worst.

The air turned sharply colder, a mixed blessing. After twelve years Rafe had grown a little weary of California's endless sunshine, and the nip in the air made his blood race. On the other hand, when he strode back into the cabin with an armload of wood, the country radio station was talking about snow, sleet and freezing rain, all combined in one big storm.

For a moment his relief was overwhelming. He didn't have to go anywhere, do anything. The place was well stocked with food, coffee and whiskey, he had a telephone and a fax and a computer, enough Westerns so that he could move on to Tony Hillerman when Louis L'Amour lost his charm.

But he didn't have Silver. She was heading into those mountains, and he was willing to bet half the profits of *Cop for a Day* that she didn't know how to drive in snow. He tried to remember the car she'd driven off in, but all that he could bring back was something tinny, imported and old. She probably didn't even have snow tires.

She probably wouldn't make it past Denver tonight, if she even got that far. She'd probably wake up tomorrow morning to find herself snowed in, and be cursing a blue streak. She'd guess that he'd come after her. He'd never made the mistake of underestimating her intelligence, and he hoped she'd do the same.

He glanced out at the darkening sky, as old memories flooded him. If he'd paid attention, he wouldn't have needed the radio to tell him what he already knew. If he had to go anywhere, do anything in the next twenty-four hours, he'd better do it now. In a little while the road would be impassable.

It hadn't taken much to find out where Maven had once lived. His plan was simple enough—head out there, post the Xerox copy of his death certificate that Bernie had faxed him on the door, and leave directions back to his place. It was up to Silver what she wanted to do when she finally made it there.

But it had been more than twenty years since he'd been in Colorado, and he underestimated the severity of the storm. He was just heading down the winding gravel road to Maven's abandoned cabin when the sleet started.

He cursed, slamming the truck into neutral as he considered his options. The cabin was another mile down the narrow trail—even with four-wheel drive and good conditions the going would be slow and treacherous. With that nasty stuff coming out of the sky, there would be no telling how long it might take. The wiser thing to do would be to turn around now, before things got too bad. Storms could be treacherous this time of year, and there were some things you never forgot, no matter how long you'd been away.

He shifted in reverse, about to turn the pickup, when he saw the lights halfway down the narrow road. For a moment he didn't move. And then he began to curse, slowly.

There were headlights through the deepening gloom. And they weren't coming any closer. As a matter of fact, they were at a crazy angle, and he squinted through the darkness, knowing with both resignation and a reluctant joy that it could only be Silver.

He slammed the truck back into first and started down the path, slowly, the four-wheel drive kicking in. He could see the sleet splatting against the window, and unwillingly he remembered the night he was eleven years old and his father had gone out on the snowplow. It had started like this.

He hadn't had any choice in the matter, he'd told Rafe's mother when she'd protested. Times were hard; he was hired to plow the roads up over Red Mountain Pass, and he couldn't just decide not to if he didn't like the looks of the weather. He'd plowed it a hundred times or more each winter—he'd make it over this time as well.

But he hadn't. He remembered his mother screaming when they'd told her. He remembered being told that he was the man of the family—it was up to him to take care of his mother.

They were right about one thing. He'd been a man from that day forward, his childhood wiped out by a winter storm. But they'd been wrong about his pretty, fragile, weak mother. He couldn't take care of her, stop her from destroying herself. No one could.

He was halfway down the narrow road when he saw Silver, and suddenly he knew the meaning of that stupid phrase about someone's blood running cold. Her car was hanging over the ledge, and all it would take was one strong gust of wind to push it over. At first he thought she'd had enough sense to get out and away from danger—there was no sign of her in the front seat.

And then he saw her, struggling to open the back door that was balanced up high, and a moment later he saw her try to crawl up in there.

He didn't remember stopping the truck, opening the door and running for her. He didn't waste time calling her—if he startled her and she jerked around it could be enough to send her car hurtling over the cliff. Instead he sprinted across the icy road, skidding in his leather boots, catching her legs as she dived inside the car, hauling her out roughly, pulling her so that she toppled over onto him just as the car lost its purchase with a hideous grinding noise and disappeared over the edge.

For a moment neither of them moved. He lay on his back in the ice and mud, with her on top of him, and her face was white with shock and surprise. He wanted to reach up and hold her tight, to press her head against his shoulder and keep her there, safe.

But of course he couldn't. He was already prepared for her rage when she shoved against him, hard, vaulting to her feet. The effect was somewhat ruined by the gathering slipperiness, and it took everything she had to keep from tumbling back down on him.

He moved more slowly, already used to the treacherous surface. "Were you trying to kill yourself?" He didn't shout, much as he wanted to, to scream out the rage and terror that had swamped him.

His bitten-off words had just as powerful an effect on her. She flinched, but stood her ground. "Do you realize what just happened?" she demanded. "That was everything, everything I owned! If you hadn't grabbed me I could have gotten my clothes..."

"If I hadn't grabbed you you'd be lying at the bottom of that crevasse, and you wouldn't be worried about clothes. You haven't got the sense God gave little green apples. How the hell did you get your car stuck up there anyway?"

"It's slippery!" she shrieked back at him in the rising wind.

"I know it is. And you should know better than to be out in this kind of weather. You shouldn't have come here at all—you belong in California, with palm trees and sunshine and your safe little life..."

"My life hasn't been safe since I met you," she said bitterly. "I should have known you'd follow me here. You've wasted your time—D. Maven is long gone."

"I know that. He died in 1973."

She just stared at him, and he knew she wanted to hit him. "How do you know that?" Her voice was low, bitter.

"I've got connections you can't even begin to imagine."

"I'm sure you do. So if he's dead, what are you doing out here?"

"Looking for you."

That stopped her. She still wanted to hit him, he could see it quite clearly in her eyes. She was also beginning to look like a drowned rat. She wasn't dressed for this weather—the cotton sweater was beaded with ice, plastering itself to her tall body, and her lower lip was beginning to tremble.

"Well," she said in a tight voice, probably to keep the shivers from it, "you found me. Now you can go back to where you came from."

He didn't move. "Are you telling me to leave you here? Alone, without a car, in this weather?"

"It's your fault my car's gone," she said stubbornly. "And I'm not going anywhere with you."

He took a deep, calming breath. For all his rage, for all his panic at the sight of her, balanced on the precipice, he felt suddenly, oddly happy. The past twenty-four hours in Colorado had been an unexpectedly peaceful blessing, the calm before the storm. Now that she was here, he was ready for anything but peace. He was ready for her. He was ready for their battles to begin again. And this time it wasn't going to end in a standoff.

"The longer we stand here and discuss it," he said evenly, "the worse the roads will get. I've got four-wheel drive and studded tires, but I don't think the truck comes with chains, and you sure as hell aren't dressed for walking. Now act like an adult for a change and get in the damned pickup."

Her eyes narrowed. "Go to hell," she said primly, and turned away from him, obviously planning on walking back to Maven's derelict cabin.

For just a fraction of a moment he considered letting her go. He had no idea what kind of condition Maven's cabin was in, but it probably still contained a roof and a fireplace. She wouldn't freeze to death, and it might teach her a lesson.

On the other hand, he had no intention of being without her for another minute. He didn't want to examine why. He just knew he wasn't going to let her go.

She slipped on the gravel road, landing on her backside with an inelegant thump. He was wise enough not to laugh, simply coming up behind her, hauling her to her feet.

She tried to yank her arm free. She was looking colder, more miserable than ever, and he wasn't too happy himself. The freezing rain had slid beneath the shearling collar of his coat, his hair was matted with ice crystals, and his hands were freezing.

"I told you, I'm not going with you," she said fiercely, tugging at his arm.

It had never come to a test of physical strength before. He'd always had the ability to cajole a woman into doing what he wanted. But this woman couldn't be cajoled, she was stubborn, furious and too damned smart. He simply hauled her up, tossing her far-from-petite body over his shoulder, and started up the slippery slope to where he'd left the pickup.

She fought him, of course. It was close to pitch-black, the sleet was coming down in earnest, and he felt a moment of real concern. "Hold still," he said, smacking her across her blue-jeaned bottom.

Her shock was so intense that she stopped fighting, rigid with outraged dignity as he battled his way up the slope, fighting for every inch. He opened the passenger door and dropped her inside, half expecting her to scramble back out again.

"Stay put!" he thundered, as she started to move.

She looked up at him, and her eyes were huge in her pale, drenched face.

"I despise you," she said.

He moved around to the driver's seat, climbed in and fastened his seat belt. "I'm sure you do," he said wearily. "Just sit back and shut up while I get us out of here, and once we get to my place you can tell me all about it in excruciating detail."

"Your place? I'm not going anywhere with you..." She reached for the door, but he simply caught her arm and slammed her back against the seat.

"I will tie you up," he said simply. "If you don't stop arguing and fighting with me, I'll strap you to the front fender like a dead deer and drive you back that way."

She looked at him for one long, startled moment, and he could see that she almost believed him. If he wasn't so concerned about the weather he would have been amused.

As it was, he nodded. "That's better," he said. "Now let's get the hell out of here."

# Chapter Twelve

At least the cramped confines of the pickup truck were warm. Silver hunched down in the seat, as far away from Rafe's tall body as she could, as she fastened the seat belt around her with shaking fingers. It was only October, for God's sake! How could they have an ice storm in October?

The heat blasted her soaked running shoes, and she could feel the prickly pain as the numbness began to recede. She tucked her hands in her armpits, shivering as the ice on her lightweight clothing began to melt in shivery droplets, soaking through to her skin. She spared a glance over at Rafe, then looked away with nervous haste. A part of her still wanted to fight, wanted to jump down from the pickup truck and stalk off in icy dignity.

Icy was the operative word here, she reminded herself. Absurd as the thought might be, she might not survive out here on her own, in weather like this. It was even remotely possible that he'd saved her life, hauling her out of her Toyota before it went over the precipice. She didn't want to think about that, either. If he'd saved her, then she'd owe him something. And there was only

one thing he really wanted, only one way she could re-
pay her debt.

She cast another brief, curious glance at him. He
looked very different from the Hollywood mogul, different and yet the same. The rough denim and suede
suited him, more than the Armani suits and custom T-
shirts. His long hair was still tied back, and she could
see the sparkle of melting ice in its dark strands. He'd
stripped off his gloves, and she stared at his hands on
the big steering wheel as he negotiated his way up the icy
slope. She'd never noticed them before, how large and
strong and capable-looking they were. The hands of a
man who could do things, take care of things. Not the
hands of a desk-bound dilettante.

And then she remembered the work-roughened tex-
ture of those hands, touching her breasts beneath the
warm water of his swimming pool, and she shuddered.

"The heat's up full blast," he said, not looking her
way as he concentrated on the driving. "Do you want
my coat?"

"No, thank you," she replied in a small voice.

"You'll warm up soon enough," he said, gunning the
motor as the truck went up and over the first rise. "Just
keep thinking about how angry you are at me and you'll
be burning up."

"I'm not likely to forget," she said, pulling her eyes
away from his hands as she huddled closer to the door.

"And make sure the door's locked. I don't want you
falling out into the night if we end up in a ditch."

"End up in a ditch?" she echoed. "I thought you
were Mr. Cowboy, able to leap icy mountain ridges in a
single bound?"

"You want to shut your mouth and let me concentrate?" he asked in a deceptively mild tone of voice. "Or do you want me to do something about it?"

Silver shut up. The white, wet stuff coming out of the sky absolutely terrified her, and while goading Rafe might take some of the edge off her panic, it might also prove dangerously distracting to the man who was supposed to get her out of there. The snow was hurtling itself toward the windshield in a mad suicide dash, and Silver leaned back, closing her eyes and swallowing the small, frightened moan that threatened to bubble up.

She lost track of time. It seemed endless, the truck moving at a maddeningly careful pace through the storm. She could feel the wheels slide on the slick surface, feel the consummate skill in Rafe's deft hands as he turned into the skid then carefully drove out of it. She'd read about that when she'd learned to drive, but the theory seemed to have no practical application. How the hell could one turn into a skid on an icy, mountaintop road?

It seemed like hours later when Rafe let the pickup drift to a halt. Silver lifted her head, suddenly hopeful. "We're here?" she asked, no longer caring that she was heading into enemy territory. She only wanted to get out of this vehicle of torture, out of the ice storm and under a roof.

"Not exactly," he said, his voice dry. "We've got one more stretch, and the road's too icy. I'm going to need your help."

She swallowed her first instinct to tell him to go to hell. Her safety depended on him, whether she liked it or not. Arguing would simply prolong it. "What do you want me to do?" she asked.

"Leave the truck in neutral," he said, reaching for his gloves, "and steer. I'm getting out to push."

"Why?" She was aghast.

"Because the ice is so bad the tires can't get any grip on the road. I'm going to nudge the car in the right direction, you simply need to steer."

"And if I start going over a cliff? Are the brakes going to work?"

"No brakes," he said. "Fortunately there are no cliffs on this stretch of road, either. The worst that will happen is you'll end up against a stand of fir trees, and you won't be going fast enough to cause much damage. Just take it slowly and carefully, don't jerk the wheel, and we should be fine."

She wanted to refuse. But he was already climbing out into the swirling storm, and she knew that there wasn't any choice. He wouldn't get out into that kind of weather unless he had to, no matter how much he wanted to terrify her. She slid across the bench seat, her fingers numb with terror, and grabbed hold of the steering wheel.

The graceful, silent glide of the truck on the surface of the ice sent a knot of fire through her stomach. She stared straight ahead, ignoring the ice that pelted in the open window as she steered the truck down the almost invisible road.

It went on forever. Her face was stinging from the icy snow, but she was too frightened to brush it away. She could only try to concentrate on steering the damned truck.

She heard Rafe shout something. Instinctively she touched the brakes, only to find the truck hurtling out of control, faster and faster, and she knew she was going to die. And then a moment later it came to a stop, slamming up against something solid.

She didn't move. The truck was still running, sending wafts of heat around her face, the icy pellets were still falling, raining in the open window.

And then Rafe opened the door, reached in and turned off the truck and the lights, plunging them into a swirl of wintry darkness. "We're here," he said.

She made a small, gulping noise as she swallowed her sob of relief. "About time," she managed in a shaky voice, trying to unfasten the seat belt. For some reason her fingers didn't work.

She felt his hands cover hers, undoing the belt, and then he pulled her out of the cab, those strong, hard hands of his surprisingly gentle. "We've got a few yards to go," he said, and his voice was emotionless. "You want me to carry you?"

"Over my dead body." She had some life left in her after all. She took a step, and for a moment her knees buckled beneath her. He caught her as she fell, but she pushed him away, using all her remaining resources to stand upright. "Lead on, MacDuff."

His idea of a few yards to go was extremely optimistic. It had to be another five minutes before the lights loomed up out of the darkness, five minutes of slogging through ankle-deep snow as the chill sank deeper and deeper beneath her skin. And then a door opened, and light and heat poured out, and she stumbled inside into safety.

"The bathroom's up the stairs to the right," Rafe said, stripping off his ice-covered coat and shaking his long hair loose. "Turn on the shower as hot as you can stand it and don't come out until you've thawed."

She moved slowly, too frozen to argue with his high-handed orders. "What about you?" she paused to ask halfway up the rough-hewn pine stairs. "You must be frozen, too."

He looked up at her, and he looked big, larger than life, and completely at home in the rustic surroundings. "Are you asking me to join you in the shower?"

"No."

"I have two bathrooms, and enough hot water for both of us. Get out of those frozen clothes."

"I'm going," she said, her teeth chattering as she continued her slow, torturous climb upward. "I don't suppose you have any suggestions as to what I can put on once I get thawed."

"Use your imagination." He had already stripped off his heavy wool sweater, and he was ripping open the snaps on his denim shirt. The fireplace behind him was huge, blazing, and even from halfway across the room she could feel the heat.

He was reaching for his belt buckle, oblivious to her watchful eyes. Or perhaps not oblivious at all. She turned and ran.

The water hurt. It made her teeth ache, her bones throb, her skin scream in pain. She leaned against the tiled wall and let the streams of water sluice down over her, as slowly, inexorably, life and awareness flooded back through her.

She didn't want to leave the cocoon of water. She didn't want to have to find something to wear, to go down and face Rafe McGinnis, knowing she was trapped somewhere out in the middle of nowhere, in the midst of a howling blizzard, with nowhere to run.

And part of her wanted to run, wanted to run quite badly. She wouldn't, of course. She was tougher than

that. She just needed a few minutes to pull herself together.

But there was a limit to how long she could stay in the
shower. The sooner she emerged and faced him, the
sooner she'd realize she was more than capable of
standing up to him.

The bathroom was flooded with steam when she finally emerged from the shower. The towels were huge
and thick, and wrapping one around her tall body pro-
vided more coverage than she would have dared hope
for. When she stepped into the balconied hallway she
could still hear the sound of the other shower somewhere at the other end of the cabin, and she knew that
for the moment, at least, she was safe.

There were two bedrooms upstairs, a smaller, utilitarian guest room with empty closets and drawers. And
the master bedroom, with ice-coated skylights, a rough-
hewn pine bed the size of Denver, and Rafe's clothes in
the closet.

She knew a moment's pang of sorrow when she
thought of her expensive new clothes lying at the bottom of some ravine, and then she forgot about it. The
longer she dithered, thinking about something that
couldn't be changed, the greater the chance of Rafe
finishing his own shower and coming upstairs, looking
for clothes for himself. It was going to take all the self-
control she possessed to keep things on a professional
basis. Standing in his bedroom wearing nothing but a
towel wasn't the way to start.

His clothes fit surprisingly well. He was lean, but
then, so was she. A little broader in the hips, a little
narrower in the waist, of course, but close enough. She
rolled up the hem of the jeans and ended up with a T-
shirt and another heavy denim work shirt, sleeves rolled

up, length reaching to her hips despite the fact that she was tall. The more layers she had, the more protected she felt, and she almost started hunting for a thick wool sweater when she realized that, wonder of wonders, she was warm.

There was still no sound from Rafe. Shoving her damp hair behind her ears, she headed back down the wide pine staircase, ignoring the huge bed and the tartan flannel-covered duvet. She hadn't seen a matching duvet in the guest room. Was she going to have to make do with blankets on such a cold, comfortless night?

He was in the kitchen, waiting for her. He leaned back against the wooden counter, surveying her, his hands cupped around a mug of coffee that smelled very close to heaven.

"You look good in my clothes," he said, and his voice wasn't much more than a low rasp.

She could have said the same thing for him, but she didn't, moving past him and reaching for the second mug of coffee that sat waiting by the restaurant-style stove. He was wearing jeans and a black T-shirt, and for once he hadn't tied back his long hair. It hung around his face, damp, curling slightly, and she wanted to tell him he looked absurd. But she couldn't. He looked very, very sexy.

She took a deep swallow of her black coffee, then choked when the alcohol hit her. "It's half whiskey," Rafe said. "I figured you needed it."

"Not on an empty stomach I don't." She took another sip anyway, letting the liquid burn its way down, warming her from the inside out.

"I'll cook something for you. We have steak, steak, and more steak."

"You'll cook?" she echoed, astonished.

"You have no idea the range of my talents," Rafe murmured, and she ignored the wicked glint in his eyes. "Why don't you go sit by the fire and I'll bring you something."

She wanted to protest. The idea of the illustrious Rafe McGinnis cooking for her was too unbelievable, but she couldn't bring herself to offer to do the cooking for him. For one thing she couldn't cook, even if he could. For another, she hadn't eaten since the early morning, hadn't slept more than a few hours in the last seventy-two, and for the most important reason, she wanted to get away from him. The kitchen was small, hot, enclosed, and he was too big. Too warm. Too tempting.

Without a word she headed into the huge living room, sinking onto the sofa, her half-drunk coffee in her hand. She put her bare feet up on the Indian-style fabric and stared around her, wondering what was causing the weird sensation just below her heart. Telling herself it was heartburn, a reaction to strong coffee and straight whiskey. Knowing it was something more.

There were no curtains on the windows, and she could see the swirl of snow and freezing rain in the darkness, hear the constant, ominous clicking sound as the precipitation beat down on the snug cabin. The fireplace was huge, taking up a complete wall, and the fire burning brightly was probably heating the whole house. The furniture was simple, rustic, surprisingly comfortable. The rugs were old and Indian, the paintings straightforward and filled with glowing colors. She wanted to feel contempt for the place, for a Hollywood producer's version of mountain chic. Instead she felt at peace.

"I hate Colorado," she announced defiantly.

"Do you?" He appeared in the kitchen door, taking her coffee mug away and refilling it. Refilling it with whiskey as well as coffee. "The weather's not always this bad."

"Then why don't you spend more time here?"

"I have my reasons." He didn't sound defensive, simply matter-of-fact. "I grew up here."

She snuggled down in the sofa, wiggling her toes. "It's hard to believe. Where did you grow up—in Denver?"

"No, I grew up here. In this cabin. It was a little simpler then. No running water, no electricity. It does happen to have one of the most spectacular views on earth, but you can't see much in weather like this."

"Is that why your parents lived here? The view?"

He shook his head. "I doubt they even noticed. They lived here because they were too poor to live anywhere else. They would have moved to Denver in a shot. Hell, they would have moved to Australia if they'd had the chance."

"Where did they end up? Some retirement home in Florida like everyone else?" She took another deep swallow of the lethal coffee. She was beginning to like the way it burned.

"They ended up dead."

The warmth left her. This was a man who'd done everything he could to demoralize her. There was no reason why she should suddenly feel distraught.

But this was a man who'd rescued her, who'd just saved her life—a man she was foolish enough to believe was possibly just a little more vulnerable than he seemed. "I'm sorry," she said, knowing it sounded inadequate.

He didn't seem to notice. "My father died on a night like this one," he said flatly. "The only job he could get was driving a snowplow for the road crew. He went off a mountain pass during an ice storm when I was eleven." He took a drink of his own coffee.

"What happened to your mother? Did she take you away from here?" She didn't know why she was asking. She half expected him to slap her down verbally, but he seemed oddly ready to talk.

"No, she left on her own. She drank herself to death, slowly, politely, not causing any fuss. I didn't leave here till my aunt and uncle caught up with me when I was fourteen and took me to live in Ohio." The way his voice curled around the name of that state made it sound like the worst profanity on earth.

"And as soon as you could you came back?"

"Nope. This is the first time I've been here since I was fourteen," he said, pushing away from the door. "How do you like your steak? Rare or rarer?"

"I don't eat red meat."

"You do tonight, sweetheart. Drink your coffee."

They ate their dinner in almost total silence, broken only by the hiss and crackle of the fire, the sound of the elements beating against the cabin. The steak was rare, the salad simple, and despite the fact that she hadn't eaten much at all in the past twenty-four hours, she could barely manage to eat half of the generous portion he'd served her.

He ate his own without the slightest bit of hesitation, and as she watched his strong white teeth tear into the rare meat, she had a sudden, unsettling feeling in the pit of her stomach. He was a carnivore, and she tended toward passive vegetarianism. Just how far apart could two people possibly be?

Without a word he cleared the dishes, disappearing into the kitchen, and she watched him go. Just when she thought she had a handle on who and what Rafael McGinnis was, just when her defenses were solidly in place, he'd say or do something that threw all her preconceived notions awry.

She could picture him so vividly, despite the matter-of-fact starkness of his words as he'd told her of his past. He would have been tall as a fourteen-year-old, and astonishingly self-reliant, living alone out here, with none of the conveniences everyone took for granted. His aunt and uncle might have thought he was half-savage. She knew without a doubt that he had been cool, self-contained, probably faintly contemptuous of soft suburban living. It couldn't have been an easy adjustment.

She drained her after-dinner mug of laced coffee and decided she wanted more. She rose from the sofa on slightly unsteady feet and trailed him out to the kitchen. "Did you get along with your aunt and uncle?" she asked, reaching for the pot of coffee.

She half expected him to snub her. But he seemed curiously open as he rinsed the dishes in the copper sink. "Nope. I kept running away." He reached over and poured a generous helping of whiskey into her mug. "They finally put me in foster care, and I discovered what restrictions were really like. I decided I didn't like having anyone tell me what to do, so I got a scholarship to the best college I could find, and turned my back on my past."

"Including this place," she said. "So why are you here now? Why do you still own it?"

"I didn't always. I bought it back when I made my first substantial amount of money. I must be sentimental."

"You haven't got a sentimental bone in your body."

His smile was small, mocking. "Maybe not. Maybe I just got tired of hunters trashing this place. Maybe I like to control everyone."

"There's no maybe about that," she said, half to herself.

He turned to look at her, and his eyes were cool, unreadable. "You want to have dessert before or after?" he asked.

"Before or after what?"

"We make love."

She just stared at him. She hadn't drunk that much whiskey, had she? "I beg your pardon?"

He leaned back against the counter. "We're going to, you know. You can play all the games you want, try to convince yourself and me you're unwilling, but sooner or later we're going to end up upstairs in that big bed. Things would be a lot simpler if we just accepted that fact."

"What if I say no?"

"You'll change your mind," he said flatly.

"Or you'll change it for me?" she asked, feeling a cold dread in the pit of her stomach, warring with the hot lick of desire that spread through her belly.

He didn't say a word. He didn't have to.

"All right," she said abruptly, setting her coffee down and levering herself up on the broad counter.

The smugness vanished. "All right?" he echoed.

"I'm sick and tired of fighting with you. I don't think you're going to leave me alone until you get me in bed. I can't imagine why you'd want to—I'm hardly in your league. You only take the cream of the crop. I'm a little long on brains and short on drop-dead gorgeousness for you, but maybe you're getting bored with beauty. Or maybe you just figure that's part of how you're going to control me. That once you get me in bed I'll be so grateful for your monumental sexual prowess that I'll give you anything, including the rights to *Black Canyon,* and then bow humbly out of the picture."

"You do have a mouth on you," he said faintly.

"So go ahead," she said, leaning back against the open shelving. "Get it over with, and then we can get back to negotiating on an even footage."

"That's a step in the right direction," he said, not moving. "A couple of days ago you wouldn't have even admitted the word negotiation was part of your vocabulary."

He was right, it was a major slip on her part. Particularly since she had no intention of negotiating any of the rights away.

"The only negotiating I'm interested in is getting you to leave me alone."

"What if I promise to do that in return for *Black Canyon?*" he asked, his voice cool and distant.

She didn't even flinch. It was nothing more than she expected from him—she told herself she never had any delusions as to what he was really after. If only she didn't have such an irrational, overwhelming response to him.

"I'd consider it," she said. Wondering if she meant it.

He moved then, pushing himself away from the opposite counter, crossing the tiny area with a pantherlike grace. He came up to her, between her legs, not touching her, and his mouth was level with hers.

"The problem is," he said in a low, beguiling voice, "that I want you both. And I don't feel like settling for half."

She fought the treacherous pleasure that swept through her. "For how long?"

"I want *Black Canyon* forever. I have no idea how long I'll want you. Do you expect me to come up with a pre-coital agreement?"

She flinched. "I expect you to leave me alone."

"Not in this lifetime, Silver," he said under his breath.

He still didn't touch her. The tension in the kitchen was at fever pitch. He watched her out of still, unblinking eyes and she knew what it was like to be mesmerized.

She was a fighter, not a weak, cowering victim. "All right," she said, managing to keep her voice brisk. "Let's get it over with." And reaching up, she began to unbutton her shirt.

# Chapter Thirteen

Rafe stood there, his hands braced on the counter, watching her as she calmly unfastened the denim shirt. She'd looked so damned cute when she'd come downstairs, dressed in his clothes, that he'd been half tempted to tell her so. And half tempted to rip those clothes off her.

In the end he'd done nothing, hoping to prolong the confrontation. He'd meant it when he told her they'd end up in bed together—he'd had no doubt of that whatsoever. And he knew from the faint, panicked expression in her eyes that she knew it, too. And wanted it just as much as he did.

The problem was, she just as strongly resisted it. For every ounce of desire that suffused her delectable body, there was an equal pull away from him. There was no way he could overpower her, wipe out her distrust when, in fact, it was very well founded. He could only keep pushing, and wait for the time when she was ready to give in to what they both wanted.

She finished with the last button and shrugged out of the shirt, tossing it on the wide pine floor. She was wearing one of his T-shirts, but obviously his pilfered wardrobe hadn't contained anything as utilitarian as a bra. He waited to see whether she'd pull the shirt over her head.

Instead she reached down to the jeans. She'd taken a hand-tooled leather belt and cinched it tightly around her waist—it gave her something else to dispose of before she got to the more interesting parts.

"I hope you're enjoying this," she said in a bored tone of voice, sliding the belt out of the loops and tossing it onto the floor.

"Not yet, but I expect it's about to get a lot more interesting. Do you think you could manage to put a little more enthusiasm into it?" He reached for his mug of coffee, draining it. It was cold, more whiskey than anything else, but it gave him something to do with his hands, something to keep him from touching her. Because he wanted to touch her, wanted to quite badly. And she wasn't ready.

"I'm not feeling enthusiastic," she said, unsnapping the jeans. "I'm feeling coerced."

"I'm not touching you."

Her eyes met his for a brief, heated moment. "No," she agreed, "you're not. But you're going to."

He watched as she slid down the zipper. "Yes, I'm going to," he said, his voice suddenly husky.

He could see the pale peach of his custom-made silk shorts beneath the open zipper. His fingers dug into the counter, and sweat beaded on his forehead. For the first time he had serious doubts as to who would emerge the victor in this little encounter. She was disrobing with an elegant disdain, seemingly unaffected by the sweep of desire that ran between the two of them. And he was so turned on he could barely stand.

And then he realized her blasé attitude was all a lie. Her hands were trembling as she fumbled with the jeans, her breath was coming just a trace more rapidly than it needed to, as if she'd just climbed a steep flight of stairs, and in the steamy hot kitchen her nipples were hard.

His mouth curved in a slow, triumphant smile as he leaned closer, almost touching her. "Are you going to take off the rest of your clothes?" he asked. "Or am I going to have to do it for you?"

She swallowed, reaching blindly for her coffee mug and bringing it to her lips.

He took it out of her hands. "You've had enough whiskey for now," he said, setting it on the counter beside him. "I don't want you to have the excuse of being too drunk to know what you were doing. I don't want you to have any excuses. I want you to know what you're doing. I want your eyes to be wide open, watching me, when I come inside you."

She made a tiny, shocked sound, staring at him.

"You aren't used to having men talk to you like that, are you?" he continued. "They're usually polite and deferential. That's what you want, isn't it? Some tame yuppie you can ride herd on. And instead you wind up with me. I told you I was more than you can handle."

She reached for her jeans, struggling to zip them up again, but her hands were shaking too hard. "I'm going upstairs to bed," she said. "Alone. I've changed my mind."

He put his hands on top of hers, holding them still, and he could feel the heat of her body, the heat of her anger, the heat of her passion. "Too late, Silver. Take off the damned T-shirt. Before I rip it off."

She sat very still, unmoving, her eyes wide and waiting. She looked as if she expected him to hurt her. He wondered briefly if she'd been hurt before. And then he realized that it wasn't so much that she expected the worst from all men. She simply expected the worst from him.

He put his hands up, to the neck band of her T-shirt, and he watched her brace herself. Instead he slid his hand up the side of her neck, his thumb resting on her rapid pulse, as he drew her toward him, drew her unresisting face toward his mouth.

She tasted sweet, amazingly so. Her mouth was parted in surprise beneath his, and she tasted like whiskey and coffee. She was too bemused to close her mouth, and he took advantage of it, pushing his tongue inside, kissing her with a sweeping thoroughness that was overwhelming without being the slightest bit threatening.

He lifted his head a few inches to look down at her. Her eyes were wide and bright and confused. "What are you doing?"

He smiled. It was entirely without mockery, and she reacted with wonder. He didn't feel mocking, or cynical. Her mouth was damp from his, soft and vulnerable, and he knew now how he was going to get her. Not with overpowering her. Not with dirty tricks or threats or lying promises. He was going to get her to go upstairs with him, willingly, by simply kissing her.

He did it again, partly because he couldn't believe how wonderful it had been, partly because he wanted to do it again. It was even better than the first time. He had never been particularly fond of kissing. He used it as a means to an end, a way to get a woman he wanted to want him back. He'd never had any particular affection for the practice—it was merely a skill that led to other, more intense pleasures.

But he found he liked kissing her, liked it very much indeed. He tugged her closer, so that the juncture of her thighs was resting at his belly, and he could feel the open zipper of the jeans. And he wished he could get her to unfasten his jeans, too. She was getting more enthusiastic, her hands resting on his shoulders, fingers digging in lightly, and he could feel the tension running through her.

He put his arms around her, pulling her close against him, and she came willingly enough, sinking against his chest with a sigh. It was easy enough to slip his hands under the loose T-shirt, easy enough to pull it up and over her head in one swift move, baring her breasts to him.

She tried to pull away, to cross her arms in front of her, but he stopped her, simply by catching her wrists and holding them. Watching her out of hooded eyes he said softly, "Do you have the faintest idea how much I want you?"

Now was her chance, and he knew it. She could bargain, offer him her body in return for *Black Canyon,* and in his current frame of mind he'd probably agree. He waited, holding her wrists, waiting for her to say the words that would give him permission to finish what they'd started, waiting for the words that would wipe out any last trace of compunction on his part.

She opened her mouth, but the expected words never came out. "You have me," she said. "I can't fight you anymore." And there was a despairing, rueful expression in her eyes, and she no longer pulled against his hands.

He placed her arms around his waist, flattening her breasts against his chest, and he wished he'd had the sense to tear off his own clothes. He wanted, needed to feel her flesh against his, the heated silk of her skin caressing his. "Come upstairs with me," he whispered against her mouth. "Come upstairs and I'll give you..."

She turned her head deliberately, silencing him. Not allowing him to make the offer that he might rescind or regret, an offer that would turn the next few hours into a transaction. She slid her hands up under his denim shirt, against his skin, and the first willing caress made him shiver. He wanted her with an intensity he'd never felt before.

But something wasn't right.

He pulled away from her, out of her arms, out of her reach, leaning down and picking up her discarded T-shirt and tossing it at her.

She caught it instinctively, and the dazed, aroused expression on her face faded, as she pulled it back over her head. He watched her breasts disappear with a feeling of chagrin, and he wondered whether he had finally snapped.

"Go to bed," he said roughly, moving away from her.

He could sense her confusion. She slid off the counter, fastening his jeans around her. "I see," she said flatly.

He turned to look at her, keeping his face deliberately blank. "What do you see?"

"That you got what you wanted. Me, vulnerable, willing to do just about anything you wanted. Just to the point where I would have sold my birthright, and then you dumped me. Very effective. You were able to get me so turned on that I would have denied you nothing, all the while you were simply manipulating me. You told me you had still more dirty tricks up your sleeve, and I didn't believe you."

"You think that's why I stopped?"

"Isn't it? You never really wanted me, you merely wanted to show me the kind of power you held . . ."

He moved across the room so quickly she didn't have time to duck, grabbing her wrist and bringing her hand against his groin. "You think I don't want you? I hate to explain this to you, lady, but what you've got beneath your hand means that I want you quite badly. I just have no intention of taking you."

She tried to pull away from him, but he held her tightly, even though the pressure of her fingers against his erection was driving him crazy with desire. "Why not?"

"Because I'm not interested in a virgin sacrifice. You've given yourself permission to sleep with me, but you've told yourself you're doing it for the sake of *Black Canyon*. That's a pile of crap, lady, and you'd know it if you really thought about it. I want you in my bed, but I don't want that damned movie there, too."

"Then give it up," she said fiercely. "You've got a million movies to make—every screenwriter in Hollywood would work with you. Leave *Black Canyon* alone."

"And then I can have you?" he supplied the next part. He shook his head. "This is a battle, Silver, and I never, ever lose. I'm going to have you, and I'm going to have *Black Canyon*. Sleeping with me won't alter that fact, even if you think you can still be in control." He released her hand, moving away from her. "When you accept that fact, come and tell me."

"Everything has to be on your terms, is that it? You'll do me the great honor of making love to me, you'll take the only thing I've ever cared about, and you'll do it when and how you want to do it. Let me tell you something, mister," she said, moving close, in her rage forgetting how dangerous he could be, "it'll be a cold day in hell before I come to you."

He pulled her into his arms, ignoring her flailing fists. "Have you looked outside, Silver? It already is." And he kissed her, long and hard and deep, until her struggles faded, her mouth softened and a deep shuddering sigh shook her body.

His hands were gentle when they released her. He wanted to touch her, to smooth her shaggy hair away from her face, to kiss her nose, to take back the stupid ultimatum he'd issued. He should have taken her any way he could. She'd been willing, and why the hell should it matter what lies she'd told herself to come to him? He should take what she offered and run with it.

He let his hands drop to his side. He couldn't do it. Not this time. He'd slept with countless women who'd gone to bed with him for what he could do for their careers. Done it and enjoyed it, and given the women the pleasure they deserved.

For some stupid, quixotic reason he couldn't be so cold-blooded with Silver. He couldn't let her make that kind of moral bargain with herself. When she came to him, and she would, it had to be devoid of any gain. She had to come to him knowing she was risking everything. And she had to come anyway.

She walked out of the kitchen without looking back, heading up the wide staircase with all the dignity of a queen. He watched her go, then turned back to the cold coffee and the bottle of whiskey. It was going to be a long, long night.

THE BED WAS COLD. Silver piled every wool blanket she could find on it, so that her limbs felt weighted down, but she was still shivering.

Part of the problem was the fact that she'd locked and barred her door, dragging a heavy maple dresser in front of it just in case he changed his mind and decided to honor her with his sexual attentions. There were no registers in her room—the heat from downstairs stopped when it came to her locked door, and the temperature in the room was dropping rapidly.

His oversize T-shirt didn't provide much extra warmth, and she'd tried to discard it, not wanting to accept even that much from him. But lying naked in a bed across the hall from him brought its own disturbances, and even a T-shirt that had once covered his body was some protection.

She wished she could sleep. She hadn't had more than a few hours rest in recent memory, and she was bone-weary. But the cold, and her anger, kept the adrenaline pumping her system, so that she lay in that narrow bed, thrashing around, searching in vain for comfort and warmth.

Why had he done that to her? Kissed her until she was half-crazy, then turned around and accused her of being willing to trade her body for him keeping his hands off *Black Canyon*. She should have punched him in the nose.

Except for the fact that he was right. She had been willing to sleep with him for the sake of the movie.

Of course, there wasn't anyone else on the face of this earth that she'd sleep with for such a reason. And the fact of the matter was, she had talked herself into it, giving herself an excuse to do something that she'd wanted to do almost since she first set eyes on him. Definitely since he'd first set his hands on her.

And now here she was, snowbound, alone, and he was making the rules. The man's ego must be colossal, if he thought she'd abide by them. Did he expect her to beg?

What did he want from her?

She slept for a while, the sound of the wet snow pelting against the windows. When she awoke she was shivering, a faint gray light filtering through the storm-coated windows.

She climbed out of bed, her body shaking so hard she could scarcely keep her teeth from chattering. She was wearing his absurd shorts and the T-shirt, and she ought to pull on more clothes if she was going to leave the safety of her room. But what good was safety if it kept you away from what you really wanted?

The hallway was bathed in heat. His door was open at the other end, and through the darkness she could see the outline of his huge bed. Could see the glow of his cigarette as he sat there, sleepless, waiting.

It was a little past dawn. For a moment she stood there, motionless, wondering whether she should turn and run back to her room, slamming and locking the door again, locking him away from her, locking her own crazy needs away.

"Come here, Silver." He said it so quietly she almost thought she imagined it. His voice was low, beguiling, and there was no way she could resist. She moved toward the room, her long bare legs moving of their own accord.

"You have more games to play?" She stopped inside the door, one last ounce of fight in her.

"No more games," he said, stubbing out the cigarette. Her eyes had grown accustomed to the dark, and she could see him quite clearly, sitting in the bed, the duvet pulled up to his waist, his chest bare. "Come to bed with me, Silver. I'll take you on any terms you're willing to offer.''

She thought about it then, the terms she could dictate. And then she knew she didn't want to think about terms. She didn't want to think about right or wrong, or her career, or her father or the future. She didn't want to think about why he wanted her. She believed him when he said he did.

''No terms,'' she said, crossing the room and climbing up onto the high bed. ''Just you and me.'' And she leaned forward and kissed him.

He pulled her down on top of him, wrapping his arms around her, and his mouth tasted of whiskey and cigarettes and desire. The darkness and heat were all around them, and she closed her eyes and turned off her mind, her doubts. All that mattered was the moment. The rest would take care of itself.

He was good, she had to admit that. He knew how to kiss, how to bite at her soft lips, how to use his tongue, his teeth, his whole mouth, until the act of kissing was an erotic mating that made her dizzy with longing. He rolled her onto her back, leaning over her, pressing her down into the surprisingly soft mattress, and pulled the feather-soft duvet over both of them. And she found he was naked. And she found he was aroused.

This time when he took the T-shirt off her he did it slowly, gently. She'd never considered her breasts to be particularly sensitive—to her mind they were too big, too cumbersome, simply a source of pain at certain times of the month. But Rafe showed her new dimensions. He didn't just take them into his mouth like a hungry infant. He kissed them, breathed on them, licked them, nibbled at them, until a fire of longing burned in a direct line from her breasts down to the center of her legs.

"You like that, don't you?" he whispered in the darkness. "Do you know how long I've been wanting to kiss your breasts?" He ran his tongue over the fiercely pebbled nipple, and she arched beneath him in dizzying response. "I want to kiss you everywhere." He moved his mouth away, down her flat bare stomach, to the edge of his silk shorts.

"Oh, no," she said, trying to move away, but his long fingers had already slid beneath the underwear, pulling it down her legs even as she squirmed.

"Oh, yes," he said, his hands strong and inexorable as he held her hips, his voice gentle. "Most definitely yes."

The touch of his mouth against her was a shock and a wonder. She still didn't want him to do it, it made her too vulnerable, too defenseless. She didn't want to accept this from him, but he was giving her no choice.

"Stop fighting me," he said, lifting his head and looking at her. "This isn't a battle anymore." And he slid his long fingers into her, as his mouth touched her again, and she let out a muffled sob as a small convulsion hit her.

But Rafe wasn't satisfied with small convulsions. He knew how to take each one, prolong it, until they grew, meshing together until she was trembling, awash with sensation that suddenly peaked into an explosion that shocked her. Shocked her enough to try to stop it, but her body was no longer under her control.

She pushed at his shoulders, her hands slipping against his sweat-soaked skin, and she wanted to tell him to stop, she couldn't take any more, wouldn't take any more, when he loomed up over her, moving between her legs, pushing into her with one deep, hard thrust that rocked her back against the soft mattress.

She moaned, deep in her throat, but he didn't make the mistake of thinking she was in pain. She kissed him, tasting herself on his mouth, and she wrapped her body around him, knowing this was going to be fast and hard and deep, reveling in that knowledge, needing him that way, needing him any way he cared to give her.

She never thought she'd come again. Never thought that when he reached down and lifted her hips, to deepen the angle of his thrusts, that the crazy tension would keep building, building. Until she was meeting him, her hips slamming up against his, her breath sobbing in her ear, her arms wrapped tightly around his waist as she held on until suddenly he was very still, and she could feel his warmth and life filling her, and inexplicably her body dissolved once more, lost with his.

He rolled off her almost immediately, sitting up on the side of the bed, his back to her. "Damn," he said, his voice coming in breathless rasps. "Damn," he said again. "I didn't mean to do that."

Even as her body still trembled in response, the cold overtook her. She pulled the duvet over her, shivering in the cool night air. "Didn't mean to do what?" Her own voice sounded like that of a stranger, raw and strained.

He turned to look at her, and in the darkness his expression was unreadable. "Didn't mean to lose control," he said flatly. "I didn't even remember to use any protection."

She hadn't even thought of it, she who carried condoms in her purse while pursuing a life of dedicated celibacy. "Is there any particular reason you should?" she asked carefully.

She could see the ghost of a smile flit across his face. "Nothing catching. Believe it or not, I have a sense of responsibility to the women I sleep with."

"Oh, yes, those four score and twenty."

"Not exactly." He turned around and lay down beside her again, his breathing regular, his reactions now under tight control. She missed his shaken response, regretted the return of the cool womanizer. Still, he felt so good, wrapped up against her, his body all fire and bone and muscle. "You have the most amazing effect on me. You know that, don't you?"

"No, I don't," she tried to say, but he was kissing her again, softly, his mouth nibbling at hers, and she was more interested in kissing him back than arguing. And then he moved his mouth down the side of her neck, and she realized with sudden shock that he'd done everything, everything to her. She hadn't been allowed to do more than kiss him.

The battle hadn't been left outside the bedroom after all. He was still trying to control everything, and she'd been a willing victim to his sexual thrall.

Except that she didn't feel like a victim. She felt warm, and sated and oddly triumphant. She reached up and threaded her fingers through his long hair, rubbing the silky strands against her palms. "Your hair is ridiculous," she said, nuzzling against it like a playful kitten.

She could feel his smile against the tender skin of her neck. "Your breasts are magnificent."

She closed her eyes, as his hands touched her once more. "You're not going to win," she said.

For a moment he didn't move, and she told herself she was glad she'd done it, shattered the temporary truce.

"Silver," he said, his voice low and certain in the velvet darkness, "I already have."

# Chapter Fourteen

Rafe didn't make love to her again. She didn't expect it. She'd reopened the warfare between them; he'd dealt her a mortal blow. There was no way they could come together again, not with so much distrust on either side.

But she slept in his arms, her body wrapped tightly against his, slept deep and well, long into the day, and if her mind and spirit rejected him, her body had its own trust.

He hadn't said another word, simply tucked her against him, smoothing her rumpled hair away from her face, and gone to sleep. She supposed she could have left him, gone back to the sterile coldness of the guest room. But she didn't want to. She needed his warmth wrapped around her. Because she knew they were living on borrowed time, and the moment they left this bed they'd finally shared, life would come crashing down on them.

When she woke she was alone, wrapped tightly in the down comforter. Her body felt peculiar—restless, tingly, pleasured and frustrated. That was the problem with breaking a celibate streak, she thought wearily. The longer you did without it, the easier it was. Now, after one night, one occasion of admittedly powerful sex, she was already craving more.

She could fight those cravings. He'd left the bed rather than wake her and start it all over again. He probably didn't realize he'd done her a favor by giving her time to pull her defenses back around her. If she'd woken in his arms, there'd be no telling what kind of fool she would have made of herself.

That was the problem with sex. You couldn't just enjoy yourself. Your emotions had to get involved, she thought with strained disgust. You had to start thinking about stupid, impossible things like relationships, like caring, like falling in love. You started thinking you couldn't live without him, and where did that leave you? Up a very muddy creek without a paddle.

Not that this had happened to her before, Silver had to admit. Her limited experiences with sex hadn't led her to the dangerous, totally mistaken impression that she might be falling in love.

Still, the only explanation for her current state of brain-melting insanity had to be the sudden onrush of hormones. She was too levelheaded a woman otherwise.

At least when Rafe McGinnis wasn't around.

She stared at the clock beside the bed in disbelief. There was no way it could be half past one. The sunlight was streaming down on her from the skylight overhead, telling her that indeed it was. The storm was over, a new day was half begun, and she couldn't hide from it any longer.

There was no sign of Rafe as she darted into the bathroom. The hot water was as plentiful as it had been the night before, and she stayed under the shower far too long, dreading the bright cold light of day. Dreading she'd do something weak and sentimental, something that betrayed how much she'd begun to care about him.

In the daylight the rustic cabin looked bright and cheerful. She dressed in his clothes again, having no other choice, shivering when she'd pulled another pair of custom silk shorts against her skin. She needed to get away from him, from this place, as soon as she decently could. Because a strong, irrational part of her couldn't stand the thought of leaving.

She found coffee in a carafe, hot and strong and wonderful. She found sticky buns in the fridge. She devoured them all, then made herself bacon and eggs, finishing up with four pieces of toast. She couldn't remember when she'd last had a decent meal. She'd barely touched the steak he'd broiled, and last night, or was it this morning, had worked up a powerful hunger, one that food might just start to assuage.

There was no sign of Rafe. She opened the front door, expecting arctic cold, and stood there in numb surprise, enchanted. The storm had blown through, along with the cold weather, covering everything with a rime of ice that was now sparkling and dripping and melting in the bright sunshine. The air was damp and warm, almost springlike, and Silver felt a strange little tugging in her heart.

She tried to remember the misery of slogging through the ice and snow. She remembered it, all right. But she also remembered the mountains surrounding them, the limitless blue sky, the smell of the earth rather than of smog, the rough-edged beauty of it all. She was a city child, born and bred in Los Angeles, and for the first time in her life she felt as if she'd come home.

It was a lucky thing for her that Rafe hated this place. Otherwise she might start weaving all sorts of impossible fantasies. Fantasies that could never come true. He was a transplant now, a man who lived in the fast lane. It didn't matter if he seemed at home behind the big four-wheel-drive pickup truck. He didn't belong. And she had the strange, certain feeling that she did.

For the time being she had no choice but to depend on Rafe. She had no car, no clothes, nothing at all. If he wanted to stay, secluded in the remote mountains of Colorado, then she'd have no choice but to stay with him. It was a shame she couldn't work up more outrage at the notion.

She was humming beneath her breath when she closed the front door again, heading back to the kitchen to wash the dishes she'd dirtied. She froze when she heard the phone ring, waiting for Rafe to suddenly materialize from the walls and answer it.

He didn't. It was up to her, whether she wanted to face reality or not. No answering machine clicked in, as it rang four, five, six times. And then the ringing stopped, and Silver told herself she was glad.

Five minutes later it rang again. "All right, there's a limit to my self-control," she said out loud, reaching for the phone with soapy hands.

She wanted to drop it again. She wanted to come up with a fake accent, pretend she was anyone other than Silver Carlysle. But she'd inherited her mother's spectacular lack of acting skill, and when Clement's well-bred tones sounded on the other end she knew she'd have to answer.

"What do you want, Clement?" she asked wearily.

"Silver, where in God's name have you been?"

"Since you're the one calling me I'd think you'd have figured that out," she said.

"You're with that man!" Clement said in a shrill voice. "Honestly, Silver, haven't I taught you anything? I thought you were immune to that kind of mindless animal attraction. I couldn't believe it when I heard you'd gone off with him..."

"I didn't go off with him. I came out here to find the author of *Black Canyon,* and presumably Rafe did the same thing. We got caught in an ice storm, he rescued me, and the rest, as they say, is history."

"I can't believe it," Clement moaned again. "The thought of the two of you together simply boggles the mind. Haven't I taught you anything?"

"Don't waste your time thinking about it, Clement," she said in a calm voice. "It's not going to happen again."

There was a gusty sigh of relief on the other end. "Thank heavens! We may still be able to salvage something from this debacle. Things haven't been standing still since you disappeared, Silver. Your handsome stud left orders before he took off into the wilderness. While he was trying to distract you, his lawyers have been very busy."

"I imagine they have." She didn't want to hear this. She tried to pull the phone away from her ear, to hang it up, but she couldn't.

"I've told Marjorie what I think of her, of course," Clement continued, unaware of her reaction. "Locking you out in the middle of the night! Why in heaven's name didn't you come to me before things got this far? I could have used certain leverage with Marjorie, stopped her before things went too far..."

"What leverage? Stopped her from doing what? How far have things gone?" she demanded, finally giving in to her unwilling curiosity.

"Your father's papers, Silver. Technically they didn't belong to you. When Hatcher died, his old will was still in effect, leaving absolutely everything to your mother, despite the fact that she'd remarried and that you'd been born. She may have passed the trunk over to you, but technically it was hers. Everything of Hatcher's was hers, with the exception of that small trust fund."

She'd drunk too much strong black coffee. Her stomach twisted, and she wanted to throw up. She stared blankly at the wall, the receiver still to her ear. "What did she do?"

"What do you think? She sold the trunk and its papers to the highest bidder. Pegasus Pictures, of course. While you were off in his mountain hideaway, Rafe McGinnis was stabbing you in the back."

The front door was thrust open, and Rafe stood there, a load of wood in his arms. His color was high, his eyes bright, he looked healthy and oddly, irrationally happy. Until he looked at her face, at the telephone in her hand, and his expression vanished, leaving nothing but blankness in his dark green eyes.

"Is there anything I can do about it?" she asked finally, her voice raw.

"We can fight it, darling. I've got my lawyers working on it already. Your father's been dead a long time— the studio's shown no interest in *Black Canyon* until you came up with your screenplay. It doesn't matter that McGinnis doesn't actually want your work—they'll have to prove to a judge they weren't influenced by your version of it, and that would be damned hard to do. We have other options. We can break your father's will, though considering the time lapse that might be tricky. Or we can settle for a huge amount of money and a lavish apology."

"No."

"No?" Clement echoed. "I don't blame you for your fury, but we have to be reasonable about this. It's not as if it's holy writ, for heaven's sake. I've already fixed your dear mother's wagon. The *Clarion* is running my piece of the worst actresses of the 1950s, and there's a picture of dear Marjorie in her little jungle leotard as she appeared in *Swamp Queen of Africa.*"

Normally Silver would have laughed. Of all the bad movies Marjorie had made, *Swamp Queen* was the worst, her major claim to fame. It turned up on everyone's list of ten worst movies, and it guaranteed that Marjorie Carlysle would never sink into polite Republican obscurity.

But she didn't feel like laughing. "Do what you can," she said numbly.

"I already have the lawyers busy earning their retainer. And Silver, come home to me. Don't let that man touch you again."

Silver shivered. Rafe still stood in the open door, and the damp warm wind carried a sudden chill with it. "Goodbye, Clement."

Rafe kicked the door shut behind him, walking across the room and dumping the logs into the wood box. He left a trail of melting snow as he walked. "So the serpent has entered paradise?" he drawled. "Why did you answer the phone?"

"I thought we agreed," she said. "This isn't paradise, it's hell."

He didn't touch her. Which was a good thing. If he touched her she would have shattered. Helpless with love and longing. Or in fury.

"What did Clement have to say?" he asked after a long moment.

"That your lawyers have been successful. They managed to get my father's papers away from my mother."

"Good for them," he said coolly. "How did they manage that?"

"It was really quite simple. It turns out that my father left me nothing. The one parental gesture, of leaving his papers to me, was in fact my mother just wanting to get rid of them. Once they proved to be worth something, she's reclaimed them." Silver managed a brittle smile. "And she's sold them to you."

She didn't want to see the look of compassion that darkened his eyes. She didn't need his pity.

He had enough sense not to offer it. "So then it's settled."

"Don't count on it," she said, her voice fierce.

She expected frustration and rage from him. It couldn't be a faint trace of relief in his cool green eyes, relief that she was still fighting him. "The battle isn't over, then?" he asked lightly.

"Not until I win."

"We might be at it for a long time."

"I've got staying power."

"So do I."

She wanted to scream at him that they weren't talking about sex. Except that they were.

She turned away from him, staring out the window into the glorious mountains, unable to deal with him.

"I'm going to take a shower. We can talk about this when I come down," he said.

"There's nothing to talk about."

"Silver..." There seemed to be a wealth of longing in his voice. If she turned and looked at him, she'd see it in his eyes, and she'd run to him. They'd end up in bed again, and she couldn't do it. Couldn't do it to herself. She was on the narrow edge of survival—one false move and she'd topple over.

She heard his footsteps, and she braced herself. He came up behind her, and his long arms reached around her, pulling her back against his tall, strong body. His long fingers threaded through her short-cropped hair, and his mouth was at her temple. "We can work this out, Silver," he said softly, and her treacherous heart cried out to believe him.

But her mind knew better. She needed to protect herself, hold together whatever small part of her still remained inviolate. She didn't move in his arms, didn't turn as she longed to. She covertly let her body absorb his heat, his strength, knowing this was the last time she'd let him touch her.

When he released her he did so slowly, reluctantly. "We'll work it out," he said again, moving away from her, up the stairs.

She kept her face to the window, waiting until she heard the bathroom door close, waiting until she heard the sound of the shower. Then she moved.

She took a pair of oversize boots from the front closet. She took a heavy sweatshirt, a couple of cans of Diet Coke, and a frozen box of muffins from the freezer. And then, quite calmly, she went outside, climbed into his huge truck and turned the key he'd left in the ignition.

It started with a throaty roar. It had the kind of dashboard that practically drove the truck itself, and she could see that the four-wheel-drive option was already engaged. Surely she could drive this boat out of the mountains. The alternative was too painful to contemplate.

At least it had an automatic transmission. She fastened the seat belt around her, put the gear into low and started off, slowly at first. By the time she'd reached the first bend in the road, she knew she could make it. And she told herself she'd had no choice at all. It was simply a matter of survival.

RAFE HAD NEVER BEEN so angry in his life. He felt like a kid, like a furious, miserable kid. He wanted to smash furniture, break windows, rip the phone out of the wall and hurl it into the fireplace. He wanted to beat his fists against the wall until they were bloody. He, who prided himself on his cool self-control, wanted to lose it completely.

He tried counting to ten. He tried counting to twenty. He stalked over to the front door and stared out into the bright afternoon light. There was no sound at all—she'd been gone for at least the ten minutes he'd been in the shower. Sound carried in the silence of the snow-covered mountains—if there was any chance he'd be able to stop her, that chance had long gone.

And he'd thought he was doing her a favor, lingering in the shower, giving her time to pull herself together. She didn't like to lose any more than he did. He couldn't really believe that she thought she'd had a chance in hell against him, but she must have thought so. Defeat had been very bitter, and he'd hoped to find some way of salvaging her pride.

Damn his lawyers! He'd told them to do what they had to do, to get those rights, but he hadn't quite realized the cost. If he'd known it would shatter Silver's tenuous faith in her father's love, would he have told them to leave it? He wished there was a way he could know.

Hindsight was always twenty-twenty. And he had to admit that there was always a solid possibility he would have told them to go ahead anyway. He'd warned her he fought dirty. And he always won.

Damn Clement Walden, the wasp-tongued little pedant! He wanted Silver as his eccentric acolyte, and he didn't care what he had to do to keep her dependent on him. He didn't want her getting involved with anyone, himself included. He probably didn't even want her working on that screenplay. The screenplay had nothing to do with the great Clement Walden, and it would therefore be unacceptable. But Silver hadn't realized that yet, realized that any form of independence would be squashed. She'd gone running back to him now, for comfort. She'd find out soon enough that Clement Walden was cold comfort indeed.

And damn Marjorie Carlysle for selling her daughter's birthright to the highest bidder. If she'd lied so long ago, why didn't she just let the lie stand? It wasn't as if she needed the money. His sources had suggested she didn't approve of her daughter's choice of career. That she wanted a junior matron.

Silver Carlysle would never be somebody's idea of a society matron. She was too stubborn, too bright, too unconventional to ever fit in with that kind of stultified society. She was made for freedom, for wildness, for fresh air and mountains and battles and love.

Damn it, she was made for him! How long was it going to take him to admit it?

And what was he going to have to pay to get her?

He picked up the phone he'd wanted to throw across the room and punched in a number. Bernie answered on the second ring, her cigarette-roughened voice sounding oddly concerned.

"I'm stuck at the cabin," he said abruptly, not bothering to identify himself. "Arrange for a car and driver, will you? Make it soon."

"Rafe, what the hell has been going on? Is Silver Carlysle with you?" Bernie demanded, and Rafe got the sudden, strange feeling that for once Bernie's concern wasn't primarily for his own tough hide.

"Why do you think my truck's gone? She took off in it about half an hour ago, and I'd assume she's out of the mountains already, heading back home. See what you can do for me, Bernie. I need to get the hell out of this place as soon as I can. It'll take someone from Denver at least three hours to get here. See if you can hire someone from Durango—they might be faster."

"I'll get Robin right on it. I need to tell you what your lawyers have done about the rights to *Black Canyon*."

"You sound disapproving, Bernie," he said in a weary voice. "I already know what they've done. Clement Walden called Silver with the happy news. That's why she took off."

There was a long silence on the other end as Bernie digested the information. "What was she running away from, Rafe?"

"I've asked you this before, and I'm asking again. You couldn't be insane enough to be matchmaking, could you?" he demanded.

Bernie had always been straight with him. "And if I was?"

"Then I'd lock you in a room with Clement Walden for a week and let you see what it feels like."

"I think there's a slight difference between the two relationships," Bernie said dryly. "We weren't made for each other."

"Oh, God, Bernie, do you have Alzheimer's?" Rafe demanded, appalled by her tacit admission. "Menopause?"

"Too late for menopause, sugar," Bernie said with her bark of a laugh. "Are you going to tell me you aren't infatuated with Silver Carlysle?"

"Yes," he said flatly.

He could hear the sudden hissing of her breath on the other end. "God, I believe you," she said, and there was no mistaking the sudden misery in her voice. "I blew it, big time."

"You certainly did," he said blandly. "You ought to consider that before you start messing with people's lives. Get me the damned car so I can get back to L.A. and see what I can do about this mess."

"Why is it a mess? You've gotten what you've wanted. She can still fight it, but it's a losing battle."

"It always was. There's just one little hitch in this whole thing."

"What's that, boss?"

"I'm not infatuated with Silver Carlysle. I'm in love with her. And I don't know what the hell I'm going to do about it."

He hung up the phone with Bernie's whoop of joy still echoing in his ears. She was a lot more optimistic than he was about it, but then, she didn't know the details about what had gone on between Silver Carlysle and the essentially boneheaded Rafe McGinnis.

Who would have thought a tough old cookie like Bernie would end up being a matchmaker? She'd given him hell when he'd made the mistake of marrying for no better reason than he'd thought it was time, but she usually kept her nose out of his romantic affairs.

But she was the one who'd brought *Black Canyon* to his attention, knowing full well it would precipitate a battle with Silver Carlysle. She'd already known he reacted more strongly to the woman than to anyone else in the past five years, including his ex-wife. Maybe it was simply that that had inspired her.

Or maybe it was her ancient relationship with Silver's father. For a moment he allowed himself the truly horrifying thought that Bernie might be her real mother, and then quickly dismissed it. Silver looked like Marjorie Carlysle, whether she realized it or not. She had the beautiful, uncluttered features, the magnificent bone structure, the same luscious mouth and wonderful eyes.

Still, Benjamin Hatcher's daughter hadn't been a random choice. And he didn't like to feel manipulated.

But in fact, all Bernie's matchmaking would have come to nothing if it weren't for the fact that Silver Carlysle made him feel alive for the first time in years.

He glanced around him at the cabin that he'd avoided for so long. She'd even made him come home again, unwillingly, he had to admit, but he'd come. And in coming back, he'd found a part of himself that had been missing for a long, long time.

It was midafternoon already. He allowed himself a brief, chilly fear that Silver might have trouble steering the huge pickup over the melting roads, and then dismissed it. Silver Carlysle could do just about any damned thing she set her mind to. Particularly if she was mad enough.

It would take hours for a car and driver to reach him. Hours to kill. The fire was blazing, the coffee was hot, and there was a reasonable amount of whiskey left over. He could stretch out on the sofa and see if there were any more Louis L'Amours to while away the time.

But he wasn't going to do that. He was going for the coffee and the whiskey, all right. But he was going to read the one thing he'd secretly carried around with him for the past week, something he swore he'd never touch.

A copy of Silver Carlysle's screenplay. He'd had Bernie get it for him. There was no stopping Rafe McGinnis when he wanted something. He'd read the script and then he'd find whether there was any way he could salvage it and give her what she wanted. Or whether they were going to have to do it the hard way.

## Chapter Fifteen

It never rained in L.A. It was raining that late Sunday afternoon when Silver drove the huge truck through the wet streets. It was probably snowing up in the mountains of Colorado again. And Rafe was probably still cursing her.

She'd grown fond of the oversize vehicle in the eighteen hours of driving. After the first two hours of sheer panic as she tried to float the boatlike thing down off the mountains, she'd learned to respect its power. The ride across Arizona was smooth and seamless, with nothing to distract her from her dark thoughts.

There was no danger whatsoever that the monotony of the landscape and the hours upon hours of driving would lull her into sleep. She'd slept long and well, wrapped in Rafe's treacherous arms. She didn't need caffeine or fresh air to keep her alert—the pain and fury in her battered heart precluded any kind of peace.

How could he have done that? How could he have made love to her, kissed her, smiled at her, all the while knowing his lawyers were doing their best to cut the ground from underneath her? She'd been a patsy, taking off to Colorado and letting herself get caught in his snare.

He'd warned her more than once, and she hadn't listened. He'd made love to her all the while he was stealing her dream.

And the final blow was that he'd stolen her father, too.

If she hadn't made the major mistake of going to bed with him, she wouldn't be so vulnerable. But somehow the fight had gone out of her. She, who never quit, couldn't battle anymore. She just wanted to run away and hide.

There was never any question as to where she would end up. Not at her mother's mansion. Marjorie had committed the final act of betrayal, and she was self-absorbed enough not to realize how it would affect her daughter. She probably assumed that Silver would come home, move into the big house where she belonged, and become the kind of daughter Marjorie always wanted.

What Marjorie didn't realize was that Silver had tried, for years and years, to be that daughter. She'd finally come to accept who she was, accept that her mother would never be satisfied. And right now she needed to go to the one person who always gave her a shoulder to cry on, a listening ear. Clement Walden.

The heavy rain poured down on his French provincial town house, making it look like an Impressionist painting. She pulled into the circular driveway, probably the first pickup truck to enter that hallowed preserve since the house was built, sometime after the Second World War, and jumped down in the rain.

He knew her very well. He must have been watching for her, knowing she'd come to him to pour out her shame and misery. He was waiting at the open door, immaculately tailored arms outstretched.

She went into them, aware as ever of the absurdity of being comforted by a man half her size, and let him lead her into the cool, peaceful confines of his living room, all the while he murmured soothing, meaningless things. By the time she was settled on a Greco-Roman chaise, a cup of raspberry herb tea and honey in her chilled hands, she was feeling both listless and unnaturally calm.

"I hate him," she said, lying back and looking at the ceiling.

"You have every reason to," Clement murmured, sipping at his own Earl Grey. "The man's unprincipled. A liar, a swindler, an artistic cretin. How you could have thought he could be reasoned with is beyond my comprehension. I warned you, Silver, I warned you..."

"I know you did," she said, her voice soft with exhaustion and strain. "I can't explain it. There was something that drew me to him, something that called to me, no matter how much my brain told me it was crazy. I thought I saw something else in him. I thought there was a real person beneath that cold exterior, someone capable of deep, abiding love. I thought there was a wounded child..."

"And you'd be the one to heal him? Don't tell me you fell for that one, Silver!" Clement's contempt would have been painful, if only she didn't feel the same contempt already. "It's part of his stock in trade. He grew up in a nice middle-class family in Ohio, went to the University of Michigan, and then on to NYU. He didn't have a deprived childhood."

"He grew up in Colorado," she corrected him. "His father died in a snowstorm when he was eleven, his mother drank herself to death. He lived alone until his aunt and uncle came and took him to that nice middle-class family in Ohio, and he hated every minute of it. Do you realize he'd never been back to his home, not in twenty years?''

"I'm really not interested," Clement said, though the quickening in his light voice said otherwise. "I must say, this is all news to me. It's never appeared on his public bio.''

"He wouldn't lie to me.''

"Don't be ridiculous, Silver, the man would lie to anyone. Still, this is something quite new. I'll have to have my people look into it.''

Silver sat up on the couch, a cold dread washing over her. "What do you mean?''

Clement's smile was the epitome of innocence. "Don't you want revenge, Silver? The man manipulated you, deceived and tricked you and stole the one thing that really mattered from you. Don't you want him to suffer?''

She could see him quite clearly in her mind. The distant, shuttered face, the flash of emotion in his cool green eyes. "No," she said. "I don't.''

"Very noble of you, darling. Quite Christian, in fact. I never knew you were so merciful.''

"You won't do anything, Clement?" She swiveled around to look at him, suddenly uneasy.

Clement smiled his wintry smile. "I wouldn't think of it, my dear.''

She leaned back, closing her eyes, listening to the rain pour down outside. Thinking about the snow, and the mountains and a man's strong, talented body. "Promise?" she murmured drowsily. And she was asleep before she heard the answer.

"GOOD GOD, look at the cowboy," Bernie greeted Rafe as he stormed into the office. It was half past seven on a Monday morning, and he hadn't been in the mood for Armani. He'd jumped into the shower, dressed in jeans and denim and boots, and only eschewed his ancient Stetson at the last minute. "Where's your earring, boss?"

"Lost in a snowdrift," he replied, grabbing his coffee. "Where the hell is Sam?"

"Awaiting your presence, oh lord and master," Sam said, appearing from the inner office, rumpled-looking as usual. "What the hell have you been doing, watching too many John Wayne movies? Haven't you heard that cowboys aren't in right now?"

"Do you really think I give a damn?" Rafe said, sinking down behind his desk and surveying his office. It was odd, but it felt like home. Just as the cabin in Colorado had, just as his house in the hills had. How could a man have so many homes? So many different homes? "We've got a change in strategy."

"Lord, don't tell me that!" Sam protested, settling into one of the leather chairs. "We finally nailed Silver Carlysle, and you want to change the rules. Or is that it? It wasn't just the lawyers who nailed her, was it, buddy? How does she stack up to Marcia Allison? She's got a great set of headlights, but she looks a little too fierce for my tastes..." His voice trailed off, suddenly uneasy. "Now why do I get the feeling that I just said something I shouldn't have?"

"You usually aren't stupid for long," Rafe said in a measured voice.

"Since when have you decided to be gentlemanly and protective?" Sam asked, more curious than defensive.

"After all, I usually get your leavings. Your advice has been invaluable to a lonely old bachelor like me."

Bernie had been listening to all this with a disapproving expression on her face. "I don't think there are going to be any leavings this time," she said in her gravelly voice.

"You mean you're going to do it so much there won't be anything left when you dump her?" Sam demanded cheerfully.

"Do you want to survive for the next ten minutes?" Rafe inquired sarcastically. "Because you're treading on very thin ice."

Sam laughed, unmoved by the threat. "There's not enough room in this town for the two of us, pardner," he drawled. "Don't worry, Rafe. I got the word from Bernie—the mighty McGinnis has finally fallen. I was just pulling your chain."

"You think I'm in the mood for that?" Rafe growled.

"Nope. You think I care? I just want to know if I get to be best man this time? I was out of town when you were fool enough to marry your first wife. I must say I think your taste has improved tremendously."

"You can hold my hand while I weep in my beer."

"I'd rather hold her hand."

"Boys," Bernie said sternly. "We're not getting anywhere with all this. What's going on, Rafe? If you want to settle with Silver Carlysle, you're going to have to do something about it. I gather the lawyers have worked up some conservative figures."

"She doesn't care about money," Rafe said, leaning back in his chair and propping his old boots on the teak-and-glass table that served as his desk. They looked good there. At home.

"Don't be ridiculous, everyone cares about money," Sam protested. "If she doesn't, how the hell are you ever going to get her to do what you want?"

"Maybe by asking her real nicely."

"Maybe." Sam sounded doubtful. "I don't know if she's going to be in the mood to listen."

"It depends on what she'll be listening to."

"Why don't I like the sound of this?" Sam demanded of Bernie. "We've got Miller working on the first draft of the screenplay, and not only has the man made us a fortune, he's also been up for an Oscar twice. He likes the book, he's got a good handle on what he wants to do with it."

"Just for the sake of conversation, what does he want to do with it?" Rafe took a sip of his coffee. He'd left his cigarettes in Colorado, and he hadn't bothered to get any more. This was the first time in twenty-four hours that he missed them.

"Oh, just a few cosmetic things. Tone down the girl, probably kill her off in the second act. Makes good motivation for the hero to go after the renegades, gives the audience some vicarious flesh and violence."

"What are we paying him?"

"We had to go up, of course. You know what an Oscar nomination is worth to an agent when he's negotiating a deal. But he's worth it, you know that."

"How much will he take in a kill fee?"

Sam looked at him, aghast. "You're kidding, aren't you, buddy? Tell me you're just paying me back for teasing you about Silver Carlysle. Tell me you don't mean it."

"I don't want Miller doing the screenplay. I don't care how good he is at *Cop for a Day* epics, I don't even give a damn how many Oscars he's nominated for. He's not doing *Black Canyon*.''

"Then who the hell is?" Sam snarled. "If you'll pardon my asking such a blunt question."

For a moment Rafe didn't answer, and the faint smile on his face was unreadable. "The person best suited for the job," he said finally. "Silver Carlysle."

"Oh, God," Sam moaned. "He's finally lost his mind. His brain went to his pants and stayed there, and we're all going to pay the price. Rafe, baby, no broad is worth it."

"Sam," Bernie warned, eyeing Rafe's still expression.

"You've already gotten her into bed. Anyone who's seen the two of you together knows she's crazy about you, no matter how hard she tries to fight it. You don't need to sacrifice a multimillion-dollar production just to flatter her."

"Sam," Bernie said again, her voice even stronger.

"At least let her assist Miller. No one ever writes a movie alone in Hollywood, you know that. Buy her draft, give it to Miller, and he'll see what he can salvage. He won't like sharing screen credit, but maybe we can come up with a compromise, like a story credit, or maybe 'additional dialogue' or something."

"You're missing the point, Sam," Rafe said with icy calm. "I've never made a business decision dictated by my sex life, and I'm not about to start now. I read her screenplay. There's no other word for it, Sam. It was right."

"It was right," Sam echoed, leaning back in the chair, an expression of despair on his face.

"I need you to get the lawyers in here, Bernie," Rafe continued, ignoring Sam's stricken expression. "Make it for one o'clock, that'll give Sam enough time to read the manuscript.''

There was no disguising Bernie's look of triumph. ''Sure thing,'' she said, turning to go, but Rafe put out a hand to stop her.

''You wanted this, didn't you?'' he asked with sudden shrewdness. ''You'd read her screenplay and you wanted us to do it. For God's sake, why didn't you just say so in the first place, Bernie?''

''Because you weren't in the mood to listen. You would have thrown the whole idea out rather than negotiate with her,'' Bernie said, her faded eyes defiant. ''I knew that book better than anyone. I read Silver's script and I was astonished. You had the word, Rafe. It was right. It was just that simple.''

He stared at her in mute frustration. ''You know what kind of kill fee we're going to have to pay Miller?''

''Take it out of my share of the profits.''

''If there are any profits. Westerns are problematic.''

''I don't give a damn. You and I both know it's going to be brilliant. We just have to convince Sam.''

Rafe turned to him. ''So how about it, Sam? You ready to rise to the challenge, or will I go looking for the new Spielberg to make *Black Canyon?*''

Sam roused himself, glaring at both of them. ''The script better be damned good,'' he said, pulling himself out of the chair.

''It's more than that.'' He tossed the coffee-stained pages across his desk. ''There's just one thing that troubles me.''

''What's that?'' Bernie said warily, as Sam wandered off toward his office, muttering under his breath.

"How come you know that book better than anyone else alive?"

And Bernie only smiled.

"I THINK it might be a good idea if you came into the office," Clement said in a gentle voice some three days later. "You can't just sit around brooding."

"I'm not brooding," Silver said listlessly. "I'm swimming laps in that pool you never use. I'm catching up on my beauty sleep. I'm wearing the clothes you've been sending home for me."

She was currently dressed in one of Clement's favorites, a white linen suit that looked just a little too much like the sort of thing he always wore. She'd accepted it with a singular lack of enthusiasm, and while it made her look stylish, elegant and daring, it didn't make her look like Silver.

"You need to work. Not that I blame you for keeping a low profile. McGinnis has been looking for you."

"Has he?" she murmured, blessing the numb feeling that didn't abate at the mention of his name. "When did he get back in town?"

"Same day you did, I gather. And actually, it isn't McGinnis who's looking for you. It's his lawyers."

Even that news didn't penetrate her cocoon of numbness. "Let them look."

"Oh, I imagine they'll find you sooner or later. There are only so many places where you might be found, and our relationship is rather well known. You may as well emerge."

"In another day or so." A sudden misgiving broke through her abstraction. "Do you want me to leave, Clement?" she asked, suddenly anxious. "I don't want to impose..."

"Don't be absurd, dear girl. I love having you here, you know that. At last my little protégée is where she belongs. I just think it's getting to be time to get on with your life."

She smiled up at him. "I will, Clement. Just give me a few more days."

"Anything, darling. All you have to do is ask."

She liked being in limbo. Clement was gone during the day, and many of the evenings, too. Like Rafe McGinnis, he was on the A-list for parties, and there was always some occasion that demanded his presence. He thrived on that attention, even though he pretended boredom with it all, and the elegant, peaceful confines of his town house were Silver's peaceful haven most of the time, her solitude only broken by the occasional discreet presence of Clement's raft of servants.

And the telephone. She never answered it, of course, but she could hear it ring, almost constantly, the bell-like tones echoing through the house. Clement had instructed his houseboy never to bother Silver with the callers, but every time the phone rang she could feel her stomach knot up.

Not that Rafe would try to call her. He didn't know where she was, and he hadn't made any effort to find her, apart from siccing his lawyers on her again. She could just imagine what they wanted. Some nice discreet settlement, to ensure that she wouldn't cause any more trouble.

They didn't know her, of course. And Rafe didn't know her. She was past the point of causing trouble. She'd lost. It was that simple. He'd always told her she would, and she'd been a fool to think she could buck the system, buck someone as powerful as Rafe McGinnis, and walk away intact.

She'd paid for it. Paid for her temerity with most of the things she held dear. The last strands of peaceful coexistence with her mother. The fruits of her creativity for the last two years. Her one loving memory of her father. All destroyed, or shown for the sham they really were.

But she'd paid with something even more dear, and she'd known it was at risk early on. All her efforts at self-protection had come to nothing, though, when faced with someone as devastating as Rafe McGinnis. She'd fallen in love with the man, and that stupid act of emotional and physical surrender had made everything else lose its power over her. She'd lost her heart in more ways than one. She'd lost her heart to him, given it to a man who would never value it. And she'd lost the heart to keep fighting. Until now she felt empty and hollow inside.

It was late the next morning when the phone rang once more, pealing through the sterile house. Silver tried to pull the feather pillow over her head to shut out the insistent noise. She'd taken to sleeping as much as she could, morning, noon and night, hoping to sleep away the ache inside. She had the drugged, stupid feeling one gets after sleeping around the clock, and she stared in disbelief at the digital clock by her bed. Eleven-thirty. And she'd gone to sleep at eight the night before.

She pulled herself out of bed, running a hand through her shaggy hair. "What you have, my girl, is a clinical depression," she said out loud, over the noise of the telephone. "Now you can wander around this place, hiding out, sleeping your life away. Or you can come back to life."

The distant ringing of the phone mocked her. There was an extension by her bed, one she'd turned the ringer off but hadn't unplugged. "Life it is," she said flatly, and picked up the receiver.

"I thought you'd be there." Marjorie's voice was accusing, but even an angry Silver could hear the uncertainty beneath her deliberately arch tones. "Do you know how worried I've been? Why haven't you come home?"

Silver considered hanging up the phone and crawling back into bed. It took all her willpower not to, to remember she'd decided to face life. "I was evicted," she said in a calm voice. "Locked out, as a matter of fact. I had no place to come home to."

"Don't be absurd, darling. Your room at the big house is just as it's always been. I've been the indulgent mother for far too long, but when your silly forays into the movie business start dragging the family name in the gutter, it's time for me to put my foot down."

"The family name wasn't dragged in the gutter, Marjorie," Silver said calmly. "Just yours. And it isn't as if you slept your way to the top. You never made it to the top."

There was a pause on the other end of the line. "Darling, perhaps I underestimated you. You do seem to have your father's way with words," she said in an acid voice. "What are you doing with Clement? Besides hiding out? He's not good for you, you know. You may think he's your champion, but Clement Walden doesn't care about anyone but himself. He's just using you to settle an old score."

"What old score?"

"I wouldn't think of passing on ancient gossip..."

"You don't talk about anything but," Silver said sharply. "Spill it, mother. What old score is Clement trying to settle?"

"Any number of them, I imagine. He's the most malicious man in Hollywood. He hates me, he hated your father, who called him a prosy old bore, and he despises McGinnis because he's everything he wants and can't have."

"What are you talking about?"

"It's really quite simple. When Rafe and Sam first turned up in Hollywood, Clement fell all over them. He called their first film the most brilliant piece of work he'd seen since *Citizen Kane*. He tried to make Rafe one of his little protégés, and you can imagine how Mc-Ginnis responded to that. He told Clement to go stuff himself, in very public, humiliating terms. Clement didn't like being rejected and humiliated by someone he'd deigned to honor with his attentions. He's been working on his revenge ever since."

"I don't believe you."

"Don't you? Ask Clement. I'll say one thing, he's usually honest about these things."

"Goodbye, Marjorie."

"Wait!" There was a sudden broken note in her voice, one her daughter knew didn't come from an excess of acting talent. Marjorie was truly upset.

"Yes?"

"I want you to come home. I know you're angry with me for letting McGinnis have your father's papers, but I checked with our lawyers and they would have gotten them in the end. We really didn't have a legal leg to stand on. It simply made sense to accept their very generous offer and get the thing off our hands. It's occupied too much of your time, baby. It's time you settled down, got married. Even—" there was a strained gulp on the other end "—have children."

Silver didn't move, deeply shocked. "You really must love me," she said finally, "if you're asking me to make you a grandmother."

Marjorie managed a choked laugh. "I didn't say you had to be in any particular hurry about it. I just want to see you happy."

"By marrying whom you want, doing what you want?"

Marjorie sighed. "I've given up on that. I want you to marry who you want, and if it's Arnold Schwarzenegger or Rafe McGinnis, I'll accept it."

"Arnold's taken."

"So he is. That leaves McGinnis. Do you love him?"

Even her uninvolved mother had seen that far ahead. "Let it be, Marjorie. This may be Hollywood, but I don't believe in happy endings. Not for me."

"Oh, baby," Marjorie said, sounding more like a mother than she had in Silver's entire twenty-nine years. "Most especially for you."

Silver sat staring at the phone, long after she'd hung up. She ought to go home, she knew that now. She needed to make her peace with her mother, who loved her despite her self-absorption. She needed to make her peace with her stepfather, a solid, unimaginative, relentlessly kind man. She needed to make her peace with herself, and hiding out at Clement Walden's town house wasn't getting her there.

It was half-past twelve by the time she showered and dressed. She knew where she'd find Clement—his was a life of unchangeable habits, and he always dined at Spago's on Thursdays, even though he decried its descent into commonness. If she hurried she'd be there ahead of him.

The rented truck still stood in Clement's elegantly curving driveway, and she knew a moment's guilt that she hadn't returned it. Except that she didn't know whom he'd rented it from. Besides, Rafe McGinnis could afford to buy that truck ten times over.

Clement hadn't arrived yet, but the maître d' knew her from previous occasions, and he ushered her to Clement's waiting table with his usual flourish. "Read your piece in the *Clarion* this morning," he said with his usual friendliness. "Nasty."

The word was said with deep approval tinged with awe, and that sudden trickling of uneasiness blossomed. She hadn't written anything for the *Clarion* in over a week, and as far as she knew, there wasn't anything on file for them to use.

She managed a faint smile. "Thanks. I don't suppose you have a copy of it lying around?"

"Someone will bring it right over," he said smoothly, and she knew he'd send a minion out to purchase one. In Los Angeles they knew how to treat their customers, especially if one was paying the kind of prices Spago's commanded. "In the meantime, may I suggest the squid ravioli in pesto sauce?"

Silver barely listened. "You decide."

She sat there, numb, waiting. Around her were faces, the famous and not so famous, and many of them were looking her way. Whispering. Sly smiles on their faces. Intimate nods in her direction.

The newspaper and the pasta arrived at the same time. She ignored the food, thumbing through the fresh paper with numb hands, the circulars already politely removed. And then she found it. Nasty indeed.

It was her byline, all right. Clement had very humbly not even taken an assistant credit. She wondered where they'd found that picture of Rafe, a tall, bony-looking teenager in a faded shirt that showed his wrists, ripped jeans that were too short, a shaggy haircut and a hurt, defiant expression on his face.

There was a grainy photograph of his mother, looking far older than her stated age, and his father, a tall, biblical-looking man with flowing beard and kind eyes.

It was all laid out for the curious in Hollywood, written in carefully malicious prose. Rich little poor boy making good in Hollywood, the American dream come true. His mother's wasted stay in a state alcohol-treatment center, a photo of the twisted wreckage of his father's snowplow. His hidden, protected past splashed all over the *Clarion* for people to gossip about.

She didn't need to feel numb with guilt. Rafe had done the same to her, of course. Worse, in the tabloid. And she was innocent—Clement had done it, Clement had concocted this mishmash of truth, innuendo and outright lies and then attributed it to her. She stared at it, the smell of the pasta rising to her nostrils, and wondered what the elegant clientele of Spago's would do if she got sick, right there and then.

## Chapter Sixteen

"Silver, darling!" A woman swooped down on her, embracing her in a Poison-scented cloud. "Where have you been all this time? You're looking marvelous! I knew Clement was lying. He'd have us believe you were sitting around, sulking over a broken heart. You know how wicked that man can be. He made you sound positively pathetic. But then, Clement always has such a nasty air about him when he talks about his little protégées. I must say, you've lasted longer than they usually do. Most people see through him sooner."

"Mavis," Silver said cautiously, finally remembering the woman's name. "How have you been?"

"Just peachy, darling, just peachy. Of course, it's no wonder Clement is slightly more circumspect around you. You have a great deal more talent than his slaves usually have. That piece in the *Clarion* today is one of the most deliciously wicked things I've read in a long time. The whole town is talking about it. We never thought anyone could make Rafe McGinnis look vulnerable, but you managed. Well, as Clement said, 'Hell hath no fury like a woman scorned' and all that. You've perfected the art of revenge, darling."

Silver looked up, across the noisy, crowded restaurant. Clement was strolling toward her, his face smug, self-confident, his immaculate white suit without a wrinkle.

"Not yet," she murmured. "But I intend to work on it."

Mavis had wandered off, espying more powerful victims, by the time Clement reached the table. "Silver, what a treat," he said, not a trace of wariness in his voice as he leaned his papery cheek down for her to kiss before taking his seat opposite her. "I was afraid you were never going to leave the house."

"Never is a long time, Clement," she said carefully. "Marc was kind enough to get me today's *Clarion*."

Her exalted opinion of Clement's intellect took a drastic plunge as her mentor smiled, not the slightest trace of uneasiness marring his genial expression. "I rather outdid myself, didn't I?" He preened.

"You did," she said. "It's a shame people don't appreciate that you're the one who wrote it."

"You needn't look so stricken about the whole thing. If you're fool enough to care about what McGinnis thinks of you, comfort yourself with the thought that he probably won't believe you're capable of writing so brilliantly. He'll probably assume I wrote it. Many people do, you know. They just assume I rewrite most of your columns for you, and I must confess, I encourage that belief. After more than thirty years I've run out of things to say. Whereas, you, my dear, are fresh and biting. I must say, in this case I really outdid myself, and you, with all your freshness and flair, can't hold a candle to an old master like me."

"Did you say 'old bastard'?" Silver inquired with deceptive sweetness.

Unease was beginning to click in. "You're unhappy with me, aren't you?" Clement said, pouting slightly. "Darling, I did it for you. The man had hurt you, and you gave me the perfect ammunition to fight back with. The man looks pathetic, and his stock in trade was his invulnerability. You should be thanking me."

Silver rose slowly, gracefully, towering over her dinner companion. "Thank you so much, Clement," she said sweetly, picking up her plate of squid ravioli, "and go to hell."

The green-speckled ravioli looked quite attractive adorning the once-pristine front of Clement's jacket. The noisy chatter filling Spago's had stopped abruptly, and all eyes were on the two of them. Clement had taken out his handkerchief and was vainly trying to mop some of the splashed pasta from his face with an air of elegant disdain. It only managed to make him appear more ridiculous.

There was a murmur as she strode through the restaurant, a murmur that swelled and rose until, when she reached the door, it erupted into an enthusiastic round of applause, sweetened by an occasional cheer. She turned, gave a solemn bow and marched out, the crowd's approval still ringing in her ears.

At least she'd left nothing behind at Clement's, only the clothes he'd bought her in his attempt to turn her into a sexless clone. She never had to go back there, never had to see him again. Her job at the *Clarion* was finished—there'd never be any choice between the Pulitzer-winning Clement Walden and a minor underling. It didn't matter.

Even *Black Canyon* no longer mattered. She'd put her heart and soul into it for two years, and now she was ready to let it go. Not because she had a sudden epiphany of mental health. But because she had something new to work on, a new idea for a screenplay, this time original, this time, of all things, a pirate epic. Now all she had to do was find a computer.

The driveway was empty when she pulled in later that afternoon. Her mother was presumably out at bridge, her stepfather at his office. She'd get settled into her room in the big house, with the ridiculous canopy bed. Maybe she'd even see if she could find one of those stupid tea dresses her mother used to keep buying for her, dresses that looked frilly and ridiculous on her long, deep-bosomed frame.

"You're a sight for sore eyes!" Wilkers emerged from the row of garage bays, wiping his hands on an oily rag. "And where in heaven's name did you get that rig?"

"It's rented," she replied with all truthfulness, jumping down from the truck. "Where's Mother?"

"Off on a mission. She'll be glad to see you home, missy. She was worried half to death about you." He tucked the rag into his back pocket. "I think herself has learned a lesson this time. Not to go interfering in her grown daughter's life."

Silver found she could laugh. "I don't think mothers ever learn that one," she said.

"Can I help you with your bags?"

"What you see is what you get." She started toward the main house, when Wilkers's voice stopped her.

"Wrong way, miss."

She turned to look at him. "You mean . . ."

"That's right. I told you she's seen the error of her ways. She had me move everything back a couple of days ago. I'm not sure that I set the computer up right, but I'd bet you could have it running in no time."

She flung her arms around him, kissing him loudly on his rosy cheek before racing past him, up the stairs to her loft.

Wilkers hadn't lied—everything was just as it had been. She stood in the middle of the room, confused for a moment, waiting for the peace and rightness to sweep over her. She was home at last, everything would be all right again.

Except that it wouldn't be. She still loved the place, her first piece of independence. But too many things had happened in the last weeks. She'd discovered the mountains, the peace and the cold fresh air. She'd been betrayed on all sides. And she'd made the very grave mistake of falling in love with a man who didn't know the meaning of the word.

It would come back to her, wouldn't it? The sense of rightness about the place. All she had to do was set up her computer, find a comfortable pair of sweat pants and an old T-shirt, lay in a supply of Diet Coke and coffee, and she'd find peace again.

The answer her apartment gave her was a resounding no. It was time to leave home, this time for good. While her mother's gesture of apology melted some of the ice around her heart, it wasn't good for either of them, this living in close quarters, never being what the other wanted. It was time to pack her Mac and her jeans and take off.

There was one thing she had to do before she left. She had to see Rafe once more, to try to apologize, to explain. She hadn't written the article, but she'd been fool enough to trust Clement not to spill out things that should have been left unsaid in the first place. How could she have been so naive—not to realize what a venal creature he was?

And he'd been absolutely right—Rafe's power in Hollywood stemmed from his invincibility. He never lost, he was never vulnerable. She'd learned to her cost how invulnerable he was. But the film colony was a fickle place. The moment they scented weakness they'd be after him like sharks at the smell of blood.

He wouldn't believe her, of course. Unless, like everyone else, he'd always assumed Clement had ghosted her columns for her. In fact, it had been the other way around. Clement had grown increasingly lax about deadlines, and he'd signed her better pieces more than once. At the time she'd been immeasurably flattered. In retrospect she felt like a bigger fool than ever. It didn't matter that Clement was a past master at manipulation. She was a past master at seeing through manipulation, having lived with her mother most of her life. She should have been able to see through Clement.

It was time to get her life in order, time to move ahead. She had unfinished business to take care of, with her mother, with Rafe.

It was past nine when she set out into the brightly lighted streets of Beverly Hills in the huge pickup. She'd accomplished a surprising amount in the past five hours, including making peace with her mother, cutting the apron strings, and even getting a start on "Pirates" before she packed up her computer along with her most comfortable clothes. Her mother was willing to let her go—sad, reluctant, but accepting—and her afternoon mission had been easily accomplished. When Mrs. Harry Braddock spoke, even the *Clarion* listened with dutiful respect. A corrected byline would run for two days in the *Clarion*, starting with tomorrow's edition. Marjorie knew her daughter better than Silver realized. She knew Silver would never betray the man she loved, and she'd taken care of the matter quickly and efficiently.

The appointment with Rafe's lawyers was set for ten the next morning. She'd tried to get out of that one, returning their endless messages and telling them she no longer made any claim to *Black Canyon.* Apparently that wasn't enough for them, they wanted legal documents and all that. They wanted money to change hands too, but at that she drew the line. She was willing to give Rafe *Black Canyon,* now that she had nothing left to fight with. But she wasn't going to be bought off. She reserved that small taste of victory for herself.

All that was left was Rafe himself. She'd saved the hardest part till last. She'd considered writing a note, but the words wouldn't come. She considered saying nothing, counting on the fact that she'd be meeting with his lawyers, not him, and with luck she might never have to face him again.

But she couldn't. She wasn't a coward, and she'd never taken the easy way out. She couldn't get away with a note, or with simply disappearing. She'd run away once, in Colorado. She couldn't run away again, and live with herself. She had to face Rafe, knowing she'd be facing his contempt and disbelief, and apologize.

She drove more slowly than she'd driven since she was fifteen years old and just learning on the crowded streets of L.A. The hills were dark and still as she steered the pickup up the narrow road, and she found herself hoping, praying he wouldn't be home. Then at least she could tell herself she'd tried.

But in fact, when she reached his outlandish little house and found it dark, deserted, the hollowness inside her spread and grew. She refused to consider whether she'd had any false hopes, whether she thought there was a chance for them. She only knew that if she drove away now, she would never see him again.

She climbed out of the pickup and walked to the front door. He had one of those electronic keypads—some password would open the door, and she couldn't for an instant imagine what that password would be. She punched in several possibilities, all to no avail.

And then it came to her with stunning clarity. The most obvious choice for anyone in Hollywood. The cryptic word from the best movie ever made. She punched in the word "Rosebud," remembering the child's sleigh in *Citizen Kane*. And the door swung open into silence.

Nothing seemed to have changed since she'd been there less than a week ago. The house was still in the midst of renovation, the Moorish architecture still bizarre, absurd and ridiculously attractive. He was probably out with some starlet, she thought morosely. After all, he hadn't been trying to find her. Only his lawyers. He'd probably forgotten all about her. Until he'd seen today's paper.

She'd wait an hour, no more. She certainly didn't want to be here when he brought some sweet young thing home. If she had any sense at all she'd leave right now rather than run the risk of being thrust into such a hideously embarrassing situation.

Except for the simple fact that she really didn't think he'd do it. His romantic exploits might be legend, but she didn't think he was going to jump into someone else's bed right away. Even if she wanted to torment herself with the possibility, she simply didn't believe it.

And she'd come too far to run now. She'd wait for him, long enough to apologize, to say goodbye. And then maybe she could get on with her life.

The swimming pool drew her like a magnet. She stepped onto the terrace in the warm night air, remembering. Remembering his body drifting against hers. Remembering his mouth. Remembering, as they sank beneath the cool surface of the water, how fear left her, and only Rafe remained.

He wouldn't be home for hours, she knew that. She stripped off her clothes quickly, without giving herself time to think about it, dumping them on the chaise. She knew how to dive. She just never did.

She looked at the moon-silvered water, and thought of Rafe. And then she dived, headfirst, splitting the water like a silver arrow.

HE WAS DRIVING FAST, too fast, his booted foot clamped down on the responsive gas pedal of the Lotus. He'd let his hair hang loose, and it was blowing in the night air, whipping into his face. He was cold and angry. He was in pain, the sense of betrayal sharp and fierce, and there was nothing he could do to release it. Nothing but drive as fast as he could, hoping to outstrip the demons that rode him. But even the Lotus couldn't go that fast.

He'd spent the day watching people's faces. The smirks of those who were in his power. The compassion on the bleeding hearts. And there wasn't a damned thing he could do about it.

If he could find Silver Carlysle he could cheerfully wring her neck. He doubted that would make him feel better. It wasn't the article, with its malicious tone and cheap shots, that bothered him so intensely.

It was that he'd been so mistaken in Silver Carlysle. The woman he thought he'd fallen in love with didn't exist. Not if she could turn around and write something like that.

He pulled into his driveway, too fast, and barely avoided slamming into the pickup. The car stalled out, and he sat there, staring.

He didn't give himself time to think, to react. He jumped out of the Lotus, punched in the code on the security entrance and walked into the darkened house.

It was empty. For a moment he was horribly afraid that she'd simply dropped the truck off rather than face him. She'd never been a coward. She'd run from him in Colorado, but he knew that came more from anger than fear. She'd hidden from him in L.A. But if she was afraid of anything, it wasn't him. It was herself.

And then he knew where she was. By the time he stepped onto the terrace he was barefoot, wearing just his jeans and a T-shirt. She was slicing through the water with graceful, steady strokes, and she probably didn't even realize he was there.

He waited silently until she could feel his eyes on her. She stopped mid-stroke in sudden confusion, sinking beneath the surface, and he knew a moment's panic. And then she rose again, shaking the water out of her eyes, and looked up at him.

"You're trespassing." It didn't come out the way he'd meant it. It sounded hostile, distancing. But then, he was feeling hostile.

"Yes," she said, treading water. "I need to talk to you."

Better than nothing, he thought. Not what he wanted, but something after all. He wondered for an idle moment whether she could carry on this conversation in the nude, whether she'd manage to maintain her composure, or whether a blush of color would cover her delectable skin. And where that blush would start.

"I'll get you a robe," he said abruptly, heading into the cabana and cursing his unruly body. How could he still want her so much? How could he still think he was in love with her?

She was waiting by the edge of the pool when he came out with the thick white terry robe, her shoulders out of the water. He dumped the robe beside her and turned away, walking into the house. By the time she followed she was wrapped up tighter than a mummy, and he handed her the drink he'd poured.

"I don't..." She tried to refuse it, but he put it in her icy hand.

"Dutch courage," he said. "Besides, it's colder than you think. You might catch a chill."

"Do you care?" The question seemed to surprise her almost as much as it surprised him.

Surprised him so much he didn't answer, simply took a delaying sip of his whiskey. He hadn't bothered to turn on the lights. For one thing, he liked his house better in the moonlight. For another, he was hard as a rock, standing next to her damp, robed body, and he'd just as soon she didn't notice.

"I didn't write the article," she said flatly. "I know you won't believe me, but I didn't. Clement did. It was my fault for telling him about your past. I can't believe I did, except that I was upset and vulnerable, and Clement has a way of getting things out of people that they'd rather not say. So it is my fault, for telling him, but I didn't know he was going to use it. If I had, I would have tried to stop him."

"Tried to stop Clement Walden in the midst of a scandal?" he said. "An impossibility."

"I know you don't believe me," she said, hugging the robe more tightly around her, "but I had to apologize anyway. To try to explain. I..."

"Oh, I believe you," he said gently. "Unlike me, you don't fight dirty. That's why you'll never survive in Hollywood, why I can't believe you've survived this long. You need to learn to swim with the sharks, Silver. To use every advantage, fair or unfair, to get what you want. Otherwise you'll be eaten alive if you stay here."

"I'm not going to stay here," she blurted out. "I'm leaving."

He held himself very still. The wrong move, the wrong word, and he might scare her away forever. "Where are you going?"

She managed a rueful smile. "Back to the mountains. I'm not sure where, exactly."

"Don't go to Montana. Half of Hollywood has already moved there. Colorado's nice, and not as trendy as it used to be."

"I liked Colorado," she said in a soft, shy voice.

"You said you hated it."

"I lied."

He set his drink down, then took her untouched one from her cold hand. "When are you leaving?"

"I said I'd meet with your lawyers in the morning. I thought I'd take off after that, sometime tomorrow afternoon."

He nodded, watching her from behind hooded eyes. "That leaves tonight then," he said.

It was all he said, but it was enough. "Yes," she said, her voice a whisper of sound. "That leaves tonight."

And she reached up, putting her hands on his shoulders, and kissed him.

Her mouth tasted cool and sweet against his, damp from the water in the pool. He pulled her tight against him, and he groaned deep in his throat as pleasure washed over him. She felt so right in his arms, her strong, tall body pressed against his. Couldn't she feel the rightness of it?

He loved the way she kissed him. Shy and bold, sensual and innocent, she used her lips, her tongue, her teeth in ways that were totally beguiling. Part of him wanted to overpower her, to kiss her back and scoop her up into his arms, to carry her into the bedroom and make love to her until she was a mindless mass of sensations.

But he didn't. Instinct told him not to. So he stood very still and let her use her mouth, telling himself he couldn't come just from a kiss, could he? Just from her strong hands clenching his shoulders, just from her robed body pressed up against his? Could he?

She moved away for a moment, and he let her go, reluctantly. "Where's the bedroom?" she asked, her voice husky and just faintly nervous.

It was that edge of fear that finished him. "Down the hallway," he said, smiling faintly in the darkness. "Do you want me to carry you?"

She shook her head. "You didn't even let me touch you last time. This is my turn." And she took his hand in hers and led him to the bedroom.

Her hand was icy cold, trembling slightly. She stopped by the bed and turned to him, and if there was shyness on her face there was determination, too. She began unfastening the snaps of his denim shirt, and then her mouth followed, down and down, to the buckle of his belt. She was slightly, endearingly clumsy as she unfastened it, and her awkwardness took ten years off his life, but when she finally freed him, the cool night air was a blissful relief. Followed by the shock of her mouth on him, shy, untutored, and astonishingly enthusiastic. He put his hands down, threading his fingers through her hair, needing to touch her, to hold her, as he felt his bones melt and legs tremble.

He survived as long as he could. When he could stand it no longer he pulled her upright, into his arms, kissing her full on her mouth. The robe was easy enough to strip off, his clothes a little more troublesome, and then they were on the bed, wrapped in each other's arms, rolling together until she lay on her back beneath him, her eyes shining up into his, luminous, vulnerable, her mouth damp and sweet.

She was ready for him, she was beyond ready. Her legs spread beneath him, her hips were ready to arch for his first thrust, and he wanted to so badly he was shaking. But she'd started it, she knew what she wanted, and he had every intention of letting her earn it.

He rolled onto his back, waiting for her. "Come here, Silver," he said, his voice soft and cajoling.

She stared at him, worry darkening her eyes. "I don't..." she said. "I haven't...that is...I don't know how to..."

He grinned. Not a smug, cocky smile. One of pure, masculine possessiveness. "I can't think of a better time to learn. Come here, chicken," he said, his voice gently teasing.

She came, sliding across the bed, a wary expression in her eyes. "I'm not sure..." she began again, but he simply took her and lifted her over him, so that she straddled his body.

"You wanted to be in charge," he murmured. "Now's your chance." He took her hips in his big hands, lifting her, and she sank slowly, inch by miraculous inch, as a look of sheer, primitive wonder washed over her face.

It took her only a moment to catch on to the rhythm. And then his hands left her hips, leaving it up to her, and instead he clenched the sheets, prepared for the ride of his life.

She was an apt pupil. She leaned over him, her hair obscuring her face, intent on drawing every instance of pleasure from him. She sank on him, then lifted up slowly, so slowly he groaned, afraid she'd leave entirely, and then she sank again, and it was all he could do not to grab her, to try to control the movements that were driving him to the very edge of madness.

Her body was covered with a film of sweat. She was shaking, trembling with reaction, and her smooth glides became erratic, jerky, even as he felt his own formidable control begin to dissolve. He caught her hips again, surging up into her, and she gasped, her eyes shooting open as he moved again and again and again, until she shattered around him, her body tight and convulsing, and he was with her, pouring himself into her, drinking in her strangled cry of completion.

She'd collapsed against him, her body limp, damp, exhausted. He didn't want to release her, but as her breathing slowed she began to pull away, and he knew that if he tried to hold her she'd only be that more determined to escape. So he let her move away, reluctantly, as she tried to pull some of her self-control back around her.

"We're going to have to do something about this," he said in a deliberate drawl.

She was lying on her back beside him, trying to control her breathing. She was flushed, and he could see stray tremors of reaction still rippling across her silken skin. "About what?" she said, and her voice was endearingly hoarse.

"About us. I didn't use anything this time, either, and we're playing with fire. I don't want you to have to marry me because you get pregnant."

For a moment she didn't say anything, and he wondered if he'd blown it. "No," she said finally. "That wouldn't be a good idea."

"So I think," he continued, keeping his voice casual, "that we'd better get married first. Because I don't seem to be able to think straight around you, and this is probably going to keep happening."

He wasn't sure what he was expecting. Some response, from joyful acceptance to outraged refusal. But she said absolutely nothing. She simply curled up against him, resting her head on his chest, and his fierce amazon felt very small in his arms, small and fragile.

As fragile as a mountain lion, he reminded himself. But he wrapped his arms around her, very carefully, and held her tight against him. She'd get used to the idea. Once she heard the lawyers' offer, once she knew what he was willing to do for her. She'd welcome his offer.

Unless, of course, unlike everyone else in Hollywood, she simply couldn't be bought.

# Chapter Seventeen

There was never any doubt in Rafe's mind that she'd be gone when he woke the next morning. Twice during the long night he woke up and made love to her, once slowly, gently, lingeringly, the last with a wild, desperate passion, with both of them afraid it really would be the last time.

When he woke the third time he was alone. Dawn was breaking over the city, a cool, clear dawn, and the bed was empty. She was gone, leaving nothing behind but the terry robe she'd worn so briefly. He picked it up and held it against his face. It smelled like her. It smelled like the chlorine from the pool, and warm skin, and that subtle, flowery perfume she wore that was both innocent and astoundingly sexy. And he wondered what the hell he was going to do if she really left him.

He tried to swim off some of his tension, lap after lap, slicing through the water. It didn't help. He still hadn't remembered to get more cigarettes, which was just as well. The black coffee was already doing a number on him, and he wished he could even entertain the notion of spiking it with a shot of whiskey.

He couldn't, not with his family history. He had no particular craving for alcohol, no need for its varied effects, but he didn't count on that continuing. Alcohol was a mild pleasure he enjoyed—if it ever got any power over him he'd dispense with it ruthlessly.

If only he could do that with Silver. For the first time in his life he was at the mercy of another human being. If she walked away from him today he'd survive. He'd always survived.

He just damned well wouldn't want to.

He dressed in his L.A. clothes. Egyptian cotton shirt, Armani suit, leather running shoes and emerald stud in his ear. Someone told him the stone matched the color of his eyes. The thought had amused him. Now he was willing to do anything to entice her to stay with him.

The others were already assembled in the conference room at Pegasus Pictures, several miles up the road from the more down-homey atmosphere of Mack Movies. He wondered what Silver would think when she saw the phalanx of support gathered on the opposite side of the table. Would she hold her ground?

He should have told her last night, but he'd been afraid to. The great Rafe McGinnis, the invulnerable power broker who chewed up innocents and ate them for breakfast, had been afraid. Of saying the wrong thing. Of saying it at the wrong time. All he'd wanted was to take what she'd been willing to give. And wait until today to work it out.

"Back to the high life again?" Sam asked when he strode into the conference room. "What happened to Pecos Bill?"

"Leave him alone," Bernie snapped, looking pale and edgy. "We don't need your sophomoric humor today. As a matter of fact, I don't see why we need you at all. Why don't you go back to the studio and find something to keep you busy?"

"Hell, no!" Sam said. "He started it, I intend to see him finish it. And let me tell you, Rafe, if you blow it now you're in deep trouble. I would have been perfectly happy to let Miller do the screenplay until I read Carlysle's version. Now I'm not ready to compromise." He plopped his ample frame down in the seat. "You know, I think part of the power of *Black Canyon* is that it's a man's story, written by a woman. Now that I think about it, I'm willing to bet you that D. Maven was a woman, too."

Bernie spilled her coffee.

Rafe just looked at her, refusing to take it in. "You can't be serious," he said.

Bernie managed a shrug and an embarrassed grin. "What can I say? I was young once. Idealistic. Too bad I only had one story to tell."

"I'm going to kill you," Rafe announced calmly.

"Am I missing something?" Sam demanded.

"Meet D. Maven," Rafe said.

"Bernie?" Sam was aghast.

"We all have skeletons in our closet," Bernie muttered, looking embarrassed.

"Unfortunately none of this matters. We don't care about the rights to the original any longer. What we want is Silver's screenplay, and who D. Maven really was is beside the point," a well-bred voice pointed out from across the table.

Rafe dropped into one of the leather chairs and stared at Jeremiah Pinkins as he tried to absorb this latest shock. As usual, Jeremiah was eminently sensible, but then, what else would you expect from one of L.A.'s most powerful and persuasive lawyers?

Jeremiah was a man who could make Clement Walden look like a cracker. He was in the prime of life at somewhere past seventy, with a full head of flowing white hair, the voice of an orator, the stance of a patriarch and the charm of a devil. He'd headed the legal department of Pegasus Pictures for more than forty years now, and now in his well-deserved retirement he only came out when the really big guns were required. Jeremiah Pinkins was a big gun indeed, and Silver probably wouldn't even realize how desperate Rafe was.

"She's late," Bernie said, looking at her watch and taking her seat beside Rafe, the tremor in her voice betraying her uncharacteristic nervousness. "Did you see the retraction in the newspaper? Walden really wrote that article."

"I hadn't noticed," Rafe said absently, concentrating on the walnut door to the outer office.

"Didn't notice? Someone spills your dirty laundry all over the feature page of the *Los Angeles Clarion* and you don't notice?" Sam said. "I suppose we have Jeremiah to thank for the clarification."

"No, you don't," Jeremiah announced in his wonderfully rounded tones. "Though I did have my people check with the *Clarion*. It seems Clement Walden has been a naughty boy. Signing the wrong name to various pieces. Nothing illegal about giving credit away, but he's also come close to plagiarism more than once. Perhaps overstepped the bounds. Apparently he's going on a long sabbatical. To write the definitive book on film criticism, supposedly."

Bernie snorted with contempt. "The definitive book on pedantry, you mean. What about Silver?"

"It was hardly my people's place to ask," Jeremiah said. "However, I was given to believe they'd welcome her if she chose to fill Clement's shoes."

Rafe didn't blink. He didn't know whether that was good news or bad news. If she took the job she'd still be in L.A., at least part of the time. Which meant she'd be close enough for him to keep working on, if she turned her back on him now. On the other hand, he wanted to take her away from all this, for at least part of the long future he envisioned. Up into the mountains, to make babies and movies and love.

"Do you think she's going to show?" Sam drawled, loosening his already disreputable tie.

"I don't know," Rafe said honestly, thinking of the light in her expressive blue eyes, the softness of her mouth, the strength in her body. Gone, run away from him. "I really don't know."

The two buzzes on the intercom startled them all into silence. "I guess they're here," Rafe said unnecessarily. He buzzed back, and a moment later the door opened.

He'd expected she'd come with her own battalion of lawyers. With Clement Walden hovering at her shoulder, her powerhouse of a mother lurking behind, and all the legal firepower her wealthy stepfather could afford. Instead she stood alone, and despite her height she looked small and fragile.

She'd dressed for the occasion, in some sort of soft knit dress that rested delectably on her curves. She hadn't done it on purpose, he knew that. She probably just wanted to look professional. Instead she looked so good he wanted to clear the room and throw her down on the table and make love to her until she couldn't fight him anymore.

He didn't move, a muscle ticking in his jaw. "Silver," he greeted her, sounding calm and almost bored. "Where's your lawyer?"

She closed the door behind her, and he could see the nervousness in her movements. "I don't need one. I spoke to Mr. Pinkins's office yesterday and tried to explain. I'm not contesting ownership of *Black Canyon* anymore. It's yours. I won't fight you. I'll sign anything you want me to sign, give you what you want. I just don't want to deal with it anymore."

Rafe started to say something, but Jeremiah cleared his throat, forestalling him, and the sound was deafening in the conference room. "That's exactly why you need a lawyer, Miss Carlysle. Making rash statements like that will only get you into trouble. I doubt that you have any idea what Mr. McGinnis wants from you, so if I were you I wouldn't be quite so ready to hand it over without a certain amount of negotiation."

She smiled then. A mischievous crinkling in the corner of her mouth, that made his body go rock hard beneath the table. "I imagine I can guess," she murmured. "He can have the rights to *Black Canyon*—I won't contest his ownership. Therefore he doesn't have to pay me anything, and it's all settled."

"On the contrary, my dear," Jeremiah intoned. "He doesn't want the rights to *Black Canyon* alone. As a matter of fact that's no longer an issue. He wants to use your screenplay."

Rafe didn't know what he expected. Tears of joy. Silver flinging herself across the table at him in love-filled relief. Something. Anything.

She didn't move. "How much?"

Pinkins was used to dealing, and used to reading the emotional temperature in the room. He named a figure, just below the top price Rafe wanted to pay, well above the amount he'd planned to start with.

Silver didn't even blink at the sound of more money than most people make in their lifetimes. "No," she said flatly.

Rafe sat bolt upright in the leather chair. "No?" he echoed. "Why not?"

She moved across the room, graceful, sexy, determined, and leaned over the table, the others in the room forgotten. "Because," she said, very calm, "you can't buy me. You can have the Western, you can do anything you damned please with it, but you can't have my screenplay. God, you're even willing to fork over a ridiculous amount of money just to salvage my pride. You don't need to. My pride is just fine, thank you. I can turn and walk away, and it won't hurt at all. You won, Rafe. You told me you would, and I didn't believe you. You proved it, in no uncertain terms. Don't try to throw the game at this late date because you feel sorry for the loser. I didn't lose. I'm letting go. It's not worth fighting for anymore."

"Sit down, Silver," Rafe said in a deceptively gentle voice. She didn't move. "Sit down," he thundered, and everyone in the room jumped. Everyone but Silver.

She took the seat, however, but there was no missing the defiance in her eyes.

God, it was the defiance he loved. Along with everything else. "We won't do *Black Canyon* without your screenplay," he said flatly. "Isn't that right, Sam?"

"Right," Sam piped up immediately, obviously fascinated by all this.

"You won't do *Black Canyon* with **it**," she said flatly.

They stared at each other across the table for a long, silent moment. And then Rafe leaned back. "That settles that."

"I suppose it does."

"If I might say something..." Jeremiah Pinkins began, but Rafe very calmly stopped him.

"We're finished here. Bernie, would you give Jeffrey Metzger a call at Regis Pictures. They've been doing their damnedest to get a look at Silver's screenplay ever since we got it away from them. Tell them they have first shot at it."

"Wait a minute!" Sam protested.

Rafe glanced at him, then sighed. "They can borrow Sam for director, and you too, Bernie, if you want to go. Jeremiah can negotiate." He rose, walking away from the table, not looking at Silver's stunned figure.

"Rafe!" Bernie protested. "You're handing it over to your strongest competitor, just like that?"

He paused at the door, looking back into Silver's shocked eyes. "Just like that," he said. And walked out the door.

THE ROOM WAS PANDEMONIUM after Rafe dropped his bombshell. Silver sat in the chair, unmoving in her disbelief. He'd outdone her, and for a moment she sat frozen in shock.

And then she began to laugh. Absurd as it was, she couldn't help it. She sat back in the chair and laughed until the tears ran down her face, until the others in the room stopped their bickering and stared at her in shock and consternation.

She'd been ready to give him everything, to make the final sacrifice, as some doomed act of love. And instead, like some cockeyed version of "Gift of the Magi," he'd made the same sacrifice, leaving her own grand gesture effectively trashed. There was nothing she could do but laugh.

It took her a moment to compose herself, with the aid of Bernie's unexpectedly feminine lace handkerchief and what little was left of her self-control.

"He always does win, doesn't he?" she said weakly.

Bernie stared at her. "Does that mean you agree?"

"Do you think I can let him make that kind of sacrifice? Give up what he's been fighting for? Give it up for me?" She sighed, not sure whether she was close to tears or laughter again. "Of course I agree. Whatever terms you want to come up with, Mr. Pinkins."

"I've warned you, Ms. Carlysle..."

"It really doesn't matter," Silver said. "He's going to be paying my bills anyway."

Bernie still stood there, her craggy face creased with concern. "It'll mean a great deal to all of us," she said. "We all believe in the project. And I wanted to do it for your father's sake."

Silver looked up at her, at the plain, horsey woman who was twenty years older than her mother. "You broke up my parents' marriage," she said, out of the blue.

Bernie flinched. "Yes."

"Marjorie could overlook the starlets and the one-night stands. She simply couldn't tolerate the fact that he could sleep with someone he respected, someone..." Her words trailed off.

"Sleep with someone so old and ugly," Bernie supplied wryly. "Your father loved my mind. He loved your mother's face, he loved a hundred women's bodies. I was just the final insult. He would have left her if it hadn't been for you. He loved you, Silver. Even if he wasn't smart enough to show it."

"Not good enough," she said fiercely. "I want a man who isn't afraid to show he loves me."

"Then for God's sake go after him," Bernie said. "Before he gets away."

Rafe was standing in the parking lot, between the two vehicles. On the one side was his Lotus, fast and sleek and very California. On the other was the rented Colorado pickup truck, mud still clinging to its axles. He stood in the middle, waiting for her.

"Did I hear you laughing in there?" he asked, sounding no more than casually interested.

"You did. You told me you always won, and I never really believed you." She came up close to him, not touching, tilting her head back to look up into his face. He was wearing shades again, and he looked very California. "I just didn't realize that we could both win. Which car are we taking?"

He didn't touch her, and she wanted him to. "The truck belongs in Colorado," he said. "The Lotus in L.A."

"Does it snow a lot in Colorado in October, or was that just a fluke?"

"It snows a lot in the mountains."

"I love the mountains."

"I love you," he said, pushing the sunglasses up on his forehead, and she didn't for one moment doubt him.

She smiled then. "Let's get snowed in," she said, "and we can spend our time arguing about it."

He put his arms around her then, drawing her tight against his strong, hard body. "Be glad to," he said, his mouth hovering over hers. "But let me warn you, I always win."

"I'm counting on it," she said. "Because so do I." And threading her fingers through his long, wavy hair, she kissed him, giving him her heart and soul and love.

Bernie stood watching from behind the thin-slatted blinds in the front office, a radiant expression on her wrinkled face. "Ain't love grand?" she murmured out loud. "This one's for you, Benny." And she let the blinds drop closed again, turning back to the conference room, secure in the knowledge that her job was done.

## ABOUT THE AUTHOR

Anne Stuart has written for the American Romance line since its inception, writing all sorts of books, from Gothics to comedies to heavy-hitting emotional sagas. This one is a hybrid of two of her favorite types, an odd combination she calls cowboy-glitz.

### Books by Anne Stuart
HARLEQUIN AMERICAN ROMANCE
311—GLASS HOUSES
326—CRAZY LIKE A FOX
346—RANCHO DIABLO
361—ANGELS WINGS
374—LAZARUS RISING
398—NIGHT OF THE PHANTOM
413—CHASING TROUBLE
434—HEAT LIGHTNING

Don't miss any of our special offers. Write to us at the following address for information on our newest releases.

Harlequin Reader Service
P.O. Box 1397, Buffalo, NY 14240
Canadian address: P.O. Box 603,
Fort Erie, Ont. L2A 5X3

ASB10

## A SPAULDING AND DARIEN MYSTERY

Amateur sleuths Jenny Spaulding and Peter Darien have set
the date for their wedding. But before they walk down the
aisle, love must pass a final test. This time, they won't have to
solve a murder, they'll have to prevent one—Jenny's.
Don't miss the chilling conclusion to the SPAULDING AND
DARIEN MYSTERY series in October. Watch for:

### #197 WHEN SHE WAS BAD by Robin Francis

Look for the identifying series flash—A SPAULDING AND
DARIEN MYSTERY—and join Jenny and Peter for danger and
romance....

---

**HARLEQUIN®**

**AMERICAN ◆ ROMANCE®**

American Romance's yearlong celebration continues.... Join your favorite authors as they celebrate love set against the special times each month throughout 1992.

Next month... Spooky things were expected in Salem, Massachusetts, on Halloween. But when a tall, dark and gorgeous man emerged from the mist, Holly Bennett thought that was going too far. Was he a real man... or a warlock? Find out in:

## OCTOBER

| S | M | T | W | T | F | S |
|---|---|---|---|---|---|---|
|   |   |   |   | 1 | 2 | 3 |
| 4 |   |   |   |   | 9 | 10 |
| 11 | 12 |   | 15 | 16 | 17 |
| 18 | 19 |   |   | 23 | 24 |
| 25 | 26 | 27 | 28 | 29 | 30 | 31 |

**#457
UNDER HIS SPELL
by Linda Randall Wisdom**

Read all the *Calendar of Romance* titles, coming to you one per month, all year, only in American Romance.